POETRY

AND

PURGATORY

POETRY

AND

PURGATORY

BUDDY GIOVINAZZO

THUNDER'S MOUTH PRESS

First Edition
First printing, 1996

Published by
Thunder's Mouth Press
632 Broadway, 7th Floor
New York, NY 10012

Library of Congress Cataloging-in-Publication Data
Giovinazzo, Buddy
Poetry and purgatory / by Buddy Giovinazzo.
    p.   cm.
    ISBN 1-56025-133-6
    I. Title.
PS3557.I58P64   1996
813'.54—dc20   96-16118
                                                              CIP

Printed in the United States of America

Designed by Michael Mendelsohn

Distributed by Publishers Group West
4065 Hollis Street
Emeryville, CA 94608
(800) 788-3123

For Bill Guest

1

DENISE WAS ALREADY TWENTY MINUTES LATE, and this wouldn't have been the first time she left me waiting never to appear. If not for the freezing rain pounding down like chains against the pavement I would have left, but instead I stayed, underneath the awning of the Lyric Theatre in Times Square, or what was left of it, with the dealers and whores of which two were transvestites.

Shivering and clutching my sides like an Eskimo, I watched a gang of kids from the welfare hotel laughing and splashing through puddles in potholes, kicking up dirty water into each other's faces as if it were a baking summer day. I leaned against the glass of the ticket booth and tightened my jacket, held both my ears as the wind and its razor blade sliced at my scalp. For seven days it had been like this, icy wet like frozen piss, and no amount of pills or pints seemed to get rid of these shivers. A dog pattered by with its tongue hanging out, swaying limply from side to side like a pendulum. A long string of dribble hung down from its jaw and its matted brown coat was devoured by grease, but it trotted along with its nose in the air as a middle-aged whore took a step to the curb. The dog ambled over and sniffed at her crotch as the others laughed and told her it was her next date. She swatted it away as a Buick pulled up—nobody gets it for free, not even a dog. Across the street a dripping beggar wearing rags was wiping windshields at the red; a sign blew off a shuttered store, "MOVED DOWNTOWN" and nothing more. I watched the cars and trucks crawl along, the sewage and papers splash up on the curb, the blinking red nipples from the shop across the way, all taking place beyond this curtain of rain, when I was suddenly aware of the strangest sensation, like I was naked and someone was touching me, not with his hands, but with his mind. Like beams of light through murky rivers. Looking over I saw the dog a few feet away, watching me closely as if it would speak. There was a glimmer in his eyes, so strangely familiar, a real recognition! like I'd seen him before but not as a dog, as something or someone else. He smiled at me, his shiny gray eyes with slivers of silver like diamonds on Mars, or scalpels in surgery, slicing through my tender skin in paper cuts so painful cold they cracked my teeth. A kid from the gutter went over to pet it and it jumped on his chest and licked at his face and the kid kicked it in the balls and the dog darted off with an agonized yelp. One of the tv girls took a step to protest till a shimmering blade cut the air and the rain. That shut her up and fast. A cop car turned the corner and drove west to Eighth as the kids moved east to Broadway. I stood there trying to look innocent as the cops eyed me up and down. All at once the reds kicked in: A hammer made of glass. Shattered my eyes as the street tilted sideways—through spinning purple acid trips of geometric tidal waves with crayon cars and rayon trucks and tv whores on holidays, in orange hats and red fedoras rat fur coats of gray angora, pictures paintings porno loops of severed limbs and lightning bolts, I tumbled down through liquid streets where children cried on dirty sheets, my throat choked up with blood and bile underneath a rotting pile, shriveled veins and black saliva swept me into paranoia—the fucking cunt of paranoia!—where I felt good as I should, so burn my heart with iodine.

I opened my eyes to a tapping on top of my head, and looking up at the leaking marquee like a Chinese torture from Brazil, I got drilled in the eye with a link from the chain, so I went into Peeptown across the street where I could still see Denise if and when she showed up. Moving through the aisles looking bored and unperverted, as I browsed through magazines the way you would in a doctor's office, leafing through the sweaty acts and feeling nothing churn inside, like a hollow tube of flesh, until Yudi with the forehead dot told me to buy it or beat it, I wanted to beat it right there on the floor and let him clean it up. But there was nothing to clean so I went up to Jackie's and hung with the regulars. Of course there was Dezmond and Wally and Paris and Harper and sitting at the bar was Wally's fat sister Camille with her big melon tits hanging out for a feel. Camille might have been cute if she lost a few pounds and cut off her head. Dezmond and Wally were playing Nine Ball while Harper stood on the jukebox changing a light in the overhead bulb.

"Hey, why don'tcha put in a seventy-five watter instead of those cheap little forties! It's like a fuckin' cave in here!" Dezmond yelled at Jackie.

"Because I ain't Con Ed," Jackie yelled back.

"Yeah, you're just a fuckin' con!" Dezmond answered and everybody laughed. I stepped to the bar and sat one stool away from Camille who asked me to buy her a drink which I did, then before she could ask for anything else I slid from the stool and went over to Dezmond chalking his cue.

"So what's up with you?" he said as my clothes pissed on the floor. "Don't you have enough sense to get outta the rain!"

As he got ready to shoot I squeezed out my shirt on the table; he scratched on the break.

"Hey Jackie! The fuckin' guy's ruinin' your table!"

Jackie looked over in that angry yet impotent way. "Hey Eddie," he yelled, "whattaya a fuckin' retard!? That felt costs money and I ain't gonna replace it so the next time it's ruined ya's can all go play fuckin' ping pong at the Y!"

"Sorry Jackie," I said, then shut my mouth cause I was shaking so badly it shivered my voice. I leaned against the wall as Dezmond and Wally shot pool and Dezmond scratched on the break again and Camille slurped her glass with scotch squeaking teeth, yelled to her brother for a cigarette but he ignored her.

"What's with your sister?" Dezmond said to Wally. "Don't she ever have nothin' for herself?! She's like a fuckin' slot machine! Why don'tcha take her up to Atlantic City?" And Paris and Harper like Heckle and Jeckle laughed as Wally chalked his cue and sank the three ball in the side. I went into the bathroom and puked up my drink. Turned on the light and saw a splash of it on my foot, wiped it with a tissue. Catching a glance of my face in the mirror all whitish and thin like a skull in the night really scared the hell out of me, so I heaved into the sink to make sure I was still alive. Dezmond came in and asked if I was okay and I told him just a little tired.

"You seem real quiet today, you alright? Hey, you gonna get some more of those reds tonight cause maybe we can go in on some. Geez, it fuckin' hurts to piss it's like an acid you know what I mean? I had Mexican last night with jalapenos and every time I piss it's like passin' a fuckin' stone. Hey, whattaya gonna be doin' later cause why don't you come over, Lucille's goin' to her sister's with the kid and we can hang out and watch some porno. I'll give ya a call. Hey, if you get any more of those reds later make sure you bring them cause I wanna buy at least another twenty. Hey, you alright? You look fucked up. Whattaya been takin' and how come you didn't give me a taste?"

I dried my face and wiped my hair then went back to the smoky cloud of stale beer bad breath body odor as Camille came up to me inches away. The bitter tang of her pussy underneath her dress cause she never wore any panties made me nauseous. I had to get out.

With nothing to do and nowhere to go I went back to the strip till the reds'd wear off. Standing next to Hot Dog Vic who lost his leg and half his dick, in Saigon, or Bayonne, I wasn't sure which, I watched a broken umbrella die in the street as a moving van started its engine and pulled away from the curb and behind it was Denise with a scowl on her face. My smile didn't remove it. Denise was looking fine in her knee-high boots and skin-tight jeans and white fake fur with long red hair, and standing side by side you'd never believe we were related.

"You're late!" she said with a frown.

"I was here an hour ago. You're the one who's late."

"Did you eat?"

"No."

"C'mon, let's get some lunch," she said and marched out from the awning with me chasing two steps behind. Denise was fast in her boots even on the slippery wet slabs of cement.

"Slow down! What's the rush?" I called out.

"It's raining! I don't want to get wet," and she walked even faster. I chased after spotting big round beads of water seeds like plastic flies on rubber webs, resting on top of her hair, while mine was soaked to the bone. I reached her at the corner as a cabbie hit the water, she gave me a laugh as she took out her hankie and wiped off my eyes.

"You still can't take care of yourself, do you know that?"

"Yes. Where are we going?"

We headed west to Show World and sitting at the corner was a broken down Toyota, a lady knelt crying over the dog who lay bleeding in the gutter, heaving and panting its eyes slowly slanting like strobe lights aflutter, I knew in another minute it would be dead. Denise yelled for me to catch up and brushing past a Krishna with a broken tambourine I wondered if he knew where the dog would be going.

Under the awning she slowed her pace and we walked side by side in silence. "C'mon, we can sit down in here," she said as she marched into a small luncheonette. We sat at a booth and I dried my hair with the napkin while Denise wiped her face.

"So, how are you doing?" she asked.

"Fine."

"Really? You're feeling okay?"

"Yes. I'm fine."

"You don't look so good," she said with concern, but Denise had a way of caring in a cold and uncaring way. When I said I was doing good she asked how my treatments were going and though I stopped two months ago I told her they were good too and I was in remission. The remission part was true.

"Your hair looks like it's coming back in," she said. "No more headaches?"

"No." I answered. She said that was good as she looked through the menu. "You'd better keep your weight up, you look skinny. Order whatever you want, it's on me."

I closed the menu without looking inside and told her I'd have soup.

"That's all you want? Soup? Eat something solid, go ahead. Order a hamburger."

"Just soup."

Denise went back to her menu and I gazed at her smooth wet face with red hair blue eyes and all the makeup washed away, tiny freckles scattered on her nose like jimmies on a cone. She closed her menu and slid it away.

"So, how have you been making out? You still on disability?"

"Not anymore. They caught me working off the books. I think I'm suspended now."

"Oh. So, what are you doing for money?"

"I've been keeping busy, doing temp work, whatever I can get my hands on, you know, odd jobs. If I'm really stuck I'll hand out flyers for the Kit Kat Club."

"That doesn't sound too lucrative. Are you making enough?"

"I'm doing alright."

"Do you need some money?"

"No, I'm fine."

"Why don't I believe you?"

"You should ask yourself that."

"How much you got on you right now?"

"I don't know."

"Well check. What do you got—twenty? Thirty?"

"I don't know. Thirty."

"You got any money in the bank?"

"A few million."

"Don't be funny!" Denise reached into her bag and pulled out a fifty dollar bill and pressed it into my palm. I now had fifty-two dollars to my name. The waitress came over and we ordered.

The soup was like a fever piss I forced myself to keep it down cause everything I swallowed these days had that same rancid flavor, ever since the radiation burned away my tastebuds. As the reds wore off I was hoping Denise would get to the point so I could go back to my room and lie on the bed.

"When was the last time you saw Mom?" she asked as she sipped from her straw and I told her I didn't know and that it had to be a couple months ago probably the last time we went together.

"That was last summer," she said with a crinkled nose. "Over six months ago."

"Well, I guess I kind of lost track of the time. Denise, to tell you the truth, I really don't see the point of going. She doesn't know who I am or if I'm even there, and sitting there watching her is kind of upsetting to me."

"Still, you should try to go more often," she said, softening. "I'll call you the next time I visit. We'll go together, okay?"

I nodded but knew she'd never call, then seven whores walked past outside and one of them stopped to read the menu on the window until she was pulled away by the arm.

I looked out the glass at people maggots whores and killers and saw a living snuff movie with myself as the star. Denise sat there sipping and slurping her soda like all of this made sense to her.

"You know who called me yesterday?"

I told her no.

"Uncle Ted," she said, and everything inside of me puked for a moment.

"What's the matter? Are you alright? You're sweating like a pig."

"How do pigs sweat?" I reached into my pocket grabbed my tube of pills and popped four with water as Denise looked around to make sure no one was watching.

"Take it easy! Are you sure you're supposed to take that many?"

"Yes. I'm fine. What did he want?"

"He needed a copy of mom's birth certificate for the hospital, they were moving her to another floor and they lost her files," she said matter-of-factly. She was so fucking cool, my sister Denise. The fact that she could live her life and function right and deal with the things in proper light made me envy her admire her if only I could be like her.

She finished her burger and talked of the weather and business and lovers and I just sat there tingling and waiting to know the importance of my presence, and maybe I took too many pills cause I couldn't hear what she was saying anymore, just a chatter of voices like chipmunks on acid. The reds were melting metal wires cooling off then starting fires, and as my stomach unwound and my head floated upward, Denise lowered her voice and told me the deal.

No matter what the light or time of day my room was always dark. I stumbled in and put the fifth of scotch on the table as the floor spun around me like a carousel. I opened the window a crack and felt the splashing drops of icy water freezing fingers still numb from the holes in my pockets. When I laid down on the chilly mattress my eyeballs dripped to the back of my skull, two raw eggs sliding along the valleys and gullies of black gooey matter. Then everything got real quiet and the only sound was the air in my lungs, so I held my breath and in the vacuum that was left, could hear myself at war: the pulsing throbs of poison plasma cells mutating congregating fighting hard and menstruating mushroom clouds of cobalt treatment tumors and their children. I trembled yellow in my bunker till the fever passed; if only I could fake it I'd survive. I opened my lids and through backward binoculars saw a man in the window, a fuzzy weird and Christ-like man just floating there and watching me. Now I knew where the dog had gone. For an hour I didn't move waiting for him to speak, but he just eyed me with that knowing mangy smile on his face. I caught him eyeing the scotch and I jumped up tripping over the table and grabbed the bottle but turning back he was gone. I splashed my face with water and that snapped me back cause I often lose my mind this way, especially with the reds and the booze and Mrs. Taylor still swears I strangled her cat and she might be right, but then why did I hear it meowing last night? I drank some tea and smoked a roach then slugged the scotch and took a pee and it's a good thing I didn't eat any jalapenos. I started remembering what Denise had said, but not about the deal, about our Uncle Ted.

2

I ALMOST FORGOT WHAT THE SUN LOOKED LIKE and now that it was back I remembered why I had. Sitting up a morning fever struck me blind with pictures of religious shrines, a scent of piss and shit and blood and AIDS and cancer made me bang my head against the broken tiles again and again to see if I was dizzy dreaming, but the red on my fingers said no. I wiped the blood and drank milk of magnesia. Opened my eyes and found an hour had passed. There was nothing to eat and no reason to eat it so I went out to Ninth Avenue looking for Lizard Len and his healing prescriptions.

The sun beat down like Astroturf on plastic bones and standing on the corner I saw colors of hunger and longing and pain but all the different colors were black.

Later from a yellow car as sweet as honey CandyBar climbed out. With her dark droopy eyes and her makeup smeared and blouse undone and stockings ripped she looked a hundred years old. I asked if she was okay and she told me she was but ready to collapse.

"Who was that in the car?"

"A friend of Zero's, some fireman, I did a bachelor party," she said in heavy chunks of Jersey, then made some kind of joke about their hoses running dry.

"I made a thousand bucks tonight and now I'm takin' off for two whole days and Zero ain't gonna say shit cause I fuckin' earned it." And she was right, as Zero Zero Minus One earned more than half for nothing done, and Zero was one of the nicer ones.

CandyBar asked if I was carrying and I told her as soon as I was I'd give her some. Then offered to walk her home and she didn't seem to mind. As the morning suits passed and they all grabbed a glance—cause CandyBar had big tits for a twelve year old—I searched through my pockets and pulled out a roach. She sat on the stoop and I noticed a line of blood on her leg but said nothing about it.

"You know," she said, taking a long tired drag on the speck in the clip, her eyes glazed over like a frog underwater, "between this year and last I bet I made over a hundred thousand bucks and imagine if I'd'a saved up that much. I'd be livin' easy, you know? I could probably start my own business and be a millionaire by now, who knows?"

"What would you start?" I asked, confused for a moment, not remembering where I was or who I was with.

"I don't know . . . I guess that's the problem. I don't think I can do anything, I don't know what I can do."

"What do you like to do?" I asked, searching, struggling to remember who she was. She wrinkled her brow and gave it a long, concentrated crease.

"I don't know, maybe I could open a nightclub, somethin' like that. Like a real high-class type of club too, with no hookers or pimps but like, you know, real people. And I could be like, the hostess, you know, the lady who greets people as they come and makes sure they're havin' a good time."

"I'll bet you'd be good at that. You're very friendly," I said as it all came rushing back.

"One time I went to this club, the john made me dress up in a evening gown, he gave me pearls and jewelry to wear, diamond earrings, and he took me to this real expensive Italian place in Jersey, you know, Fort Lee, right over the bridge, and they parked the car for you and everybody was nice as shit and they lit your cigarette and held your chair I'm tellin' ya, they made you feel like a million bucks. And the whole time I felt like I was his date, you know, he didn't treat me like a whore, it was like right outta Pretty Woman or somethin'. Until we got to his place."

Then searching her head with her fingertips, "I still have a lump from it somewhere."

"Yeah, I remember, that was last fall, wasn't it?"

"No, it was July. July 3rd, I remember the exact day. Anyways Zero got him back good, went to his house and beat him to a fuckin' bloody pulp with his face battered purple and his lips puffed up like Tyrone's. Then Zero took pictures and showed me in the hospital and it felt fuckin' good to see him like that. But anyways, that's the type of club I'd open up, a really cool one."

"Well, you should then."

"Yeah," she sighed, "who the fuck knows. I go through money like water, I don't know. Can't seem to hold onto it. I guess I have no direction in my life," she said with a giggle, then turning serious as something popped into her mind, "Shit, I better get off the street cause if Zero drives by and sees me he's gonna ask me to work."

CandyBar got up and took a step then turned to me and said, "Hey, you wanna come up for a minute, have a cup of coffee or somethin'?"

I stood there saying nothing cause she caught me at a loss, CandyBar never invited anyone up to her place. "Sure," I said nervously, trying to figure the deal. "That'd be nice."

Inside the lobby the rickety stairs went up into darkness and passing the coffin closet elevator I figured it was only up a few floors. But after the fourth flight I was gasping for air and CandyBar asked if I was alright and I told her just a little tired. "Do you want to rest for a minute? You don't look so good."

"No, I'm fine, I really am. Let's keep going. I'll just hold onto the banister," and we continued up the stairs. "This is a real fine banister," I said, tapping it with my knuckles. "Must be made of oak."

"Yeah? I don't know much about wood," she said, and in the darkness I heard a voice call me an asshole. She opened her door on the eighth or ninth floor and we went inside. The place looked like a normal home with a couch and some chairs and a tv and bar and a stereo paintings and rugs on the floor; a bookcase and coffee table and the coffee table had a razor blade and dried out stains from ice-filled dripping glasses; off to the side was a table for two and a small kitchenette just behind it, to the left a pink-tiled bathroom with frosted glass doors on the shower and a fuzzy gray rug at the bowl.

"Why don't you make yourself comfy, I'll be right out," she said, then turned and went into the bathroom. Standing in the middle feeling awkward out of place, I browsed around the stereo where she had a cassette deck and CD player and next to it were dozens of CDs and I tried to open one but my fingers were shaking so badly I couldn't. My stomach started growling but not for food for something else. I was hoping CandyBar would offer something to drink and not coffee. The toilet flushed and she came out wearing a red silk robe with the belt hanging down and her face all washed and her hair tied back made her look a lot younger than she did a minute ago.

"Do you like Harry Connick, Jr.?" she asked, taking the disk from my hand.

"I don't know, I've never met him."

She gave me a look and said, "C'mon, you know what I mean."

"I've never heard of him, to tell you the truth. I, um . . . I don't much follow music. Sorry."

"Don't apologize. It's not a crime."

Using her robe she wiped off the disk and turned on the player. "He's like Frank Sinatra," she said as if she had something to do with it. Then suspiciously, "You have heard of Frank Sinatra, haven't you?"

"I may be an idiot but I'm not a moron," I said with an edge, but then changed my tone. "My mother loved Frank Sinatra, he was her favorite singer."

She smiled at that, and as Harry Connick, Jr., the New Frank Sinatra, started crooning from the speakers which were mounted in the walls, I heard the screechy scratchy squealings of a subway going backwards; the speakers in my ears were ripped, I couldn't hear music anymore; so I didn't tap my foot or nod my head, and CandyBar didn't seem to notice as she swayed to the sounds like a tree in the wind. I turned and faced the window as she opened her eyes.

"What's the matter? Don't you like him?" she asked.

"Sure, he's great. Sounds just like Frank," I said but didn't turn around.

CandyBar went into the kitchenette leaving me there on the train. I stepped into the doorway where I watched her scooping coffee into a filter at the counter.

"Uh, you know, CandyBar, I really don't want any coffee. Don't go to any bother over me."

"It's no bother. I want some for myself. I'm so wound up after workin', it takes me an hour just to unwind."

She measured water in the pot and carefully poured it into the top of the coffeemaker, I watched her nickelodeon. Simple sunlight hands and face her ponytail with crimson lace, pink foam lips mouthing words from songs that I would never hear, like silent movies far from my existence, or prayers of love and affection, I wanted to laugh.

Instead I told her, "Listen, I know you're tired, maybe I'll just be going."

"You sure?" she said looking up, and when I nodded my head she didn't insist.

Lucille stepped in holding Ben and went to the refrigerator, took out a baby bottle and put it in a pot on the stove. Dezmond finished the joint, "Hey, you want anymore of this?" I shook my head and he let the roach fall in the tray. Lucille stood there holding their kid and rocking him gently as the water bubbled in the pot. Dezmond ignored her and she ignored him then Dezmond counted out his reds and scooped them up in his palm leaving three on the table and none for Lucille. Finally Dezmond turned to her, "Don't you have something to do? Like make the bed or something?!" Lucille took the bottle and squeezed a drop of formula on her wrist, then put it in Ben's mouth and walked inside telling Dezmond to go fuck himself. Dezmond gave me a smile and we sat there sipping and toking and popping our pills as he flipped through the channels stopping on the sex ads where some big tit blond was squatting on the floor and taking a pee. Dezmond asked if Denise ever ran ads on tv and I gave him a look. After an hour Dezmond talked me out of working so we went up to Jackie's where I sat at the bar with Harper who showed me his new blue tattoo of a snake eating cheese and when I asked him why the cheese he told me it was cheddar. He flexed his arm and the snake did a dance like a cobra in heat, but underneath the ringing in my ears I heard it talking to me, its voice in a whisper saying over and over, "Beware of the man with the soviet plan." I turned around and saw Dezmond scratch on the break. Camille came tripping out of the ladies room and Harper called her a klutz. She sat at the bar as I stared at my glass and the ice melting smaller. "Beware of the man with the soviet plan"—it had to be code. Then Harper started talking in one ear and Camille in the other and I sat in between letting sentences joust as the syllables fucked and gave birth to a curse, till Harper got up and went to the back leaving me with Camille who was drunk and fucked up.

"You know, Eddie," she slurred with a slobber, "I don't know why everybody hates me so much, it's not like I did anything to them." The gin on her breath mixed with pot gave me cravings.

"Camille, nobody really hates you," I said. "You're just being paranoid."

"No, they do. Even my own brother hates me. You know how many times he tells me he wishes I was dead, he tells me all the time, all the fuckin' time! I'm his fuckin' sister, for Chrissakes, his own flesh and blood and he treats me like a piece of garbage, the shit he says about me to his friends . . ."

"Look Camille, that's how brothers and sisters are, they always say things they don't mean." But glancing over at Wally bending over the table with a bridge under his cue and the crack of his ass bursting out of his pants like a forty-pound ham, I realized that he really did hate her. He hated everybody. Camille sat there crying on the bar and no warm words of wisdom could have changed that—sometimes Camille just needed to cry—so I stepped over to the pinball game which Jackie kept for old time's sake, while Jackie stayed behind the bar yelling at Camille for crying and upsetting the customers. Camille wiped her face and grubbed a sympathy drink from Old Man Costello who had one fucked up eye that faced in a different direction. Wally was clearing the table in order while Dezmond was scratching his balls, Camille stole a cigarette and a dollar from a guy sleeping on the bar and Harper came out from the back room carrying a keg of beer on his head; faded tattoos stretched across his arms like Sunday comics silly putty. Dezmond tried to distract Wally by ranting of yuppies and drugs and of militant lesbians, but Wally just ignored him, "Nine ball in the side," then sunk it and won. Dezmond threw down his cue and whirled around with nostrils flared as Wally snatched the fiver from the table and Jackie chortled from behind the bar. Camille slid from her stool and flabbed to the jukebox with a dollar in hand as Dezmond caught sight and spun around clocked her hard WHACK! cold crisp snap like breaking bones across her brittle pock-marked face. Everybody turned as she dropped her drink and almost toppled over. She stood there for a moment, stunned and somewhat pleading, touching the cut on her cheek from his ring. When she let out a wail from the tip of her spleen my legs buckled. Dezmond told her to quit faking it and that he was sorry and it was all a big misunderstanding. Wally stood at the bar watching his sister sob on the cigarette machine as if she had cancer, then he ordered a drink for himself and the loser. Dezmond bought me a scotch but I told him I didn't want it, so he held it out to Camille who sniffled, wiped her wet and puffy eyes, and took it like a guilty fearful child.

What amazed me more than anything else was at that moment I hated Camille more than I hated myself.

3

THE TEMP AGENCY TOLD ME TO REPORT AT 8:30 to the law offices up on Fifty-Fifth. All I had to do was answer the phone, the receptionist was out sick. I jumped at the offer. I wore my dark cashmere jacket white shirt and tie, black pants made of something not cotton and my black suede sneaker/shoes. I thought I looked somewhat conservative, in a leftist sort of way. The second I stepped through the door I knew I was mistaken. I took two reds to take off the edge and as long as I didn't come into contact with too many people I'd be fine. Some friendly guy named Albert, an awkward gawk with slightly crossed eyes and a six-hundred-dollar suit, told me to sit over there and answer the phone. Four seconds later it started ringing. "Hello, Garbus, Frankfurt, Brakowitz and Jacobson," I said, trying to sound receptionly.

"Who's this," said the gruff, fuck-you voice on the line.

"Uh, I'm answering the phones today, the receptionist is out sick. Who would you like to speak to?"

"Give me Brakowitz!"

"Hold please."

Looking down there were no names for any extensions, just numbers. I didn't know how to get Brakowitz or even if he was in. I quickly looked around for a directory when the phone rang again. I felt my stomach jerk, pushed the button on the third ring.

"Hello, Garbus, Frankfurt, Brakowitz and Jacobson."

"I'm already holding for Brakowitz! Connect me through!"

"Oh, I'm sorry, I must have punched the wrong line."

The phone kept ringing, I looked for Albert who was nowhere to be seen, all the other cubicles were manned with faceless figures, none of whom glanced up. As the phone

continued ringing I reluctantly punched another line. After a
pause, "Hello?"

"Hello, is this Garbus, Frankfurt, Brakowitz and
Jacobson?"

"Yes it is, how can I help you?"

"Let me speak to Marc Brakowitz, please."

"Sure, please hold, I'll see if he's in."

As soon as I put down the receiver another line was ringing. I punched it and my stomach twisted tighter.

"Hello?"

"Hello, let me speak to Jason Frankfurt."

"Please hold and I'll see if he's in."

Three blinking lights and no idea of how to connect
them, I started pushing buttons. The phone rang again. I
punched in line three. "I'm sorry but Mr. Frankfurt is not in
yet, we expect him shortly. Can I take a message?"

"Yes, tell him Robert Jennings called, and to call me
back."

"Very well, I'll give him that message." Then as I was
about to hang up, "Wait a minute, aren't you going to take
my number?"

"Oh yes, of course, I'm sorry."

The phone kept ringing but I took down the number
first. I punched line four. I shouldn't have.

"What's going on over there!? Connect me through! Who
is this!?"

"Oh, I'm sorry, I was just about to get back to you. Mr.
Brakowitz is not in yet, but we expect him shortly. Can I take
a message?"

"I know he's there, I just spoke to him! Where's Albert?!"

"I'm sorry, I don't see him, uh, could you hold please?"

I quickly punched in the ringing line, "Hello, Domino's
Pizza."

"What?"

"Domino's Pizza," I repeated.

"Oh, I have the wrong number."

I immediately opened all the remaining lines, then stood up looking for Albert. A barracuda paralegal skirted past my desk carrying a folder. "Excuse me, do you know where Albert is?"

"No, I don't," as he didn't break stride. The blinking red lights of the switchboard acupuncture stomach pouch, tea and toast about to make an appearance. A young woman with long brown hair was approaching my desk so I stepped into her path.

"Excuse me, can you please help me? I've got these lines on hold but I don't know how to connect them through. Do you know how to do it?"

She stopped and looked at me with a wry smile. "Drives you crazy, doesn't it? I don't know the extensions myself, Carole has the system down by heart, but she's not here, obviously." Then she looked down at the switchboard. "Say! you don't have any lines open. Nobody can get through!"

"I know, I'm sorry, but I couldn't keep putting people on hold."

"I'll tell you what, open up those lines again and I'll get Albert, okay?"

"Thanks, I appreciate it."

I opened the lines and the phone rang immediately.

"Hello, Garbus, Frankfurt, Brakowitz and Jacobson."

"WHO THE HELL IS THIS!?"

I slammed the receiver down.

"What seems to be the problem?" Albert was standing over me with the woman behind him, she gave me a sympathetic smile then went back to her desk.

"I've got three people on hold but I don't know how to connect them."

"Didn't I give you the directory?"

"No, you didn't."

"Oh, okay, let me clear this first." Albert then took each call starting with the third one.

"Sorry about the delay, we're having a problem with our switchboard, it's the phone company, you know how they are . . . Sure, he's expecting your call, I'll connect you through."

Line one was still blinking and every blink was a jab in my eye. "You'd better get to that first guy, he sounds pretty upset."

Albert punched it on. "Hello? . . . Oh, Mr. Garbus, I'm terribly sorry about that . . . Carole's out sick, we're using a temp and he's not familiar with the system yet. Surely, I'll take care of it, I'll connect you right through." Then Albert took two new calls, wrote down messages on a pad, and cleared the lines. My shirt was soaking wet and it wasn't even 9:30 yet. Albert leaned down over the console.

"Here are the names and extensions for the partners, here are the research departments, word processing, in case anybody wants it; personnel, graphics, accounting, but most calls will be for the partners, and always intercom them before connecting; we get a lot of kooks trying to get through. If there's any problem, my office is right over there, call me, extension 514. Okay?"

He looked me right in the eye and gave me a big toothy grin; there was something weird about it. The phone continued ringing and didn't stop until lunchtime, by then I knew the system. As everybody filed past me to lunch, I looked for the woman with the long brown hair and friendly face but she never left the office. A black pinstriped suit walked in and shot me a look that froze the film in my eyes. Garbus went straight into Albert's office and closed the door. I popped two reds to fight the throbbing and answered the phone on the second ring.

"Wow, you sound very professional."

"How did you get this number?"

"I called your agency, told them it was an emergency."

"How did you know which agency to call?"

"I tried them all until I found it."

"That's a little neurotic, don't you think?"

"What are you doing later?"

"I don't know. Why?"

"Why don't you come over for dinner?"

"Dinner? I don't know, I mean, talking twice in the same week . . . Is everything alright?"

"Don't be a wiseguy. I just want to talk to you some more. You were, shall we say, not completely lucid the other day."

"I know. It wasn't a good day."

"So, come over. We'll have a bite to eat and talk for a bit, alright?" After a pause, "C'mon, it'll be fun."

Garbus and Albert stepped out of the office.

"Sure, okay, I gotta go. I'll see you later." I hung up without waiting for her to reply. Garbus walked into the executive offices in back as Albert stepped smiling to my desk. Too friendly, this guy Albert.

"Listen, Ed, I'm afraid we won't be needing you after lunch after all. I'm sorry, but I didn't realize that we had made arrangements to pull somebody from word processing to work the phones. So, if you could stay on until one?"

"Sure," I said, knowing one o'clock was the minimum amount of hours they would be charged through the agency. "I'm sorry about this morning, it was just . . ."

"Don't give it another thought," he interrupted. "That was my fault, I didn't give you the directory numbers, and besides, this has nothing to do with that. It's just a surplus of personnel."

"I'm sorry anyway."

"Thanks for helping out," he said and shook my hand, squeezed my shoulder, then signed my work form and added, "Sometimes we need people on short notice, would you be interested in filling in when that happens?"

Albert wrote down my number and put it in his pocket. He waited for me to shake his hand but I kept it at my side. Finally the phone rang and I answered it.

At 1:00 exactly I got up to leave, Albert didn't show his face to say good-bye, maybe he checked that number I gave him. I left the lines unmanned and headed out the door. Let Garbus answer them.

Standing on Fifty-Fifth Street Halina's Beauty and Jewelry Store was sealed and shuttered tight, a sign out front read STORE FOR RENT. I turned and headed up Broadway, reaching the corner as an open flatbed roared past with seven single PortoSans tied down with rope, behind it came the Absolut girls speeding through the light. My stomach yelled for something hard but food and reds don't mix so well so I'd have to hold off on the food. By the time I reached Columbus Circle I had passed an army of bums with dirty cups and squeegee sticks but kept on moving straight ahead and nobody gave and nobody got as misery like weeds grew everywhere and I've always felt sorry for weeds, but there were just too many, and too many scams.

The concierge checked my name and let me pass and stepping out of the elevator Denise was waiting in the hall. Faded jeans snug on her thighs, an oversized tee shirt with the pocket hanging off and her bare feet green paint toenails sinking into the plush gray rug, she gave me a smile and went inside.

The place hadn't changed much since my last visit: a wide open luxury loft with beige white walls and shiny wooden floors, fancy modern fixtures shooting light from severed tubes pointing up at the ceiling; glass tables on each side of the paisley pattern couch, and a mangled piece of metal standing in the corner. The dining table near the plate glass windows with the view of the park was all set for dinner, and Denise was using real china not glass; her stereo wall—for it took up one whole wall—seemed to be growing in stature and volume. I was glad she wasn't playing music.

"Why don't you have a seat, make yourself comfortable."

I sat on the couch and studied the crunched up metal in the corner. "Were you in an accident or something?"

"No, why?"

"I noticed your car all smashed up."

She grinned. "Can I get you something to drink?"

"Do you have any scotch?"

She scratched her chin as she went to the bar and disappeared behind it. Came back with a glass of scotch sans ice. I gulped it.

"So, how was work today?"

"Alright."

"How long have you been there, at that firm?"

"Just for today. I might be back, I don't know."

"They're a big firm, I've heard of them."

"This couch is new, isn't it? Did you have this last time I was here?"

"I don't know, when was that?"

"Last Christmas."

"Oh, you've been up here since then," she said defensively.

"No, I don't think so."

"You were here for my birthday, remember?"

"No, we met at that restaurant downtown for your birthday; Marion's. Actually it was a week after your birthday."

"But still, you've been up since Christmas."

"I don't think so."

"I'm sure of it."

"If you insist."

She gave me a weary frown like mom used to do, then sat up with her hands on her knees. "Well anyway, I got the couch in September. But it's going back."

"Why?"

"There's a rip in the back, the movers must have ripped

it bringing it in. They think cause they put it against the wall
I wouldn't notice."

"Well, if it's in the back who's going to see it?"

"That's not the point. When you buy something new you
should get something new."

She tucked her left leg under her right and watched me
finish my drink. I didn't ask for another.

"I'm making roast chicken. You like chicken. I bought a
lemon meringue pie for dessert; your favorite."

"There used to be a painting over this couch. I remember
a painting of a gray thing with a fence around it. What happened to that?"

"Barbara took it with her."

"Oh. I was sorry to hear about you and Barbara."

"Don't be . . . there's nothing to be sorry about."

"I thought you were serious about Barbara."

"Me and Barbara?! Never. She was nothing special,
believe me."

"You got to keep everything else in the apartment
though, right?"

"It was all mine to begin with. She came with a suitcase
and that painting. That's all she took when she left."

"You should be lucky she's not suing you for alimony,
or palimony, or whatever it is you can get sued for these
days."

"She won't."

"Can I have another scotch?"

"You drink too much."

"I know."

She got up to get the drink anyway. Brought it back.

"How long has she been gone?"

"I guess it's been four months."

"Well, I haven't been over in at least four months cause I
would've noticed Barbara being gone."

Denise gave me a hard blue look, then got up from the

couch and went into the kitchen. I snuck two reds in my mouth and gulped the burning metal scotch.

"Why don't you take a seat at the table?" she called from inside. "The chicken's ready."

"Do you mind if I smoke?"

"Since when do you smoke?"

"Not cigarettes."

"Oh . . ."

"It makes me eat better, relaxes my stomach."

"Well . . . okay, but at the window."

I lit a joint as Denise clanged around in the kitchen, blew the tender tired smoke onto West Fifty-Seventh Street below, watched the sun sear it's poison rays on the skyline of New Jersey. Denise came out with the steaming bird smelling of linoleum and sitting at the table I begged it not to talk to me.

We ate in silence broken occasionally for a word or two of mom and food. Denise jabbed a chunk of chicken on her fork and asked before putting it in her mouth, "Did I tell you who called me yesterday?"

"Uncle Ted."

"No, that was Tuesday."

"What day is today?"

"Friday."

There was silence as Denise sat there waiting.

"Well, aren't you curious who called?"

"Okay . . . Who called?"

"Elizabeth." She stopped and waited for my response. "She asked how you were doing. I told her you were doing well."

"Why did you tell her that?"

"Because it's true, isn't it?"

"I didn't know you still stayed in touch with her."

"We don't really, she just called out of nowhere. We talk once in a blue moon."

I couldn't eat anymore, chicken flesh and machinery paste, I spit it into the napkin and folded it into a ball.

"How is she doing these days?"

"She's fine. Did you know they bought a house on Hatfield Place. Remember the old Sparanza house, near the corner?"

"Whatever happened to all her big plans? Her career. I mean, it seemed to be the only thing that mattered to her. Or was that all bullshit?"

"No, at the time I'm sure it wasn't. I don't know what happened. Well, yes I do. She got pregnant. Once you have kids, and worse, a husband, it's hard to have a career. Your life becomes your children's life, and your husband's life. After a while you don't have one of your own."

"Other women seem to do it."

"Other women swallow cum!"

I looked up from my plate.

"You've barely touched your chicken," she said, a wicked delight in her eyes. I had to smile, she could always do that to me.

"I hope you have room for dessert," she added. Then went inside with the dishes and I slipped two more reds with scotch, got up from the table and strolled over to the window. The view of Central Park and parts of Harlem and the Bronx with lights and buildings clouds of claustrophobia, I turned and found myself in the bedroom. Huge, you could fit my room in here twice. I sat on the round bed as my palpitate heart popped like buttered popcorn. Barbara watched me from the dresser; still turned on by her masculine/feminine/androgynous charm. Denise had her facing the headboard, which was very unlike Denise.

"What are you doing in here!" she snapped, and no matter how young she looked when she was smiling there was no hiding her age when she wasn't.

"I'm sorry," I said, putting down the picture. "I just kind of strolled in."

"You shouldn't touch things that don't belong to you."

"I know. I'm sorry."

"C'mon, let's go inside. I got a pot of coffee on."

"Denise . . . I liked Barbara, I thought she was nice."

"Barbara was a fucking cunt! Now let's go inside. C'mon, I got some new CDs you might like."

"I'd rather not hear any music. If that's okay with you?"

"Whatever you want."

She turned and left the room and I followed after, wondering what Barbara thought of the whole thing. We sat on the couch one on each end when Denise asked if I wanted another drink and being a bastard I told her I did.

She came back with my drink and sat back down. "So, how are you doing these days? You seeing anybody?"

"What do you mean? Women?"

"No, farm animals! Of course women. You seeing anyone?"

"No, I'm not."

"Why not?"

"Well, it's kind of difficult, given the situation, don't you think?"

"No, not at all. You should at least be having sex. You certainly don't have to worry about getting infected with anything."

"Well, that's the damn truth," I said with a chuckle, then took another sip. "What about you?"

"I got my eyes on a few prospects. There's a fashion designer on the fifth floor of this building I'd like to get my hands on."

I smiled.

"What's the matter?"

"It's funny to hear you talk that way."

"Why?"

"I don't know, it just is."

"I've seen her with some guy though, I doubt she goes both ways. Hey, speaking of which, I have a friend . . ."

"No thanks."

"You didn't let me finish."

"You are finished."

"But this one's very nice, you'd like her."

"Let's change the subject."

Denise grabbed her flaming hair squeezed into a pony tail as burning candle cinder licks fell brightly on her shoulders. I gulped another mouthful of gasoline.

"Why did Elizabeth call you the other day? Tell me the truth."

"It's like I said, we talk once in a blue moon."

"Was the moon blue the other night?"

"It was sort of an aqua color."

"I must have missed that."

"She calls sometimes just to bullshit. She sounds bored out of her mind out there, stuck in that house. I could hear the kids screaming and running around, her yelling for them to behave, it was right out of a bad sitcom. Poor asshole."

"If that's how you feel, why do you still talk to her?"

"I'm not saying anything bad about her, that's just the way it is. I feel sorry for her in a lot of ways."

"Maybe she feels sorry for you, you ever think of that?"

"Why would she feel sorry for me?"

"Well, she has a husband and kids, a family, she's got people in her life. People that love her."

"Do you really believe that?"

I took a moment to think about it. "You ever see your kids? When you're visiting Mom?"

"I haven't in a while."

"Jerry can't stop you from seeing them, can he?"

"I can see them whenever I want. That's not the problem. It's the things he tells them when I'm not there."

"What things?"

"I don't know. Vinny wouldn't come near me the last time I visited, he was holding onto the couch bawling, you'd have thought I was Frankenstein. Cindy doesn't say two words to me, she just sits there like a zombie. They're terri-fied of me. And it's all because of that . . . bastard. I want to kill him sometimes, I swear . . ."

"Jerry was always a jerk."

"Anyway, what am I going to do? I can't force them to like me."

"Well, maybe when they're older," I said.

"Yeah, maybe."

Neither one of us spoke for a while, peeling thoughts like falling leaves from artichokes so green and heartless, the forks in the road. When I opened my eyes Denise was look-ing at me.

"You know, Eddie," she said with a softness and warmth I hadn't felt in years, "the reason I wanted to see you tonight was to explain a few things about the other day."

"Denise, you don't have to explain."

"No, I do. Because you must think I'm a horrible person. After all, it sure did come off that way."

"No, I didn't think that."

"What did you think? Did you think at all about what we talked about."

"Well, I gave it some thought, but I still think it's a bad idea."

"It's not something that came lightly to me, Eddie. I would never even dream of something like this if I wasn't in so much trouble. You're the only one I could go to for this. There's no one else. Do you think it was easy for me to ask you?"

"No, I'm sure it wasn't."

"I even asked Uncle Ted for a loan."

"You asked Uncle Ted for money?"

"That's how serious this is. Eddie, I'm in real trouble."

Denise turned on the light and I was struck by the darkness. The entire room was black. The walls floor and ceiling painted, shadowed, hidden in tumorous black. Hanging from the ceiling in the middle of the room were two chains at the bottom of which were leather ankle binds. On the cement floor right under the chains was a drain. I noticed a garden hose coiled on a hook against the far wall; against another wall was a standing wooden X with leather straps at each limb, on the adjacent wall was a wooden rack with pegs and hanging from the pegs were assorted whips and handcuffs, a cat o' nine tails, a riding crop, dozens of small metal weights and hooks, buckles, clamps, and a leather Eigel Vesti mask impaled with a peg through the eyehole. Behind me near the door was a makeup table and mirror, next to it a wardrobe rack with dresses and evening gowns, outfits like waitress, nurse, cheerleader. I took an evening gown from its hanger.

"That's for feminization," she said. "I dress them up sometimes. Show them what it feels like to be a woman. Actually, a lot of them really get off on it. Here, take a look at this."

Denise stepped over to a large wooden cupboard and swung open the doors revealing a row of multi-sized dildoes ranging in size from a few inches to the size of a muscular forearm. There were cock rings and lotions, oils and piercing pins, gags, a large tube of KY, sitting on the top shelf was a small jar of Midol; on the shelf below were needle nose pliers. I picked up the pliers and rubbed my finger along the nose.

"What do you do with these?"

"Oh, whatever needs to be done," she said with a smile.

I turned to the middle of the room, taking it all in, when I was suddenly aware of the strangest sensation, as if my nose had been clogged with the flu disappearing, or cyanide incense melting cerebellum.

Denise watched the fascination on my face, the sick sense of wonder; she always got a kick out of that, from when we were very young. Out in the yard near the fence next to

Whitson's, I was five years old when she showed me her body for the very first time; when she lifted her dress and pulled down her panties, the trauma and shock of that moment, of having the floor ripped out from under my feet with my stomach crunching egg shell omelettes in lost remorse of ignoramic bliss; knowing that nothing would ever be the same. Then Denise squatting down and showing how she pees with the lemon drop splashes beading up on her knees, my face turning white as she giggled and told me not to tell mommy now that I knew the secret of girls.

"So, what do you think of my office?"

"Huh? It's right out of a Vincent Price movie."

"Is that bad?"

"It depends on how you feel about Vincent Price."

"C'mere, I want to show you something."

Denise stepped over to the wall directly opposite from the rack and binds. She put her hands on the surface level with her waist and slowly pushed it in, lifted up a four foot square of plasterboard revealing a chamber the size of a small closet.

"I found it by accident," she said. "I always thought it was unusual that all the walls were cement except for this one. See? this inside wall was built a few feet in front of the original wall.

"I'll bet whoever had this place before me was a dealer or something. We could set up everything inside here, cut out a little hole, put a screen or some gauze over it, nobody would know anything. I could play music to drown out the camera, I could put fucking ear plugs in their ears if I wanted, I mean, don't you see, that's the perfection of it, it's what they want!"

And the gleam in her eyes shining dollars like flies shook me down to the bone.

4

YELLOW POLYESTER TIED AROUND MY WAIST like some eunuch clown from the Circus of De Sade, announcing "Girls Galore at the Kit Kat Club," I was handing out flyers on Forty-Sixth and Seventh. The monte boys were flipping their scams and as the crowd around them grew I took a break and watched from the curb. Flyers at my feet and the cabbies in the street the smell of piss and trash as yellow sun puked down like vomit from above, my eyes burned red from all this yellow.

Two dark suits came running up with cheap tin shields and the monte boys scattered like mice in a field. The bald one shaped like Mr. Clean stood on his toes peering over the heads of the crowd. The other suit craned his neck in all directions. I kept handing out my papers of perversity, when behind me in the alley saw the object of their pursuit. A platinum blond with a scowl on her face and a tiny dancer's body wearing black skirt black shirt black shoes black tights. She leaned against the wall trying to keep out of sight. I gradually strolled down the street bringing the suits' attention with me and when I glanced back she knew what I was doing. A suit talked into a walkie talkie while the bald one came up and asked me if I'd seen her. I took a step toward the corner and pointed east to Lexington. Once they crossed the street the platinum blond darted out of the alley and gave me a pinch on the arm. Before I could speak she disappeared around the corner.

Now that me and Denise were friends again she was taking me to a party tonight, the last one was a high-class master/slave sort of thing with nude butlers and guys pretending to be furniture. To prepare I went to see Lizard Len to pick up my prescription. Lizard Len had doctor scam insurance jobs all over the city and for a piece of the scrip I'd visit doctors and pretend to be different people. I went to Sixty-First Street and Lizard Len approached with his green eyes tan skin neck pouched out, his tongue whipping his lips with a layer of lotion, I imagined him stuck to a tree in Peru. Of course he was jumpy and nervous and checking his back as he took me into the alley where our business began.

"Yo Eddie, today I need you to make two visits then pick up two scrips and on the second scrip you gotta deliver it to a friend of mine, okay?"

"Sure."

"Okay, first go down to the Fink and tell him to refill your last one, tell him you can't sleep and you're in pain. Tell him if he doubles the count you'll double his fee."

"He won't do that. I asked him the last time and he said he couldn't do it."

"He's full of shit. He just wants you back for the extra visit so he can feel important, fuckin' jew bastard."

"Well, whatever he is, he won't double the scrip."

"Ask him anyway, if he says no then drop it, okay?"

"Sure."

"After that you got an appointment with the chink at two o'clock and don't forget your name for that one."

"I know, Peter Thomas."

"Peter Thomas? I thought you were Jerry Morton for the chink."

"No, I'm Peter Thomas for him. Lobster Harmon is Jerry Morton."

"You sure?" then Lizard Len flipped open his book of charts and schemes and numbered names. "Shit, you're right. Peter Thomas. Okay, then take both scrips to Sav-Rite after four-thirty and see Jeremiah. He's expecting you."

"Sure . . . Len, you think you could give me another couple to cash in? I'm running low this week."

"From now on we can't do more than two at a time.

Jeremiah says they been watching the cameras. We're gonna have to start hitting the outer boroughs soon. You got an address in another borough you can use?"

"Sure, I got plenty of them."

"Good, how you feelin'?"

"If I could just get some more reds."

Lizard Len licked his lips as wheels on windmills churned up thoughts of charity. "I'll tell you what," he snapped, "I'll try and get you an extra fifty on Wednesday, if you could wait till then."

"Sure, that'd be great."

Then Lizard Len slipped me a hundred and twenty for the visits and scrips and patted my back like a friend from the past.

The second I walked into the room I knew I'd be late for my appointment uptown. Every chair was taken up with dirty scratchy scrip refillers like myself and stepping to the glass-enclosed reception window she told me to take a seat and wait. Somebody got up to go inside and I sat down next to a bloated lady with a colostomy bag. Four of us were from Lizard Len but made believe we didn't know each other. I sat on the cold metal chair thinking of that blond in the alley. I wondered why they were after her, I should have asked. One by one the room emptied out and I went in where brittle Dr. Finkelstein put on his stethoscope and told me to take off my shirt. We went through the motions of coughing and breathing and heartbeat aerobics, at one time Finkelstein was a real doctor. Then he took off his glasses and the lines etched deep in his face like razor slices made him collapse in his seat.

"Is everything alright, Doctor?"

"Uh? Yes, everything's fine. I'm just so tired lately."

"You should take it easy. Get some rest."

He looked up at my blinking eyes like pizza pies and started chuckling to himself. "It's funny, you sound like the doctor and I'm the patient," he said.

"Sorry about that."

"You should really be in chemotherapy. How much longer do you think you can go on like this?"

"I'm doing fine, considering."

"Considering what?"

"Look, Doctor, do you think you could double up my prescription this time so I won't have to come back so often? It would really help."

"No, I can't do that." He wrote something down on a pad then handed me the paper. "I want you to consider seeing this friend of mine, a specialist."

"I really don't want to do that."

"I know, but I just want you to consider it. What's the problem, is it money?"

"Well yes, that's part of it."

"I'm sure we could work something out with him."

"Dr. Finkelstein, I appreciate your concern, I really do, but if you could just help me get through the pain . . . that's all I want right now. I'm not going back for chemo or cobalt or health foods or any of that other shit, please."

Dr. Finkelstein looked at me with gray slit eyes like peepholes from Portland but no matter how good his intentions I wasn't going back to the treatments. He wrote up my scrip and I went uptown where the chink never checked me or cared to, just shook my hand and within three minutes I had the scrip and was gone.

"You were supposed to be here at four-thirty," said Jeremiah through the glass, a skeletal face of teeth and bone.

"I got held up on the train. What's the matter, you got a date or something?"

"Yeah, I do."

"What's his name!?" And Jeremiah chortled stalling engine chugging helpless. I handed him my scrips and he disappeared behind the counter as I watched the condom

boxes ribbed and greased with lamb for ham as cleanliness
like godliness infected the entire country.

Not to be expected. Not what I expected at all. With everyone
looking so neat and attired like mannequin marvelettes I
wished that I was sober. Denise led me into the room where
her friends surrounded her with cries of elation while I stood
back against the wall, drinking two vodkas chewing ice cubes
thinking they were my teeth. Denise worked the room like a
visiting pope with the men acting normal and the ladies playing their wives—I'd rather have the nude butlers and human
coffee tables. The hostess with the mostest who Denise introduced as Lucinda was greeting her guests with a smile and a
kiss while her son Lamont, a fifteen-year-old preppie brat, was
drinking his own piss. Lucinda had a dog that was sniffing the
floor and I stood at attention till I saw in his eyes that he was
just a dog. Drank two more vodkas and stayed away from the
champagne unless it had bubbles.
  "So, you're Denise's brother?"
  I turned to see a dark blond skirt with eyes like walnuts
wrinkled brown.
  "Uh, yes, I am."
  "She says you're very shy."
  "Oh?"
  "She tells me you work for Garbus, Frankfurt, Brakowitz
and Jacobson."
  "I used to. I don't anymore."
  "Oh. I've had some dealings with them. I'm a lawyer.
Corporate mergers."
  "Really?"
  "Business is dead right now."
  "Everything is."
  "So, where are you working at the moment?"
  "Denise didn't tell you?"
  "No."

"I hand out flyers for a strip club on Broadway and Forty- Sixth Street. The Kit Kat Club."

"Oh."

"If you like I could see about getting you a job there, they're always looking for dancers."

"Denise warned me about you."

"What did she say?"

"She said that you would try to be antisocial."

"Have I been?"

"Not yet."

"The night is young."

I sipped from my glass but found it empty with no cubes to chew. The dark blond was looking across the room then snuck a glance at my face and caught me looking back.

"Your name's Eddie, right?"

I nodded my head and she looked back across the room just as a business suit came walking up with a smile. The suit whispered something in her ear and they both giggled, then the suit went back into the moving sea of people eating people.

"You see that character over there?" she said pointing to a greasy slick-back lawyer type in dark suit pinstriped blue. Her seven orange freckles moved into a geometric box. "Yes," I answered.

"He's an analyst for Dean Witter. He makes sixty thousand dollars a year. You know how much his bonus check was this year?"

"No, I don't."

"Two hundred and seventy thousand dollars. Just for a bonus. Can you believe it?"

"Dean Witter must be a nice guy." The dark blond gave me a look to see if I was kidding.

"The market is collapsing and he's making a fortune off it. Go figure."

"Like catfish."

"What?" she said, and now she was really confused.

"Like catfish," I repeated. "Catfish always eat the shit at the bottom."

She nodded her head and saw an emergency friend across the room, ran over to say hello. I stood there calm and pain-free shrinking violets color of the wall chewing my lip until I tasted blood. Denise came out of the smoke with Klaus Nomi in hand and a Screaming Hibiscus that played in a band; through the screeching of the train I heard the song of Frankie Teardrop.

"Are you having a good time?" she asked.

"I think I just scared away your friend."

"I saw her leap across the room. That was quick, it only took you five minutes."

"I could of done it in three but I'm pretty drunk."

"Try not to embarrass me."

"Maybe I'll throw up on the hostess."

"Puke on her son, he'd enjoy it."

"He smells like a urinal."

"Some people like the smell of urine," she said with a gleam.

"If you don't mind, let's not discuss body fluids tonight."

Denise popped out a giggle such a small and harmless thing like a child watching cartoons, then she touched my cheek and drifted into fog. I stepped into the hallway looking for a place to hide when sitting in a bedroom was a penguin tux from New Year's Eve getting head from that analyst from Dean Witter, maybe that's how he got his tips.

After the party Denise dropped me off at Jackie's cause I didn't want to go to after-hour clubs with her and her friends. Dezmond stood alone at the table while Old Man Costello sat at the bar with one eye up on the tv screen. Lying unconscious on the floor was Paris but Wally Harper and Camille were nowhere to be seen. I grabbed a cue and shot some pool with Dezmond.

"So what's up with you?" he asked.

"Nothing."

"Why not?"

"Huh?"

"Go ahead, rack up, I'll play you some Nine Ball. Yo Jackie! Set us up with two over here." And Jackie poured two double drinks and left them on the bar. "I ain't a fuckin' waitress, you want your drinks, you come and get them."

"Is that any way to treat your best customers?"

"My best customers pay their tabs."

Dezmond touched his heart as if stabbed in the back. "Jackie, you're hurting me."

"I'll hurt you alright."

Dezmond went over and got the drinks. I gulped mine down in two swallows.

"What's up with you and your sister all of a sudden?"

"What do you mean?"

"Why are you guys so chummy? Goin' to parties and shit; I thought you didn't get along."

"I never said that."

Dezmond started clearing the table in order and didn't scratch on the break. I chalked my cue and watched as he sunk the nine.

"Yo Jackie! Two more over here!" And the whole thing started up again with waitresses and customers and Jackie and Dezmond like positive/negative, it's a wonder they didn't implode.

I asked him, "Why aren't you at home with your family? You guys have a fight?"

"No. I gotta stay out and get as fucked up as I can. I got a physical tomorrow morning, if I'm in any kind of decent shape they're gonna make me go back to work. Which reminds me, do you have any more reds? I'd love to go in completely blitzed so when they take my blood I'll be out for another six months."

"How long you been out so far?"

Dezmond chalked his cue and looked up at the ceiling, "Almost a year-and-a-half now." He started chuckling coins and dollar bills, gulped his double scotch and scratched on the break.

Denise showed me all her new gadget toys and for some-body in deep financial shit she spared no expense.

"Well, what do you think? Can we work with this stuff?"

"Yes, but you didn't have to spend this kind of money. I told you to get the low-end equipment, all this other stuff we don't need."

"Eddie, I'd rather spend a little more to have everything go right. Besides, it's an investment, you don't go into a busi-ness venture without spending money."

"Denise, I don't consider this to be a business venture. As for investments, that's how you got into this trouble to begin with."

"Alright, don't rub it in."

"I still don't know why you didn't just get a video cam-era, it would've been so much easier."

"Because with a video you have to have a VCR to play the tape. With pictures you can just mail them around, the threat of them turning up at the office or home is much more of an incentive."

"I thought you said it would never come to that."

"It won't. I said 'threat.' Don't worry, I know just who to pick."

"It's still a felony."

"Are you backing out on me?"

I picked up some sort of developing tank. "I don't know what a lot of this stuff does. It's been about six years since I touched any of it; a lot of new things have come out. The heaters you don't need, that's only for color photography."

"Oh, the guy at the store told me I'd need them."

"What did you expect him to say?"

"How's the camera? I got the quietest one I could find."

"Minolta's a good brand." I put on a zoom lens and scanned the room trying to focus on things with great difficulty. I told her about it.

"But the guy at the store told me it would focus automatically, it's supposed to have some kind of automatic focus."

I checked and it did.

"See, you don't even have to look through the camera if you don't want to."

"What kinds of things will you be doing to these guys?"

"There's no sex at all. I won't even be naked. Some of them might be, but it's all planned ahead of time and they can end a session whenever they want."

"I told you to get Tri-X, you got Plus-X."

"They were out of Tri-X, all they had was this Plus stuff. The guy told me it was just as good."

"What do you expect him to say?! The Plus-X needs a lot more light, or else a flash. I don't think you want a flash going off, do you?"

"Maybe I could tell them it's a strobe light."

Looking at her laughing sapphires I had to smile.

5

I AWOKE IN A FIELD OF TALL HIGH WEEDS with flower pods and pumpkin seeds. Leading me through the brush by the hand with golden hair and thick black rims her college eyes so smart and brown, was Elizabeth. With ruby lips and ivory teeth her smile melted cancer meat as withered branches dying leaves smacked my face like leather sleeves. I tried to speak to call her name but silent words and feet gone lame held me there as she disappeared inside the medicine chest. Looking down at my hands they were small and young as fourteen years had been removed. Elizabeth ran deeper into my brain, past apple trees of oleander cherry blossoms coriander, caught my gaze as body hairs and epidermis sucked inside a coffee thermos made me ten years old, yet still in love with Elizabeth; her deep voice husky as autumn winds through fallopian tubes of oak calling me to follow. Catching sight of bridal trains of brittle lace and blackened brains like an unwanted guest at a party of saints, I felt myself shrink even smaller; Elizabeth laughed as the chasm between us grew wider, and taller. She turned around and I fell flat on my stomach, limbless in my infancy. I gazed into her maiden eyes and begged her to try to love me again, to take me away from the steel and cement from the cells eating matter like moths in a tent. When she stepped out of my dream with her face in the clouds and a bulge in her belly, it was clear why she could never love me. Why mothers and sisters and hookers with blisters despise us all to loneliness. It's what we deserve.

I opened my eyes to the crack in the ceiling, growing larger with each roar of the trucks rumbling past. Poisonous vessels and bloodshot veins. Madness painting my thoughts with graffiti, images jabbing disjointedly, flashing my eyes with Fantasia and Blue Velvet at the same time on the inside of my brain. Elizabeth. Rot in Hell.

I sat at the table, broken chairs and furniture from the curb, but then, I wasn't proud. I made some tea and lifted the pot and noticed a roach had fried. Clouds hung over the windows and I certainly felt as gray as they looked but my head wasn't pounding yet, so I held off on the reds. Watched her picture sitting across the room. Looking back at me. Like Barbara. The loneliness. The hollow holes in stomach pouches lurking underneath, the melting capsule pesticides of memories and grief. Elizabeth. Rot in Hell.

*   *   *

I was walking along the strip near Ninth Avenue when that platinum blond with the guilt-ridden face came by in the opposite direction. I followed staying close behind but nothing weird just passing time. She headed east with something strong on her platinum mind and pushing through the revolving doors I waited for the glass to stop spinning, then slowly eased through.

Aisles full of squinting housewives in consumer spasms bartering for prices long ago recessive, she moved past the winter coats and thermal clothes past mannequins on skis through hoops of plastic flame. Standing in the socks department feeling polyester, she dropped one to the floor but bending down was gone. Above my hair was Plastic Clair in winterwear as sales machines rang in the air with jingles of the jungle. Clair's green eyes reminded me of home, the emptiness of sterile houses, while in aisle three more socks were lifted from the shelves. With Clair and I as man and wife in spite of all the black inside, I'd come home to find her waiting happily in the kitchen with her fresh baked bread and loving kisses, our children playing gaily in the yard, then sneaking off to the living room her dress flowing velvet to the floor and making love and passion Catholic fashion while through the window Tommy and Susie flew up with the birds.

But Clair looked down with joking glee her teflon eyes and hair with fleas, again! to be tricked by that dog in the street. Shadows in shadowville, lips on my windowsill, ripped out hearts on spears deceitful. A lady ran up with a run in her stocking to see if I needed help. I bolted out the doors and waited in the cold.

The platinum blond came out of the mirrors and into the vessel of cells. I jogged up and walked directly next to her.

"One of these days you're going to get caught," I said.

"Fuck off," she spit, without glancing over.

"I'm not a cop or anything."

"Still fuck off."

"Yeah, you're probably right." I dropped back as she went on seven paces then stopped and turned around, came back wearing question pupil corneas.

"What's your problem? You like following people?"

"No, I was just . . ."

"You've been following me for a while now."

"No, I haven't. You're being paranoid."

"I've seen you before."

"The other day when those two guys were after you, up on Forty-Sixth and Seventh, remember?" She didn't. "I was handing out flyers and they asked me if I'd seen you?"

"So what."

"I saw you walking past just now and thought I'd see what's up. I didn't mean to bother you."

"I don't like people following me."

"Look, if I'm going in the same direction as you and I walk alongside, that's not following, is it?"

"Do what you want."

She whirled away and continued on as I caught up.

"Yeah, this is definitely not following," I said.

"You should still fuck off."

"I will as soon as I get to Ninth Avenue."

We reached the corner red light district, porno theaters crowded stores, fire trucks screamed through the red as cabbies stopped at the curb. All this commotion like riots in Baghdad as the light said walk and so we did.

"How come you're not handing out flyers today?" she asked.

"What, oh that? That's just a hobby, I'm actually a wealthy investor."

"I could tell from your shoes."

Looking down at toes and rubber worn out socks in canvas Converse, I said, "Maybe you could steal me some sneakers if you get a chance. Size nine."

A tiny smile bubbled through. I felt her eyes blanket warm like soup on my face and the shivers were gone. Popped two reds just to make sure.

"What's the matter, got a headache?"

"I can feel one coming on."

"Look, I got some things to do so I'm going this way. Ninth's another block west."

"Yeah, I know."

She stepped into the street waiting for the flow to stop.

"Say, what's your name?"

"I don't have one."

"What do people call you?"

"They don't." And with that my platinum blond moved in between the traffic melting into yellow paint and numbered cars.

The wall was all fixed up with thin white gauze and Denise hung a painting just to make sure. I stood in the office browsing through papers and prices and weird advertisements, a hundred thousand business cards from wealthy slimy lawyer types. Files in the cabinet. Denise came in and saw me reading a file but didn't tell me to stop.

"Do they know that you have these things?" I asked.

"Some of them."

"It's amazing, seeing their lives laid out like this. Some of this stuff is pretty weird, you've got to admit."

"I don't know if I would use that word."

"How about this guy," I said reading further. "He wants you to walk in dog shit then he wants to lick it off your shoes."

"You would have to pick that one. Besides, it's not real dog shit. I use chocolate fudge."

"It's funny, all these files like this."

"Why?"

"I don't know . . . it's like the Nazis."

"So now you're calling me a Nazi."

"You always wanted to be German."

Denise gave me a smirk and sat behind the desk, looked through files as the business of sexual blackmail took place.

Me and CandyBar sat on a chilly stoop watching daylight break, sharing a cigarette and three reds each. The purple sky and empty streets were quiet for the city. CandyBar stared with foggy eyes up into space or God or nothingness.

"It's starting to get cold," she said.

"Yeah, I know. We haven't had any sun for weeks now."

"No, yesterday was a sunny day."

"Was it?"

"Yeah."

"Oh." Then sat there watching nothing.

Denise paid for the cab to the ferry and we boarded just as the doors slid closed. I stood outside with whipping winds across my cheeks, smoked a joint till a homeless beggar asked for a hit and I gave him the roach. Shoeshine men ate pretzel bits on soot stained knees with dirty pillows under arm in broken-English poverty grunts. The Statue of Liberty moldy and green snot metal leaf but that's what the French get for eating truffles. Denise came out with my hot dog and soda, red hair scorching off her shoulders as a tear crawled down from her lash.

"How can you stand it out here? It's so cold."

"It wakes me up."

"I hate the cold."

"Go inside, I'll come in a little while."

But she zippered her jacket and turned up her collar, hands in pockets of black leather and boots and damn she looked so high-class wealthy New York.

When we got off Denise tried to hail a cab but cabs didn't hail on this side of the water. I told her to take the bus.

"I don't take a bus even when I'm in the city."

"This isn't the city."

"I don't have any change, they don't accept bills, do they?"

"Not for thirty years they haven't." We went to get change and waited on the platform counting moments like cigarette butts. Finally it came. I moved to the back with Denise following and we both sat facing front. Busy streets of stores and malls and colored balls as men in hardhat mobster suits poured another foundation. The bumpy ride made sister squirm but I felt lightheaded until the Seaview Home and Hospital came into view.

The bus squealed dead and seven gray cadavers jerked with a start. Denise marched through the crowded halls past roaming folks of loneliness I followed steps behind.

Mom hadn't moved an inch in seven months as Denise sat by her side and I stood in the doorway. Watching Mom just waste away a rancid leg of lamb. Denise became a rigid mask but underneath the fragile glass a crack came etching through.

"You don't have to be so tough all the time," I said. "It's only me here. Cry if you want to cry." Then drips and drabs and liquid scabs came trickling from her eyes. She sobbed on my shoulder and I patted her softly with kindness fraternal.

"It's okay, Denise. You were the best daughter anyone could ever have, and she loved you very much. So don't feel bad." I held her head and kissed her scalp, squeezed her coated catapult. She gave me a look that shuddered my skin with her eyes sharpened blue and betrayal within . . . He won't leave me alone, wherever I go . . . if only I could kill him somehow.

I snapped back doorway standing no time passed as Denise was pulling down the blankets.

"What are you doing?"

"I want to make sure they're taking care of her."

"What can you tell from looking at her legs?"

Denise rolled her onto her side as a withered woman wearing white came wheeling past the door.

"See, this is what I mean. Look at this!" Denise pulled

back the faded robe and sitting there like a cherry gone bad
was the object of her contempt.

"I'm paying two thousand dollars a month for her to be
here and they allow her to get bedsores!"

"Two thousand dollars a month?"

"Yes, between the medication and all the extras."

"I thought it was only a couple hundred."

"Eddie, let me know when you land on earth."

"It might not be a bedsore, you should ask before you go
and make a scene."

"I know full well what a bedsore is. As for a scene . . .
Where is the supervising nurse?" With that Denise charged
into the hall, past the crutches and chairs with her voice
falling weakly on swollen, deaf ears.

I sat on the bed next to mom and the dead, noticed the
crucifix nailed above her head. Her lips had dried like
leather strips I wet them with my fingertips. Sitting there
with my guts in a knot as the peeling foam ceiling snowed
down around my shoulders, I wondered which way it would
be for me, snuffed out soft and swift like a wisp of smoke, or
long and lethargic like a snake in the desert. Then quality
and quantity pecked at my eyes like fighting roosters. The
numbers always won.

Mom, is this what's in store for me?

Denise came in with the supervising nurse up to the bed
pointing her finger and blame. Mom just lay there feeling
kind of embarrassed. I kept my tongue as the nurse gave
back as good as she got, excuses jabbed like javelins and I
could see Denise about to call her a nigger.

"Alright, wait a minute," I said. "Let's not fight about it.
That's not doing anybody any good."

The nurse turned to me with reason in her eight-ball
eyes and said, "That bruise is not a bedsore. That's from
injecting her medication. We can't give her every injection in
the arm."

"How can a bruise that size be from a tiny little needle?" Denise said and not as a question.

"The skin is very soft, and weak, she's unable to exercise. We're doing the best we can, your mother is getting very good care."

"For the fees that I'm paying I expect more."

The nurse turned to me as if Denise wasn't even there and said, "If you would like to speak to Dr. Awnbey, the executive director, I'll be happy to show you to his office."

"No, that'll be alright," I said. "But if you could just check in on her more frequently . . . ?"

"Yes, I'd be happy to."

"Thanks." And with that the friendly nurse left.

Denise gave me a look that needed no words. She started fixing Mom back up in the bed, leaning inches away and kissing her cheek and forehead, whispering words to a ghost in a tomb, while I stood there trying to feel something, anything. Empty bags in taxicabs had more life and translocations. I went into the men's room to piss and pop some reds. Waited out front.

Quiet thoughts on the bus ride back watching school kids toss their books high in the air and high school girls who never lose their thighs.

"Do you want to make a stop on the way back?"

"A stop? Where?"

"We're not too far from the old neighborhood. We could drop in and see some old friends."

"Who's still there?" And then I felt a burst of sweat as vacuum cleaners sucked my lungs, but maybe this was Mexico.

"Well, what do you say?"

"No, I'd rather not. Let's just keep going."

I felt her lasers warmly understand. "You're still in love with her, aren't you? . . . Eddie, if I would have known, I would have told you. I didn't know, she didn't confide things in me. I would have never let you get hurt if I could have helped it."

"It wasn't anybody's fault, it just happened. She didn't want to hurt me either."

The bus turned right and both of us looked at the stores and the houses of yesterday's memories, simple as children.

"You know, we should probably get started this weekend."

"Started on what?"

The view through the lens was as dark as a closet with candles and floodlamps and pockets of polio. The room was empty as I heard them talking, Denise laughing and playing polite. The voices grew louder my stomach wrenched tighter and the pounding began but I was too frozen terrified to reach into my pocket. I couldn't see the door as it opened, held my breath as they came into view; Denise in black leather tight pants squeaking shapely thighs, long leather gloves up to her elbows. Her friend was a broker in real estate; mansions and brownstones and homes in the Hamptons, a wife and two kids and a country club membership, I'd read his file. Built like a thumb on a midget with a deep rolling voice and a suit made of tar, he leaned his briefcase against the far wall and turned to the painting his face facing mine.

"I see you've put some artwork up," he said as my eyes turned to stone.

"Do you like it?" she said coldly.

"Yes, it's beautiful, you should put a light over it though."

He took a step closer and she snapped, "I didn't give you permission to go over there!" He stopped in his tracks and turned around. Denise stood there angry determined, hands on hips and that gleam in her eye.

"I think you're getting a little too independent around here. I don't like the way you take it upon yourself to do whatever you like. It's disrespectful. I don't know who the fuck you think you are!"

"I'm sorry, I didn't mean . . ."

"Sorry doesn't mean shit to me! You've been here for three short minutes and you've already offended me. Take off your pants!"

The broker undid his belt and lowered his pants where his tight blue bikinis were squeezing his cheeks.

"What are you, some kind of a faggot?! You want to wear panties—I'll give you some real panties to wear. You should be ashamed of yourself!"

"Yes . . . yes mistress."

Then Denise went to the rack and took a long leather strap.

6

SAY, DO YOU HAVE A NAME YET? The last time we spoke you didn't."

"No, not yet."

"Well, keep looking, I'm sure you'll find one soon."

She rolled her eyes and briskly kept her pace in the opposite direction.

"Who was that?" Dezmond asked then turned to watch her shapely legs in black stretch stockings bouncing from her skirt.

"I don't know."

Dezmond chuckled candycorn and stalked on daddy-long-legs. I spit out my gum and puked in the gutter.

Lizard Len sent me to Queens and the Bronx with my new names and symptoms and in Queens I forgot my name till I found it written on my sleeve. Now the trips took hours longer, but Len gave me that extra fifty we'd talked about.

*　*　*

It was really late just moping along Ninth Avenue bumping into puddle soaked employment wipers waiting at the tunnel. Walking past Forty-Fourth a streak of white blurred into a stoop and just as quickly streaked back. She was filling a shopping cart with boxes as I approached and for a second she almost looked pleased to see me.

"Hey, can you do me a favor?" she asked.

"That depends, what?"

"Watch this cart till I come down. Make sure nobody takes anything."

Without waiting for a reply she disappeared inside as I stood there reading Chinese letters printed sideways on tattered cardboard boxes. She came down a minute later with bags of clothes and folding chairs, fit them in and started down the street with the cart.

"What did you do, just empty somebody's apartment?"

"For your information this is my own stuff," she said with a snarl.

"Oh, sorry, I didn't mean anything by that."

"Then why'd you say it?"

"Well I had to say something . . . Where we heading?"

"I don't know where *you're* heading. But I'm taking a train."

"With the shopping cart? I don't think they allow those on trains."

"Report me."

"I'd like to see how this is done, I think I'll tag along."

Wheeling on the crooked sidewalk, one wheel locked and three at war, I pulled from the front till we reached the stairs. I bent to lift the wheels when she pulled them away.

"No. Go down first and make sure the booth is closed."

"Oh." I crept down and the coast was clear. We reached the gates shuttered closed with chains and warning exit

threats, no one in sight, just dirty pavement stained with souls
of fatal mugging victims. I looked around and the chain
clanged hard upon the ground. My platinum blond was holding a huge pair of clippers with that look of guilty satisfaction
on her face. She truly loved her work.

I sat across the car and watched her read the signs above
my head, her light blue eyes like milky ink in muddy water.
Pale skin yellow, rigid nose and forehead round, pert lips
with frown lines etched beside them. Barbed wire seemed
more inviting. Yet underneath that tough veneer I saw the
child hiding there. No more days of birthday dresses holding
dolls with orange tresses, look up fine and swallow hard
with easy teeth, but don't tell mommy or secret cells and jingle bells will never be the same. I waited for the dog to
appear but my platinum blond yawned and scratched at a
scab on her knee.

Wheeling down on St. Marks Place my platinum blond
leaned her arms on the cart with tired steps barely awake,
limpid lids and jaundiced cheeks, I wanted to carry her if
only I could. We reached Avenue A and she stood up aware,
made a left at dark bodegas broken glass from shattered win-
dowshields, a tire sat in our path, I picked it up and rolled it
into the street, it spun three times then trembled quiet.
Watched it die as I would die.

A big white door in a wall of gray was opened and I followed the cart inside, up the steps and holding onto the rail
which was weak and made of rust.

"It's only up two flights," she said. "Help me bring it up."

She got in front and pulled on the cart with me underneath as the stairs cried under my weight. We passed doors
with colored lights and voices whispering behind them. On
the second flight she wheeled over to a door at the end using
her key to let herself in. I stood outside gasping for air and
reaching for reds, noticed I was being watched from down
the hall. Eyes of sharpened steel to stab the night.

"I need some water," I said rushing inside.

"The kitchen's over there, I don't have any glasses yet. Use your hands."

I did. Then turned and saw two small rooms like stuffy closets, even my place was bigger. She started unpacking the shopping cart.

"Help me unload this stuff. I gotta get back up there for the rest."

"Why are you moving so late? It's after three o'clock."

"That's the best time to move," she said with that smile.

"Oh, I get it."

"C'mon, help me with this box."

"Before I do anything else I'd like to know your name."

"Why is that so important?"

"It's not, I'm just curious. I've lived three blocks up from you all this time, so that makes us neighbors. I'm entitled to know your name."

"But now that I'm moving down here, we'll be complete strangers again."

"We won't be complete strangers, just distant."

"That's the same in my book."

"And what book is that?"

"My book."

"Does your book have a name?"

"Yes."

"What is it?"

"Complete Strangers!"

"What's the author's name?"

"She uses a pseudonym."

"Let me ask you this, is it people in general that you dislike, or just me?"

"Just you."

I started lifting boxes out of the cart when she said, "Kaval."

"What?"

"Kaval. If you want to know it so badly, that's what it is."

"Kaval? Is that your first name or last?"

"Just Kaval."

"My name's Eddie. I wish I could come up with something really clever like Kaval, but it's just Eddie."

"Just Eddie, do you think we could hurry up so I can get the rest before sunrise?"

"Sure . . . Kaval." And she gave me a look as the reds warmed my neck.

Denise spread the pictures out on the table as if they were in some sort of order. Grainy black and white eight-by-tens with not much detail. Most of them were still wet.

"What do you think?"

"I think they're horrible," she said with a wrinkled nose. "You can't make out faces. They're too dark, even with the added lights."

"I tried to lighten them up. They're not that bad."

"We've got to make them lighter."

"I don't think we can. We're using the fastest film there is."

"What if I put more lights on in the room?"

"Well, sure, that would help. But you don't think these are good enough?"

"No! You can't make out the faces. What good are they if you can't see who it is?!"

"Alright, calm down. It's just . . . you told me two or three sessions and that's it. I thought you really hurt that last guy. He was crying like a baby."

"Did you see how quickly he stopped once it was over? It's all part of the drama. They completely let themselves go, then afterwards they go back to being who they were."

"What about the welts on his legs. They weren't a fantasy."

"Look, there's this one client that would be perfect, he's not into pain and he's completely guilt-ridden by the whole thing."

"Denise, I don't want to photograph every nut that comes through your dungeon. All it takes is one of these guys to go to the cops and we're both fucked."

"That's why I'm being particularly careful who I choose. Believe me, this last guy would rather jump off a building than admit to his scene. It would completely destroy him. Personally and professionally."

"Thanks for sharing that with me. I feel much better now."

"He's a multimillionaire, I'm asking for a pittance. He'd never even miss it."

"How much are you asking for exactly?"

"Two hundred and fifty thousand dollars. That's what I need. Of course you get a piece of that, you could move into a better place, get better care and not have to worry about the city hospitals . . ."

"Don't worry about me. This isn't about me."

"It would be nice to live in a nice apartment, wouldn't it?"

"I'm comfortable where I am."

"You're difficult, that's what you are."

"Two hundred and fifty thousand dollars will take care of everything? After that it's over, right?"

"After that, I retire from this whole miserable business. Promise."

"So what's this last guy into?"

I stood in the doorway and rang the buzzer. A fuzzy metal voice scraped through the screen. "Who's there?"

"It's me, Just Eddie."

"Just Eddie who?"

"C'mon, you know who it is."

"What do you want?"

"I was in the neighborhood and thought I'd say hello."

"So say it."

"Kaval, I want to come in and visit."

She buzzed me in and I went up the stairs. Her door unclicked several times then opened a crack till she saw my face, stepped aside to let me in.

"This is unexpected."

"I hope I'm not bothering you."

"Well . . ."

"Good."

"So, what brings you to this neighborhood?"

"I came to pick up some heroin. I've been running low."

"That's not funny."

"I know. I hadn't seen you in a week, I was curious how you were doing."

"You're a pretty curious guy."

"I see you're all settled in, the place looks nice."

Boxes stacked against the walls, books lined up on the floor, a small record player sat under a white metal folding chair, plastic milk crates formed a table, in the bedroom a lumpy mattress lay naked under a window crossed with bars.

"Yeah, the place looks lovely," she said. "Can I offer you some caviar?"

I chuckled for she caught me off guard, then looked at the nearest chair to my right. "Do you mind if I sit down? I'm kind of tired."

"Go ahead," she said, then sat on the chair opposite mine.

We sat there silent looking at each other, tension holding chess opponents bishoped in between, perched eye hawkish as she tried to scope the deal. I tried to reassure her. "I was really in the neighborhood."

"Oh. So this is just a chance visit?"

"Well, now that I know your name, I figured what's the big deal if I stop by and visit once in a while? To talk."

"And what will we talk about?"

"Well . . . we can discuss the latest shoplifting techniques."

"Why do you keep bringing that up?" she said with eyes shining hard. "You get your rocks off on small-time criminals or something?"

"No, I don't."

She folded her arms and stretched out her legs.

"You don't have to be so defensive. I don't want anything from you. I had nowhere else to go, so I wound up here."

"You don't want anything from me?" she asked but more as a challenge. "Why not?"

"I don't know."

"You don't want to fuck me?"

"No."

"How come? Are you gay?"

"No! I don't see what that has to do with anything."

"Pretty sensitive there, aren't you?"

"I'm not being sensitive at all."

"What do you have against gays?"

"Nothing."

"Then why did you react so strongly?"

"I didn't react strongly."

"Some of my best friends are gay."

"I feel sorry for them."

"I can't believe you just said that."

"I had to say something."

"Did it have to be something stupid?"

"It's not stupid, it's true."

"Why do you feel sorry for them?"

"I feel sorry for anybody who has to go through this with you."

"Nobody's forcing you to stay. The door's right there."

"It's a nice door too. I like what you've done with the gray."

She gave me a smirk, reloading for the next barrage. I tried to deflect the attack.

"Did you hear about the guys who got beat up in our neighborhood?"

"Where?"

"Ninth and Forty-Sixth."

"That's not my neighborhood anymore."

"Oh. So you didn't hear about it then."

"No, why would I?"

I shifted my weight in the seat, the cold rigid metal ached in my bones. "So what happened?" she continued. "You started a story then left it hanging."

"I thought you didn't want to hear it."

"I didn't say that, I just said it wasn't my neighborhood anymore."

"Oh. Well these two guys were walking along Ninth Avenue holding hands when this car from Jersey pulled over and a bunch of kids got out swinging baseball bats. Beat the hell out of them. One of them really bad, at least it looked bad, the blood and all."

"Did you do anything to help them?"

"No, I didn't."

"Why not?"

"Because I'm a coward."

She let out a laugh like a sheet being ripped.

"Maybe this was a bad idea, visiting like this."

"That's the first intelligent thing you've said since you've been here."

"Do you mind if I get a drink of water before I go? I'm thirsty."

"Help yourself, you know where the kitchen is."

Getting up I felt her lasers burning through my clothes. Out of sight I felt a little cooler. In the cabinet over the sink was a line of medicine bottles, pills and tablets and liquids galore and reading the labels one fell to the floor. I picked it up and Kaval was on me like a virus.

"What are you doing?!" she fumed with her face tense and swollen and red. She ripped the bottle from my hand but not before I could read three letters.

"Get out of here! Now! Get out!" And she pushed me aside with her palms in my chest.

"What's the matter, Kaval?"

"You know what's the matter!"

"No, I don't."

"I don't need fuckheads snooping in my life."

"I wasn't snooping. I was looking for a glass to get some water."

"I don't care! Now get the fuck out before I hurt you! Get out you bastard!!!"

"Alright, I'll get out."

She shoved me hard toward the door and cried, "Now you know why I don't want you near me! Why the sight of you makes me sick to my stomach!"

"Alright, great, I make you sick. But you're wrong about everything else."

"Just get the fuck out!"

"I'm getting out!" But stopped at the door and turned around. "Kaval, look at me for a second."

"Get out!"

"Just look at my me! My hair, my face, the shape of my head. Do you think I always looked like this? . . . I have brain cancer. Inoperable, untreatable, terminal!"

"STOP IT!" she screamed with her face scrunched up and distorted. "Get out!" She grabbed a knife from the drain as slasher films and psychotronics flashed before my eyes, but something held me tight.

"Alright, you don't believe me? Take a look at this!" I turned around and lowered my head. "You can see the scar. Go ahead, look! They tried to get it out but it was too big, and it had spread."

I felt her breath warmly brushing the hairs on my neck, the room seemed to enlarge.

"Don't you understand?" I said turning to her. "It's perfect this way! Where's the harm? Tell me, where's the harm?"

Kaval searched me with her eyes, saw me as someone else but I didn't know who.

"It's true?" she asked, the scratch gone from her voice. "What you just told me?"

"Why do you think I keep taking these red pills? It's the only way to keep my head from exploding."

Kaval sniffled and wiped it away, sat on a chair with the knife on her lap. I went to the other chair. Voices from Jamaica oozed in through the closet.

Denise warned me to be on my toes cause this one was important. I waited in my cubbyhole like a rat in a box with my lens open wide. Denise came into view with Mark Number Two who was short and soft like poor Number One, forty years old and impeccably dressed in pinstriped gray with shiny shoes and fancy hair all strands in place, and it occurred to me how normal they all looked. Denise had set up a table near the wall in perfect proximity of the lights and the lens. A dinner setting for dignified dining was laid out with a candle and silk and a high-backed leather chair. Mark Number Two stood off near the back wall talking on a foldable phone, mumbo-jumbo market daggers dipped in poison profit. Denise wore a short black waitress dress with a white blouse and thick black suspenders crossed in back; with a pin in her hair and pink full lips and dark blush eyes she looked anything but what she was. Then she turned on the stereo but not too loud. He said good-bye and folded his phone into a cute little square.

"What's with the music?"

"I thought we'd have some dinner music for a change."

"You've rearranged things, as well."

"Do you mind?"

"No."

"Then we'd better get started, the management can't hold your reservation indefinitely."

He smiled at that, then fixed his tie and smoothed back his hair, stepped over to Denise waiting at the table.

"Good evening sir," she said real polite, too polite. "Will you be dining alone tonight?"

"Yes, I believe I will be."

Denise held out his chair and he sat down. My finger poised and ready on the button steady shaking, I felt a presence close behind, watching over my shoulder, but I didn't dare move or turn around.

Denise took leather straps and started tying the mark's hands to the arms of the chair, tight so he couldn't move.

"How's that?" she asked warmly.

"Fine."

She stood upright and took a pad from the pocket on her apron. "We have a few specials tonight . . . Would you like to hear them?"

"No, I think I'll have the usual."

"The usual."

"Yes."

"You're our most consistent customer," she said as she wrote on the pad. "You always know exactly what you want."

"When you find perfection you stick with it," he smiled.

"I'll be right back with your order. Would you like a cocktail before dinner?"

"I'd like a cocktail, but with dinner please."

"Surely."

Denise took his plate and glass and went out of view for a moment. The mark sat there taking deep breaths and looking straight ahead, concentrate intensity as beads of crystal rolled down his cheeks. Denise came back with his plate and glass and put them down in front of him, he looked up at her with fear and desire as he let out his breath. Tried to lift his hands tied tightly to the arms of the chair.

Denise said, "You seem to be having some trouble. Would you like me to assist you?"

"That's very kind of you."

Denise brought over a chair and sat down next to him, the pink floodlights overhead made her smile look young and girlish.

She said, "Looks like the chef was very generous tonight."

He didn't answer, just looked at her helpless and pale. She took the fork which tinkled the plate, then raised it to his lips which he opened wide like choirboys in church.

"That's it, nice and wide." She put it in his mouth as his chin started quivering, slowly and surely he chewed like a dog eating bones. Now I knew who was behind me.

"Well?" she said. "How is it?"

He gulped and coughed and swallowed slowly. With unsteady words he said, "Very tasty. My compliments to the chef."

"She'll be happy to know that," she said with a smile as she lifted the fork to his face for another.

I hadn't snapped a shot. Frozen stiff by words and manners never seen before. All these things inside of her, all these things complex, to see her softly stroke his cheek and wipe his sweaty brow, sincerity like baby pictures made me burn with green.

"So, how is everything at work these days?"

"Fine," he said with glassy eyes as he chewed.

"That's good. The family fine?"

"Yes. They're very well, thank you."

"That's good too. Oh, you're dribbling. Let me get that for you," then she scooped it with the fork and put it back in his mouth. "You don't want to waste any bit of it, do you?"

"No, I don't."

"That's right, not a morsel. Tell me, how is the texture tonight?"

"The texture? Oh, uh, it's very soft and creamy, smooth. Practically melts in my mouth."

"Good, but make sure you chew it real good. I wouldn't want you to choke on it. Mush it around on your tongue, squeeze it between your teeth, savor every nuance . . . that's it. Let me see, open wide."

He opened his mouth and Denise leaned close to peek inside. "Hmm, it's still a little chunky, chew it a bit more. With every chew you get more flavor . . . That's it. You're doing wonderfully. It's a pleasure to have such a cooperative guest . . . By the way did I tell you, I decided to sell those Florida water bonds you advised me to buy."

"You did. Why?"

"Don't talk with your mouth full, please. Chew it some more then swallow." Two loud gulps. "Very good."

"Wha . . . why are you selling?"

"I wanted to liquefy some of my assets, there are some opportunities I'd like to get into in the near future. I needed to have some cash ready and available . . . Speaking of liquefy, open your mouth please."

He did and received.

"Tell me something, do you notice a change in flavor after you've been eating for a while? Does the taste get weaker?"

"No, not weaker, but you do acquire an appreciation. Just like with caviar."

"That's good."

I started clicking shots one after the other, zooming in on lips and teeth to get it over as soon as possible. Slithering snakes had climbed up my throat and wrapped around my tonsils, I couldn't even swallow as saliva spilled down my chin. Slowly all the sounds outside grew dim like outer space sucked inside a funnel. Watching through the lens the mark and Denise moved in slow-motion pentathol. I felt my left side die. Novocaine on tender flesh or rubber made of fiberglass I couldn't feel a thing, from my eyes down to my toes. I tried to hold my balance when through the lens the mark looked straight into my soul. That jab of recognition, he knew I was there! He let out a laugh from his nose to his tail, then he spoke to my mind: Evil as evil can be! My stomach squeezed a sailor's knot as breathing stopped and legs gave out. I fell forward against the wall and dropped to the cement spewing snakes of bloody afterbirth. The mark started shrieking like a woman in labor.

"Somebody's here! Somebody's HERE! Untie me! You fucking bitch! UNTIE ME!!!" He started hopping away from the wall on the legs of his chair as Denise tried to quiet him down.

"Untie me! Get me out of here! Somebody's watching me! You fucking bitch! You fucking BITCH!!!"

"You're crazy," she yelled, yet tried to be calm. "There's no one here but you and me."

"There's somebody behind that wall! UNTIE ME!!!"

His voice wriggled through my ribs, a ticklish tinge like feathers made of razor blades. I couldn't move.

"Alright, just calm down and I'll untie you."

"Do it, now!"

"Alright! There's no one here for god's sake. I don't know what's come over you."

"Shut up! Someone's behind that wall. I heard him. I'm going to the fucking police! I'm going to report you to the police!"

"Think about what you're saying," she said, and the surgical way of her words . . . The police were not mentioned again.

"Just untie me!"

"Alright, you're untied."

"I should fucking kill you, I should fucking kill you!"

"Keep threatening me."

He suddenly doubled over choking and heaving out wads of black intestine.

"Would you like something to drink?"

"FUCK YOU!"

A chair came crashing against the wall, then a door was opened and slammed shut with cursing and crying behind.

A second later Denise's voice came punching through the wood. "What the fuck happened back there!?"

The panel was pulled and light burst in with Denise in silhouette and leaning over. "Shit! What happened?! Are you alright?"

"I . . . I fell. Help me up. I can't feel anything."

Denise climbed into the hole and sat me up against the wall. The cool moist air brought me back to sanity.

"Look at this mess. God, are you alright?"

"I think so. I'm sorry. I just blacked out."

"Did you get the shots?"

"I believe so."

"What about that?" The camera was on the floor but not broken just covered with goo.

"Don't worry, the film's still good. Help me up, please."

The room was reeking rancidly, at the table the plate was still in place and on it lay the fork with webs of syrup connecting the teeth. The overgrown leech began to throb like rubber lungs on Barbie dolls.

7

W HERE'D YOU GET ALL THIS MONEY all of a sudden?"

"What money?"

"This money on the bar. You never have any money. What'd you do, win the lottery?"

"No. I've been doing some freelance work."

"Freelance work? What kind of freelance work?"

"I've been working as a photography assistant. Denise got me a job with a friend of hers. He's a fashion photographer."

"What do you do?"

"I assist."

"You assist?"

"Yeah."

"Don't you mean *insist*."

"What do you mean?"

"You insist on telling this lie!"

"I'm not lying." But Dezmond chortled proud obnoxious. "Buy me a drink, ya fuck."

Kaval and I were heading to some eastside vegetarian place with sprouts and plants and trees in water and the moment I stepped through the door I started nibbling on a fern. Kaval called me a jerk. We sat at a table near the back, the waiter lit our plastic net mosquito jar and shook out the match as silver sulphur burned inside my eyes. Kaval opened her menu and so did I. Fancy typeface ribbon twists weaved across the page as sticks of ink came dancing on my lap. I closed the menu and looked at Kaval.

"What are you going to have?" she asked.

"I don't know. I'll have what you're having."

"You're going to order what I'm ordering?"

"Sure."

"That's not very independent."

"It all tastes the same to me. Do they have hamburgers here?"

"I told you, this is vegetarian. They don't serve meat."

"Alright, then I'll have a hotdog."

"A hotdog is meat!"

"Not in New York City it isn't." She ignored that.

"I'm having the sesame soup with tofu, and an order of broccoli stalks in cream sauce."

"I'll have the cream of crabgrass, and an order of sod on the half shell."

Her smile flashed but quickly snuffed out; she hated to show amusement. "If you didn't want to come here you should have said so."

"I can't read the menu."

"Why not? It's in English."

"I know it's in English! I mean my eyes, they can't stay focused on the letters."

"Oh," she said then wrinkled her brow and like autumn rain her face fell softly. "I'll read it to you."

"No, that's alright." But she started reading anyway. "Please, don't read it to me. I'll just have what you're having."

"Why don't you have a soyburger. It tastes just like meat, it really does."

"Alright, that sounds good. Soyburger."

The waiter stood there tall and thin like Mr. Pretzel salted skin as Kaval gave out our wants.

"I'll have a papaya juice," she added. The waiter looked at me in the dark flickering light with eyes of glowing red almonds.

"I'll have the same."

He turned and walked away as dancing shadows found her cheeks.

"I always ate healthy even before I was diagnosed."

"Really? Why?"

"Because you feel better when you eat better. I don't see how you can eat half the junk that you do."

"It's simple. You put it into your mouth and chew."

"You know what I mean."

She looked down at the candle and stopped speaking. Picked at the peeling plastic web of the glass. Her face was hazy orange, licking flicks from burning tongues like sunsets in New Zealand. I pinched her stubby fingertip and held it in my hand. I'd never touched her before, not like this, and she didn't seem to mind.

I told her, "I never thought we would be here."

"Why? It's a pretty popular restaurant."

"No, I mean us here together. Me and you. I never thought you would like me."

"Who says I like you?" she said with edge, then just as quickly softened. "I like you very much. There's a lot to like."

She looked into my eyes as two lost dogs on rainy highways hit by cars and laying sideways appeared inside the candle flame.

We walked to Second Avenue and made a left. The wind ripped through the side streets as traffic lights swung wildly in arcs. Kaval zippered up her leather but halfway up it jammed, I tried to help but only jammed it worse. Popped two reds to ease the pain.

"Where do you get all these pills? You can't be getting them legally."

"No, I do. It's kind of legal. A friend of mine runs an insurance franchise."

"Insurance franchise?"

"Yeah, we get prescriptions from doctors, then cash them in."

"That's not legal."

"I said it was kind of legal."

"Who's this friend of yours? That creep at the bar?"

"No," I chuckled, "that's Dezmond. I get the pills from a guy named Lizard Len. His real name's Leonard Witkowski, but if you call him that or even just Len he gets pissed. I never asked him why."

"How did you get involved with him?"

"I met Lizard Len about four years ago. He was going with this girl who lived on my floor and one day we got to talking. One thing led to another, I copped some weed from him, then he asked me if I wanted to earn some free drugs, that's how I got started. I'm real good at it too, the doctors take one look at me and start writing before I even open my mouth."

"But they have to know that's it all a setup."

"Sure. But as long as it looks halfway legit, they don't care. It's all about money."

"And that creep at the bar? What's his story?"

"He doesn't have one. He went to school with my sister; that's how I know him."

"I don't trust him."

"Good. You shouldn't."

Kaval sat with her legs folded under her pillow on the floor. I sat against the wall. Streetlights cut the room in half and night put dirty ashes on her face.

"When was the last time you had sex?" she asked.

"What? I don't know."

"Was it a month? Six months? A year?"

"I don't know."

"For me it's been a year and three months."

"Is that a long time to you?"

"An eternity. I was a very sexual person. I wasn't promiscuous, but when I was involved with someone I liked to have sex with them all the time . . . What's the matter? You look a little uncomfortable."

"No, I'm fine."

"Does this bother you, talking about sex?"

"No, it's the floor, it hurts my bones."

"You want a pillow?"

"No, I'm alright."

She slid over a pillow which I put underneath my back.

"I used to live down here before I moved to Hell's Kitchen. On Avenue C, Avenue C and Thirteenth. With this guy Troy. He was a singer in an industrial band. Maybe you've heard of them . . . Bastardization? They have a CD out."

"No, I really don't much follow music."

"Well, anyway, Troy wasn't a very good singer. He wasn't very good at anything."

"Why? What did he do?"

"It was what he didn't do. He didn't give a shit, about me, about anything. He was a junkie, maybe that was the problem."

"Is that how you got infected?"

"I don't know. He was bisexual too."

"Did you shoot up with him?"

"No. I snorted, but I never really liked junk. Mescaline was my drug of choice."

"I like mesc. The last time in the hospital they had me on morphine but I didn't like it. I've always preferred barbiturates and weed."

Silent flashbacks filled the room as silly mushrooms tripped before my eyes. I held the floor to keep from tipping over.

"Do you think you would ever want to have sex again?" she asked, her head and eyeballs melting black.

"I don't know. It's not up to me."

"What if you had a willing partner?"

"That's not what I meant. I . . . I'm not in control of my body."

"Because of the pills?"

"That's part of it. It's just . . . so much bullshit, don't you think?"

Kaval nodded her head as voices from the street called for more weapons.

I heard his panting lungs of fire slurping tongues and lips on wire. Kaval laid peaceful sleeping as I sat up in bed. Wiped my eyes and saw him sitting on hind legs with charcoal eyes like drops of feces, watching me.

"What do you want?" I asked softly. He licked at his nose and his tongue dripped spit to the floor.

"Why do you keep following me?"

In a fluid voice like Jesus dipped in water, he said, "I follow to watch."

"Watch? What are you watching for?"

"I know who you are."

"So what? . . . Who am I?"

"The tick of the clock knock knock."

"What does that mean?"

"I know what you are."

"Why don't you leave me alone? I didn't do anything to you."

"I know what you've done . . ."

"I haven't done anything!"

"And what you haven't done."

The dog on his paws with his woodscraping claws gave a devious laugh. "Evil as evil can be," he chuckled. "Did you fuck her?"

"That's none of your business!"

"You wanted to. Why didn't you?"

"Just leave me alone, please."

"Listen to the tick of the clock knock knock. Wrap your hands around her throat. Squeeze all the evil as evil can be, out of her heart and down through her knees."

His face was serious sincere with eyes on mine as something grabbed my wrists and lifted them from the bed. "Evil as evil can be!" he growled.

"You're the one that's evil! Not me."

"I know what you are, tick tock said the clock."

"You're insane!"

Kaval rolled over and opened her eyes. "What's the matter? What's wrong?"

"Nothing," I said. "I was having a nightmare. Go back to sleep."

And she did.

8

OUR PLANE TOOK OFF AT 10:15. We sat in the terminal with our bags at our feet, two strange creatures from alien places and we hadn't even left New York. Kaval stayed buried deep in glossy picture photo spreads of artists models sound mechanics while I sat watching Krishna dancers handing out salvation. Comforted by the fact they were weirder than we were. We took our bags and boarded as plastic smile nameplate robots greeted us inside. Taking off I gripped her hand and squeezed it tight, imagined bodies mangled on the runway in bloody strings of interwoven flesh.

Before we landed Kaval reminded me of what they knew and what they didn't, what to say and what to keep. I practiced at the baggage claim. Kaval said there'd be a car waiting but all I saw were faceless drivers holding up cardboard strips. She stepped to one and turning back I saw the name was Erikson. He took her bag and turned to the exit with both of us following close behind. Blinding sun knives sliced my eyes with air as warm as toast. The driver opened the door and Kaval disappeared in the back and I stood there shaking reds until she ordered me inside. He drove us past the streets and stores and wretched poor but no one here did windows. Kaval started goofing on the things in the car like the tv and bar and soundproof windows and phone and fax and champagne and snacks and I just looked at her in awe.

"What did you say your father did?"

"He's a production geek at Sony," she spit out.

"Production geek? Is that the technical term?"

"I believe that's what it says on his resume," she said with a scowl.

"C'mon. What does he do?"

"He's a vice president, I told you this already."

"But what does that mean?"

"I'm not sure what he does exactly. I don't really give a shit." She turned to the window as boiling water bubbled in her mind. I kept my mouth shut and watched the gold and silver Bentleys on each side, till we pulled into a winding gravel driveway that ended at a mansion. The driver got out and opened our door. Kaval walked past without a nod or a glance as her mother came out on the porch in designer jeans and white silk blouse with hair sprayed stiff for wind resistance, face caked with red and pink, sparkling gems on hands and neck and spreading her arms she looked like Liberace.

"Nancy!" she exclaimed. "My, you've lost so much weight. Aren't you eating in New York?"

Kaval-as-Nancy stood there stiff as wood as mother wrapped her arms around. I stayed with the bags. Finally she released and looked into my eyes and saw her disappointment.

"Oh, you must be . . . Edward?" she said with trepidation.

"No. This is Eddie, Mother. Call him Eddie."

"Hello Eddie," she said with extended fingers pointing downward fancy nails with two tone stripes and rhinestones on the tips. "It's good to have you here with us. Is this your first time in L.A.?"

"Yes, it is, Mrs. . . . ."

"Erikson," she offered.

Kaval interjected, "Lillian. You can call her Lillian."

"Well . . . yes, Lillian is fine," she said as livid lashes fluttered falsely. "I know you've had a long flight, why don't we go inside and you can both freshen up."

"We're both pretty fresh as it is, Mother."

"Yes, that's obvious!" she snapped then started into the house.

"You, uh, have a beautiful home here, Mrs. Erikson." As she swept through the doors without a word Kaval-as-Nancy took a step then gave me a glare.

Kaval's house was marble tile works of art and fancy lamps and furniture, running water from Italian landscapes near the winding stairs as shaggy carpet swept across the floor. Kaval's mother-as-Lillian led us up the staircase and through the hall.

"Eddie can stay in the south guest room, and Nancy, your room is all fixed up with new linen."

"Why can't Eddie stay in the main guest room?"

"What? Oh . . . I thought he might be more comfortable in the south room."

"Why would he be more comfortable in the smaller room on the other side of the house?" she asked and not too nicely.

"Oh, uh, I thought it would be cozier."

"Eddie doesn't like cozy. He likes big and roomy."

"Oh, well then, the main guest room would be fine," she said with a hand to her hip. "It's right over here, next to Nancy's room. The main bathroom is down at the end of the hall for bathing and showering; there's a small bathroom in your room . . . for your . . . personal needs. I'll have the bags brought right up."

"Thank you, Mrs. . . . . uh, Lillian."

She turned and headed down the stairs, Kaval-as-Nancy stood there cold as dirt.

"What's the matter?" I asked.

"You're acting like a fucking butler! You're a guest, not an employee!"

"I'm just trying to be polite."

"Well knock it off. It's degrading!"

"What are you so pissed off about?"

"Nothing. Just forget it."

"How come you never told me your name is Nancy?"

"That's not my name. You call me that again and I'll stab you in your sleep!"

She spun around and flew away with slamming doors and gusts of wind behind her. I stood there puzzled pissed and dizzy, senses throbbing swollen fingers, burning up like fields of grass.

Dinner at the Erikson's was eerily subdued, casual glances in between formal courses, clinking silver china chatter, and that empty place for Mr. E. Kaval seemed tense and silent solid, gripping fork on scraping plate like human bones in bio classes. The clock rang eight with tubular bells and Lillian cleared her throat and scowled at the doorway.

"God, this is so like him! He gets caught up at the office and forgets he has a family!"

Kaval let out a burp and slurped her European water as Lillian pretended not to hear. She cleared her throat, sat up straight and clasped her gleaming fingers underneath her chin.

"So, Eddie," she began, "Nancy hasn't really told us much about you. What do you do for a living back in New York?"

"Oh, uh, I work with my sister."

"How nice. What does she do?"

"She runs her own company."

"Really?! What kind of company?"

"Uh, it's a photography studio."

"Oh? Is that how you met Nancy? She's a wonderful photographer!"

"No, I, uh, we met . . . we lived in the same neighborhood."

"Oh? You were on Park Avenue?" she asked with amazement, I looked up with the same.

"Uh, excuse me?" I said as a shoe came jabbing into my shin. "Oh! Park Avenue!? Yes, of course. I mean, no, not anymore. I had to move."

"Oh, that's too bad," she said with tilted head. "I guess the recession is hitting everyone."

"Uh, yes, it is."

"Nancy, did you bring home any pictures to show your father and I?"

"No. I forgot."

"Forgot? After the camera we sent you for Christmas?!" Lillian turned to me as if telling a secret, lowered her voice to reveal it. "It was several thousand dollars, top of the line. Japanese."

"Mother, we really don't want to hear about the cost or the ethnicity."

"I would think you'd show a little more gratitude . . . Speaking of which, now that you're home you don't have to wear black all the time. I know in New York it's the state color, but out here we could be a little more cheerful in our wardrobe."

"Mother, I'm old enough to decide what I wear."

"I was only suggesting . . . you have such beautiful clothes upstairs, it would be nice if you wore them once in a while."

"Those aren't my clothes, you bought them."

"Yes, but I bought them for you."

"I would prefer to buy my own clothes."

Lillian turned to reveal another secret. "She's so difficult sometimes. I think she just likes to disagree."

I didn't dare open my mouth as Kaval fingered her knife.

Later. "You seem very quiet tonight. Tired from the flight?"

Kaval stared at the hunk of uneaten meat rotting in her plate.

"How about you, Eddie? How was your flight?"

"Excuse me? Oh, it was good."

"Have you flown in first class before?" she asked with a studied gleam.

"First class?" I asked and felt that shoe again. "Oh uh, yes. Thank you for sending us the tickets."

"Nancy can come home as often as she likes, we'd send her the tickets anytime, but . . . I guess she's too busy in New York. We get a discount on airfare through the studio. My husband plays golf with the chairman of the airline."

Kaval let out a yawn but Lillian went unfazed.

"What were they serving on the flight today?"

"Um, we had . . ."

"We weren't very hungry," Kaval jumped in.

"Oh? You didn't eat?" she persisted.

"No, we didn't."

"Oh, that's a shame," Lillian said to me as if Kaval wasn't even there. "The food in first class is usually very good."

"We weren't hungry so we didn't eat," Kaval confirmed.

"You should be eating more. Look at yourself, you're becoming nothing but bones. You've barely touched your food."

"I'm not hungry."

"So what were they serving on the plane?"

Kaval answered, "Prime rib."

"You should have at least tried it."

"It still had marks from where the jockey whipped it!"

"Well, if it looked tough you could have ordered the lobster."

At 10:35 a car pulled into the driveway and Lillian announced, "Well, it's about time!" Tires crunched the gravel and the engine ceased and a door slammed and Lillian rose to meet the enemy.

"Benjamin, so nice of you to join us!"

"Stop it, Lillian. I'm exhausted."

"You were supposed to be here at seven."

"I couldn't leave, there was something at the studio."

"There's always something at the studio! You'd think it was the Pentagon!"

"That's enough, Lillian. I'm starving. Is there anything left for dinner?"

"Yes, your plate's in the oven. Nancy's inside with her . . . friend." And as her voice fell to a whisper Kaval gave me a smirk. A second later he stepped around the corner and into the living room, a shortened five-foot-six in shiny shoes designer suit with loose silk tie and grease slick hair, every strand in place. Seeing the tired smile on his simple face I felt relief. Until he looked into my eyes. Watching, he's always watching.

"Nancy! You look beautiful!" He said with his arms opened wide. Kaval stepped into them like zombies on parade. Gave him a peck on the cheek, then turned to introduce her friend.

"Dad, this is Eddie. Eddie, this is my father."

"I'm gl . . . glad to me you, Mr. Erikson." And shook his hand but felt a paw.

"Please, call me Ben," he said with a chuckle.

Lillian chimed in, "Oh Benjamin, I hate to hear people call you that."

"Why? It's my name."

"No, your name is Benjamin."

"Everyone at the studio calls me Ben."

"And I don't like it."

Kaval moved in for the attack. "Let's not get too pretentious about it, Mother."

"It's not pretentious to call your father by his rightful name!"

"Why don't you just give him a number!"

Benjamin yelped, "That's a good idea! Call me number seven." Then number seven went inside as steaming Lil retrieved his bowl of chow.

Twenty after midnight Kaval and I sat in the tv room as

right above our heads the fighting commenced. Muffled voices jousting gibberish. Reds on fire baked desire. Kaval steamed slightly furious.

"See? They don't even give a shit that there's company in the house."

"What are they fighting about?"

"Everything! They don't need a reason, they'll fight about the weather."

"It is a little chilly in here."

"Maybe they're fighting about you?"

"Is that why you invited me here? To piss them off?"

Kaval looked hurt, forehead lines sank down in curves. I felt good as good can be.

"No, I really didn't want to come back alone," she said. From overhead scraping wood and scuffled shoes played out in scratchy counterpoint.

"Now they'll throw the furniture around."

"Maybe they're just remodeling." And with that came a familiar smirk. Kaval shot up and kicked off the tv.

"C'mon. Let's get outta here."

"Where we going?"

"Out."

Kaval drove through the hills and onto the highway, pointing out the streets and the landmarks, shootings and stabbings and stars overdosing, showed me the field where she lost her virginity. Seeing her white little head peeking up through the arch of the wheel made me laugh.

The Boulevard looked like nothing I'd expected. The stars and stripes and lowlife types as Dianetic diarrhetics flowed from every hole, the lights and the colors and tourists with dollars as beggars reached out with their cups, the dealers and pimps and the children with limps, runaway whores hustling their bodies like vending machines, all reminded me of home.

"I knew you'd like it," Kaval said reassuringly. "It's the only part that resembles New York."

A city gets into your blood, I thought.

Kaval drove off to darker parts where woods and weeds deserted streets and burnt out buildings sprang like moldy bread. She turned the corner and cars and limos lined both sides of the curb.

"What the hell's going on?" I asked.

"You'll see," she quipped and parked up the block.

Kaval led me past a line of grumbling fashion junkies down to a stairway and a huge metal door behind a velvet rope where a crew cut blond with pins and needles stopped us moving further. Kaval yelled in her ear and slipped something into her hand. The blond pulled out a hammer and hammered on the steel door. A moment later it exploded open with pounding rumble earthquake tremors bouncing off my chest. Kaval took my hand and led me into the black smoky room where a city filled with freaks and weirdos circus clowns with mohawk hairdos, leather wearing masochists knelt chewing bits of boot. Pushing through the sardine crowd as sweat and musk and pot tobacco hung like spirits of the damned, Kaval edged up to the bar and squeezed her way inside, disappeared in the bodies closing up around her. I stood outside waiting for low tide. Watched the stage where bouncing Catholic girls gave head to Boris Karloff.

Kaval drove up some blackened mountaintop where tiny lights spread out as far as we could see. She parked the car and turned it off. We sat there watching glimmer thoughts below, my mind with pictures flowing on a stream. I blinked and treaded back on shore.

"I'm sorry," I said. "Guess I bugged out for a minute."

Kaval watched me lenses boring in.

"It's beautiful down there, isn't it?" I said but still, those lenses. She put the car in neutral and let it roll up closer to the edge. Cracking gravel underneath rubber tires as the drop opened up before us, Kaval jammed on the brakes just at the edge and put the car in park. Looked at me with vinegar.

"You're really something, you know that?"

"What do you mean?"

"You make me sick!"

"What? Why?"

"Because it's like being with a cadaver!"

"What are you talking about?"

"I practically drive us off the cliff and you sit there like you fucking want me to."

"I knew you weren't going over."

"How did you know that?! You didn't even look at me! What are you, a fucking psychic!?"

"Kaval, what's wrong with you? Why are you saying these things?"

"Because you're a fucking brick wall. Tonight! In the club. Didn't you see me with that guy at the bar?"

"Yes."

"Did you see what I was doing?"

"Yes."

"Didn't that bother you?"

"Nobody forced you to do it, you did it cause you wanted to."

"And how do you feel about it?"

"I don't know."

"See what I mean!? You're a fucking imbecile!"

"If I make you sick, fine! But don't call me a fucking imbecile. If you want to fuck around, that's your business."

"Maybe I don't want to fuck around. Maybe I want somebody who gives a shit about me."

"I give a shit!"

"You sure don't act like you do!"

"What was I supposed to do?! Maybe he was an old boyfriend or something."

"He was a stranger, I never saw him before in my life."

"You just walk up to complete strangers and jerk them off in public!?"

"Yes! I did."

"Then why didn't you suck his cock and let him fuck you up the ass too?!"

"Cause I didn't want to. But you wouldn't have cared either way."

"Look, Kaval, I'm not your fucking guardian, or your father. You wanna be a cheap fucking slut? Then go ahead!"

"And when it's over you'll pretend that nothing happened."

"What do you want me to do?"

"Act like a man, for God's sake!"

"Alright, here's a man for you . . . you're a fucked up fucking cunt! And if you don't give a fuck about me or my feelings, why should I give a fuck about you?! You can fuck all the fucked up people in this whole fucking miserable city for all I fucking care! So just go fuck yourself!"

I sat back steaming violent, thoughts of murder mixed with pleasure . . . where was the dog when I needed him?

Kaval watched with smirking eyes, then sat back and let out a sigh. "Well, it's about time," she said. "I'm glad to see there's something inside of you. At least now I know you're still alive."

"Look, I don't like to lose my temper."

"Why not? It's normal. You should lose it more often. Live a little. While you can."

Live a little. While you can. Advice like rice at Vegas weddings. I turned to her, "Kaval, it broke my heart to see you with that guy. It broke my fucking heart! But what can I do? Sex means a lot to you, it's all you talk about. So what should I do if I can't give you what you want?"

"You can give me closeness. And friendship. Don't be so agreeable all the time, yell at me when I'm wrong. Take me by the shoulders and shake the hell out of me . . . You can hold me. I need to be held sometimes." Glassine packets melted from her lashes and for a second I forgot who she was, so out of character, cold Kaval.

She looked away and with trembling swollen lips tried to speak. I said, "It's okay. Everything's going to be fine."

"How is it going to be fine?"

"It just is."

She started bawling. "All I do is hurt you, and everyone else. I don't want to, but I can't help it."

"Well, don't worry about me. I'm not hurt."

"How could you not be? You said I broke your heart tonight."

"No, I didn't mean broke, I meant chipped. You chipped it a little, but that's it. Just a small chip."

"I'm sorry."

"Forget it. So what if you jerked off some guy. It didn't mean anything to me."

"Well it should mean something to you."

"I figured you were only doing it for the exercise." Kaval choked out a laugh, wiped her eyes, and forced a wretched smile.

"C'mon Kaval, don't be upset. Cheer up and I'll yell at you again. I'll call you a whore, will that make you feel better?"

"No," she said, drying her eyes with her sleeve. Taking a deep breath and letting it out slow. "I'm okay. I'm not upset anymore."

"Good."

"How can you be so calm about it? Aren't you afraid?"

"I'm scared shitless. But what can we do?"

"We can fight it."

"I don't like to fight . . . Besides, who are we gonna fight? Each other?"

"No. I don't want to fight with you."

"I don't want to fight with you either."

Kaval gave me a squeeze and I kissed her silky hair and she put her head on my lap, closed her weary eyes and tried to sleep. Petting zoos and sheepish shepherds baahed at the moon as I stroked her fuzzy cheek.

At sunrise the main guest room seemed somewhat smaller as Kaval crawled into my bed. Snuggling on my chest her hands rubbed along my side and down my thigh. I felt nova-numbness throbbing pulse-like. Reached over for my bag of pills when Kaval took my hand and asked me, "Why don't you do without them? Are you in that much pain?"

"No, but I feel it coming on."

"Please, see what happens if you don't."

I put my hands behind my swelling head. Stared up at the woodwork above. "Kaval, can I ask you something?"

"What?"

"What's this shit with your name? Why did you tell me your name is Kaval?"

"Because that *is* my name."

"Then why does your mother keep calling you Nancy?"

"Because she's an asshole."

"C'mon, tell me the truth. Do you hate the sound of it? Maybe you knew somebody named Nancy that you hated?"

"No."

"Then what is it?"

"When I was born I was one of two. My mother had twin girls. She had names already picked out. Nancy and Caroline. Whichever one came out first was to be Nancy. Well, Nancy was born almost an hour before I was. I was Caroline—it's even on my original birth certificate. Nancy died the next day. But when my mother was told the news, she pretended not to know what they were talking about. She denied there had been another birth. Just like that, it didn't exist. So, when they brought me to her she called me Nancy, my father went along with it, and that was that."

"But you were an infant. How do you know all this?"

"When I was twelve I came across a birth certificate with the name Caroline on it. I asked what it was about and my Aunt Trudy told me the whole story. When my mother found out she threw Aunt Trudy out of the house and to this day they haven't spoken to each other. It's been eleven years."

"That explains why you're not Nancy. Where did you come up with the name Kaval?"

"When I was a kid my father brought me to see this play in a garage. He was scouting an actor that his agency was interested in—he was an agent back then. So I go along and I don't even remember what the name of the play was, but the actress, shit, that bitch was something else. She was writhing on the floor, screaming in people's faces, grabbing her tits. I'd never seen anything like it! After the performance my father went to introduce me to the actor but I told him I wanted to meet Kaval instead. So he goes up to her, introduces himself, but once she hears who he is and where he works, she tells us both to fuck off. I thought that was the coolest thing I'd ever seen in my life."

"No wonder you like New York so much."

She looked up at the ceiling, wistfully. "Kaval. She was everything I wanted to be. I didn't care what her real name was, I never even looked it up. She was Kaval to me."

"That's a very bizarre story, and you were a troubled child."

"At least I got to pick my own name."

Kaval gouged her head into my chest and squeezed me tight with her arms around my neck. Out of the quiet she said, "What was it like with Elizabeth? When you had sex with her?"

"It was . . . difficult."

"Why?"

"It just was. Elizabeth used to think I didn't find her attractive. She felt ugly when she was with me. That was pretty much the way it was." Kaval kissed me with dry lips on my chest. She took a deep breath and feathers brushed my nipples. Black dots circled a foot above my eyes. Blond hair and eyeglasses. "The thing of it is, I was very attracted to her, she was beautiful."

"Did you two ever talk about the problem?"

"No. It was something we never discussed."

A minute later her spidery fingers crawled along the seam of my distractions, edging underneath. "Do you mind if I hold it?"

"No, go ahead. It doesn't bite."

"How does that feel?"

"It feels good."

But tears filled up my passion cup and lonely holes replaced it. Erogenous zones I bleed for you.

I heard the voices coming through the wall. Popped two reds and stepped into the hall. Ben and Lil were screaming shrill with bedroom doors ajar. Kaval was out of the house and I stood listening to the volume shred my ears as Lil was ranting ravenous over something done or about to be. Ben tried to calm her with reassuring reason until he finally let go with north suburban mistresses and moving away from the pressure and tension and tired congestion, so exhausted working hard with Lil to keep it all intact. Lil shot back with threats and crimes and prison time for crooked book embezzlements. Ben stepped out the door and gave me a nervous smile and I went into my room. A second later Lil went nuts and spilled her guts, smashed the furniture against the walls like Orson Welles in Xanadu. Trembling on the floor my brain cells floated helpless free outside my skull.

Kaval and I came strolling out of the Galaxy into lights and colored neon pipes, across the street the Capitan screamed of

hidden old-time treasures. Kaval pulled me past the homeless hustler porno patrons where some old lady was kneeling
on the pavement with a toothbrush scrubbing somebody's
star. Walking past the pharmaceuticals I stopped and turned
around. "That guy back there is dealing acid."

"What guy?"

"That guy we just passed. See him?"

"Who? Charles Manson?"

"He looks like Jesus Christ to me."

"Do you really want acid? And from him?!"

"I haven't had acid in months. It's hard to get in New York.
Besides, it gets rid of the throbbing for at least eight hours."

"But you don't know this guy from Adam, he could be
dealing sugar."

"No, he said it's blotter, on paper. C'mon, let's get some.
It'll be great. We could relive the sixties!"

"I was born in 1970."

"So, you can see what you missed!"

Kaval gave me a sideways glance. The guy saw me coming and started immediately spewing out pills and pot and
coke and mesc and crack and ice and something called
Beetlejuice that I wasn't too comfortable with trying. For all
her healthy-eating ways Kaval watched with amazement as
the deal transacted. Afterwards she took me to some poster
place where monsters watched from every wall. Browsing
through the magazines of death and bloody homicide I felt
myself ignite. Kaval stood flipping past the movie posters
stopping on Alex and his pyramid.

"You ever see this movie?" she asked. "It's one of my
favorites."

"You just like the sex and violence."

"What's wrong with sex and violence?"

"Nothing."

"I'm gonna buy it," she said and went to get the guy as I
stood looking through the sheets and pictures, windowsills

and movie fixtures opened up before me, colors changing
psychedelic poverty. Outside my body watching from the
street, something changed it wasn't me but some rich yuppie
eating brie. Nipple knees and throbbing gristle graveyard
grievers sucking pistols, I grew nauseous as Kaval came up
with her poster in hand.

"What's the matter?"

"Nothing. I feel sick."

"See? I told you not to take it! C'mon, you can throw up
in the gutter."

Back at the house her father said he wanted to talk to her
about something and would I mind and when I said I didn't
they both went out into the den. Lillian was nowhere to be
seen but her presence felt like German soldiers on patrol. I sat
on the couch and stared at the fabric. Minutes later Kaval
came back with weeping eyes and went straight up to her
room. I sat there soft as tissue paper.

Ben and I strolled along the garden hedges, tall green walls of
twigs and leaves. At the end was a metal shack and inside were
tools and mowers plug-in blowers shovel rakes and things with
fancy wire handles. Ben was showing off his new tomatoes.

"See? Right over here," he said proudly. "This whole bed
of soil has been flown in from Italy. That's the key, Italian soil.
I had the plants shipped in and have been watering them with
natural spring water. This is the one spot I won't allow the gar-
deners to touch. My own little plot of land, so to speak . . . My
father was a farmer, not professionally, but he always had a
vegetable garden. I'll never forget eating fresh food from his
garden. Lettuce! Home-grown lettuce, the softest, moistest
vegetable you could eat. Not like the store-bought stuff; all
preservatives and chemicals, God knows what else. I got some
pumpkins planted over there, just a dozen or so. If half of
them come up I'll be happy. You and Nancy could use more

vegetables in your diet, you're both pale, you need to get some color in your skin. Drink some juice."

"Why do you have the garden so far away from the house?"

"You mean out here near the shed?"

I nodded.

"Well, Lillian thinks farming is beneath me. God forbid we act like peasants," he chuckled with a gleam. Shifting shapes and morphomatics, the gleam transformed the chuckle changed, pawprints where his feet had been. I looked around with no one else in sight.

"Ben?" I asked, hoping to hear an answer. The dog just laughed. "Ben's not here," he said in growling voice of gravel.

"Ben, please come back. Don't leave me here."

"Ben was never here. It's been me the whole time."

"What do you want?" I said as weakness mixed with foolishness.

"Evil as evil can be," he snickered. "Remember that clock? Knock knock."

"I don't know about any clocks. And I don't want to be evil. I'll be good, I swear, I'll be good from now on."

"It's too late for that. Too late for that indeed. You fucked her, you plucked her, and now you'll induct her."

"No, I love her!"

"If you love her, then shove her. Bring hands above her, fling them down so heavy blunt, squeeze her throat, the little . . ."

"Stop it!" I cried as tears of terror stung like angry bees. "Please, I'm begging you, stop it!" I tried to run but frozen stiff the dog laughed his frigid laugh.

"You'll do what I want you to do, knock knock. Tick tock. Do you like lettuce?"

"What?"

"Have some lettuce." He looked over at the muddy patch and twinkled harmful.

"That's nothing but dirt," I said.

"Dirt is lettuce, don't upset us. Eat it and need it as evil can be." I was flung down with my hands pulled free as fists of soil punched into my mouth.

"Swallow as you wallow, listen to the clock, knock knock. Time runs dry as big boys cry. Ease the pain, smash her brain or go insane."

I choked delirious, chewing dirt and bleeding gums with tonsils raw and open wounds. Bits of teeth and freezing nerves, crying like a baby left alone, the dog jumped on my back and pushed me deeper into the soil, scratched my neck with his sandy paws. I rolled around and felt his teeth as razor blades cut fleshy meat. Finger bits and lukewarm liquid pouring down in streaks. Hot breath, putrid and musty like sewers in summer infiltrating sinuses. Then deja vu came back to school with beating rain and yelping dogs on Forty-Second Street. I freed my leg and kicked him hard, clean crunch golf balls as he skirted off with an agonized yelp. He stopped a few feet away and licked his battered balls on hind legs limp with palsy. As the strength flowed back into his eyes I saw a shovel in the shed and grabbed the wooden handle. The dog got up and charged at my face, teeth and fur exploding into space, I raised the shovel up again and cracked it down his two front paws snapped off like broken breadsticks. The dog lay moaning on his side but convinced it was a trick, I took the blade and rammed it on his flaccid neckbone stamping down with all my might. Severed heads and simpering cries, helpless as I've known myself, and yet I couldn't stop. Flesh and tendon Turkish taffy stretched out with the shovel, still the lungs expanded. It wouldn't die, and now I cried in terror, twisted with rage, plunging the blade down into squirming tubes of stomach as I choked on muddy saliva dripping whiskers from my chin. The dog was oozing foggy matter, steaming guts and bloody splatter, covered in crimson moldy fur, loose teeth at my feet with nerve endings still attached. Slithered snakes of blue intestine Lucifer with indigestion, moving toward my legs till I chopped them into tiny bits of macaroni. I waited for the tricks to continue, but after a minute, I knew, finally, the dog was dead. The sun went down over the hedges and by the dim approaching twilight sky, I dug a four-foot lettuce hole, scooped the grizzly fragments in, followed by the tubes and snakes, then covered it all for the next generation. Filling in the final pats of dirt, a man's shoe sat sideways near the shed but looking around, Ben was nowhere to be seen.

That night nobody said a word as Ben became a forgotten mystery, but Lil kept eyeing me eerily and I wondered if she was in with the dog. Kaval just nibbled her shrimp and spun on the moon from the mesc we had taken. She was quiet and frighteningly so.

After dinner Kaval took me outside to the heated pool with lighted water. We laid there watching stars and making dead celebrities. Kaval laughed when I showed her John Lennon. All the time glancing at the lettuce graveyard waiting for something to happen. When nothing did I thought of telling her about my little accident. I studied the trees and the twigs in the hedges, looking for his eyes to shine like turpentine from Palestine, instead the hits of mescaline made me cough in fits.

"What's the matter," she asked with closing lids. "Are you alright?"

"I just thought of something funny."

"What?"

"I don't remember."

Kaval waved her hand in front of her eyes and the trails and their shadows made her blink repeatedly. I watched her with binoculars, waiting for a crack, that one slip-up that would reveal the truth, like Kennedy conspiracies and evil twins where Oswald is the good one. But Kaval stayed put, and I thought she can't be wise cause why would the dog want her dead so badly? But then the cleverness of that deduction struck me hard cause what better way to avoid suspicious insecurities with love and friendship filling in the cracks?

"Kaval? Are you the only one in there?"

"In where?"

"In your body. Is there anyone else in there with you?"

"Sure, there's lots of people. Wanna speak to Elvis?"

"Elvis Presley?"

"No! Elvis Costello."

"What about dogs, you got any dogs in there?"

"I hate dogs."

I woke to voices talking in the hall. Hushed annoyance right outside my door. The sun hadn't come up yet, just a purple bruise on the horizon. I sat up as Kaval crept in with hair pushed out in all directions.

"What's wrong?" I asked.

"You got a telephone call. It sounds important."

"Telephone call? Nobody knows I'm here."

"You better answer it. They asked for you, and said it was a personal emergency."

I got up and dressed and outside the door Lillian stood waiting near the stairs. I went to use the hallway phone when Lil grabbed my limpid wrist and whispered, "Use the kitchen phone. And try to be quiet, Benjamin's still sleeping." Then she gave me a glare. I went down into the kitchen and taking the phone heard Dezmond on the other end.

"What the hell are you doing calling me here at this hour?! How did you even know how to find me?"

"I got the number from Caroline's landlord."

"Who?"

"Caroline. Your girlfriend."

"You mean Nancy, uh, I mean Kaval?"

"I mean Caroline! That's what her landlord says her name is. Anyway that's how I got this number."

"Well, what's up? Why are you calling me?"

"A detective came into Jackie's looking for you last night. He knew you by name and where you lived. I told him I didn't know you. I asked him what was up and he mentioned Denise. Said he had to speak to you personally."

"Denise? What about her?"

"He wouldn't say. He said he had to talk to you, that it was important. He left his card. Do you want the number?"

"Yeah, give it to me. Wait, let me get a pen."

Kaval was right behind with pen and pad and cordless phone, hearing every word.

"Okay, what's the number?"

"His name is Webster. Detective Frank Webster, he's at Midtown West, the number's 698-1645. Give him a call and then call me right back."

"I'll see you in another week or two."

"No! Call me back tonight, let me know what's . . ."

"Good-bye Dezmond."

Kaval hung up as I hung up then leaned against the counter.

"What do you think happened?" she asked.

"I don't know. I'll call and find out. What time is it in New York?"

"Three hours ahead, it's about 8:30 there now."

9

I T'S TRUE. They do serve lobster in first class.

Detective Webster led me by the arm through hollow walls of cinder blocks as echo drops and water plops dripped down from leaking ceilings. Tick tock of the clock knock knock as shoes and sneakers scuffled on cement. The hallway ended at swinging glass doors and pushing through the stench of body fluid castor oils melding in my clothes, I felt myself go faint.

Her face was battered brutally, more than shovels can do. Purple skin and jagged curves with twisted lips and bloated nerves, scalp tore back on forehead bone, exposed and white, sunken eyes with blackened lids and nostrils stretched wider than should be possible, dried blood caked up on the edges . . . This was Denise.

Detective Webster stood beside me watching for reactions but none came forth, just blurry thoughts on celluloid, even I was left surprised.

"Yes, that's her," I said and Webster motioned for the attendant to roll her back into her dark little chamber.

"She was found in a basement on Fifty-Sixth Street. The lease was under a corporation in her name. Do you know the type of business she was conducting there?"

I told him no and nothing else.

10

THEY FIXED HER UP AS BEST THEY COULD but still the lid stayed closed. Alone and waiting for her friends to arrive and pay their final respects I questioned if she was even in there. What a crock this whole thing was; if only she could speak the things she could tell. The rotting stench of florid flowers made me want to puke. I heard the ticking of the clock knock knock out in the hall. Seven ticks later footsteps stopped in the doorway. She came in and knelt on the pew and even from the back so much like Denise. Maybe

that was the problem I thought, as both played men with neither acting weaker and sex like politics needs that soft sub-
mission. Barbara came over wearing jeans and boots with
flowing shirt underneath her black suede leather jacket.
Taking my hand and kissing my cheek she gave me a look of
despair.

"I'm so sorry, Eddie."

"Thanks for coming, Barbara."

"I cried when I read about it in the papers."

"It was quite a shock."

"Do the police know anything? Do they have any suspects?"

"I don't think so."

"What a tragedy. God . . ."

"I was really sad to hear about you two breaking up. I
only heard about it a few months ago."

"It was painful, on both sides."

"I can imagine."

"How have you been? It looks like you've been taking
care of yourself. You're looking better. You have a tan."

"I've been in L.A. You can't help but get some sun."

"It looks good on you. Are you living out there now?"

"No, I was visiting with a friend. She has family out there
. . . Here, please, sit down." She did, then wiped away a lash
or a tear from her eye. I watched her staring at the sealed oak
coffin with her windblown face still smooth as vinyl. She
blew her nose and wiped it with her handkerchief.

"I need a cigarette. Would you come downstairs with
me?"

"Sure."

Down in the lounge Barbara sat on the couch and lit her
menthol filters. "Was she beaten badly?" she asked.

"Yes, she was. That's why the coffin's closed. They could-
n't fix her up enough."

Barbara let out a whimper then quickly sealed her lips. I

wanted to tell her how much Denise loved her and about her picture in the bedroom but I didn't.

Instead I told her, "The police think it was a client. All the papers and books were missing from her office. It was definitely somebody who knew the deal."

"How did you like L.A.?" she asked flicking an ash in the tray to her right.

"I didn't."

"No place is like New York."

"I guess . . . Are you still with that firm? Accounting?"

"I'm a partner now."

"Oh. Congratulations."

"It's no big deal," she said with a wave of her cigarette. I noticed her looking at me strangely, bloodshot eyes about to spill their guts.

"What is it?" I asked.

"Listen, there's something I have to talk to you about. I don't know what to do, if I should go to the police or what."

I sat down intrigued to see what she would spill.

"About three months before we split up, Denise wanted me to help her with something, it was something I couldn't do. And it involved her work . . ."

As Barbara poured out her story I listened dumb as dogshit. "Shit," I said rubbing my chin. "I mean, I knew Denise was having financial trouble, but I never thought she would . . ."

"Financial trouble?! She wasn't in financial trouble, she was making a fortune."

"That can't be true. She told me . . ."

"Eddie, I kept the books. I knew what she was making. Right up until the end there were no money problems, believe me. We were doing great! Our portfolio was never stronger. That's what was so troubling about it. Your sister became obsessed. That's one reason I left."

"This is . . . kinda hard to believe."

"I don't know if it was just another one of her crazy schemes or what. I don't know what to do about it."

"Don't do anything. Don't say a word to anyone. The police haven't mentioned anything about this to me."

"What have they said?"

"They haven't told me anything. And I told them I did-n't know about the dungeon."

Barbara puffed on her burning half-ash cigarette looking at me sideways now. Barbara was no fool.

Back upstairs his silhouette towered over the coffin. Before I could turn away he called me back.

"Eddie."

His gentle purr sent slingshot shivers up my throat. I slowly went to greet him and he gripped my hand in macho mayhem, gave his tender green violation.

"I got a call from the hospital," he said. "They told me the police went to see your mother, then they told me about Denise. Why didn't you call me?"

"I'm sorry Uncle Ted. I guess I was so overcome, I didn't think."

"How are you doing? Holding up?"

"Yes."

"I talked to a detective last night, he told me they're still searching for clues."

Uncle Ted looked down at the wood and through his oat-meal tan and parted lips I saw the glimmering gold tooth still intact. Thinking demons I snuck a glance back to his eyes and waited . . . Could he still be alive?

Uncle Ted turned away from the coffin and sat on the couch in the front row. I stood there feeling naked and invis-ible. Trembling in fear and loss cause now without Denise there was me and me alone with the secret of Uncle Ted. He had conned them all supreme. If only I could see her face to see if she were crying sad as blood rushed through my aching head where pounding sounds and sensurround like fuckers fucking fistfuckation fought inside my brain! I was eight years old and peeking in her window, she didn't see me only there a second before running out to the tree in the yard with its tire and rope and sticking my head in the rubber to block out her choking disgrace, I couldn't block out that look on her face. Until a short time later I crept back to the window and heard her singing softly a song I can't remember but she sang it over and over in dead singsong till Mom came home from grocery shopping. Denise went inside to help her with dinner and I ran to the garage and cried against the side, forever kept my tongue.

Uncle Ted sat mournful with his private eyes and Catholic lies and now I wanted that shovel again. I turned around but he was looking at the flowers. I noticed the flower stand thick solid brass just out of reach, one clean shot a dizzy burst of grisly matter all debts paid in full. My fingers touched the frozen grail until he gave his Cheshire smile.

"Say Eddie, you still playing the piano?"

A kick in the balls as everything turned to stone.

"Uh . . . no, I don't."

"That's too bad. You were really good."

"Yeah . . . well . . ."

"You used to play for hours and hours, remember? Your mother loved listening to you practice. You used to play that classical stuff, Beethoven and those other guys."

"I don't much follow music anymore."

"That's a shame. So, what are you doing with yourself these days?"

"Nothing."

"Are you working?"

"Uh, Uncle Ted, I'm going to step out for a minute, okay?"

"Sure, go ahead Eddie. I understand."

Standing on the outside steps I questioned my existence,

the worthless ways I drank from life. My eyes flickered darkly, burnt-out lights with loose wires attached, maybe now I'd
go blind—it was always a possibility. If the dog was still
alive I'd succumb this time.

When I went back inside Uncle Ted was standing near
the coffin with his hand on the lid, even dead she feels his
molestation. I stepped up close and Uncle Ted turned around
with reddened rings on rusted eyes.

"It's a shame," he sniffled. "A goddamned shame. Thank
God your mother's not here to see this. It would destroy her
. . . This frigging crazy world we live in."

Uncle Ted reached for a box of tissues on the stand and
wiped his wet and veiny nose, blew it like a foghorn.
Looking at the empty room he asked, "Where are her kids?
And Jerry?"

"They didn't come. They sent flowers. Those blue ones
over there."

"He only sent flowers?!"

"Yes."

Uncle Ted looked away with gritted teeth. Dezmond and
Lucille stepped in the doorway and I went over to greet them.

Nine days later Kaval came back and told me about her
father missing and all this scandal following his departure.
The police and the feds were looking for all the wrong reasons and when his mistress disappeared two days later that
only pointed the finger further. I asked about the farm but
Kaval didn't know what I was talking about. I told her about
Denise and what happened and the wake and the services
and Kaval turned angry pissed annoyed.

"Why didn't you call me?!" she said with offensive intentions. "I would have come back."

"I didn't want to bother you with it."

"Bother me with it?! I can't believe this! You . . . You're
unbelievable, you know that?"

"Yes."

A pause. "God, I'm sorry. I didn't mean that. I just . . . I would have liked to have been here for you. There was no way to reach you, I didn't know what was up. It must have been a very hard time."

"Yes, it was."

11

I SAT DOWN ONTO CREAKING SPRINGS listening to her lungs fill up. Tired lungs. A curse to watch so helplessly lost in this maze of emergency. Living now as she lived her life where every pointed fuck-you finger had a logical explanation. But scars don't heal so logically. I leaned in close and gave my deposition.

"Ma, I know you can hear me in there, so don't pretend that you can't. There are some things that I have to say to you, and I'm going to say them whether you want to hear them or not."

Pawsteps scratched along the floor and I jumped up only to see the faded gray tiles and nothing else, the radiator spit out its steamy laughing raspberry. Alone with my cadaver, still I heard those paws.

"It's not going to work, Ma. Not this time. Go ahead and play your little game. Your fucking stupid little game. It's easy to be dead, isn't it? Safe to be dead . . . Your whole fucking life has been one long coma!"

"Don't talk to her that way!"

I whirled around and leaning on the window sunlight soulful bathed her face in butter cream, yet angry ultraviolet.

"Who are you to judge her?" she said.

"I . . . I . . ."

"I could say a few things to you too, you know."

"That's right, you could! And I don't have any rightful answers for you. But I've paid for that, I pay for it every day."

"And she's not paying for it every day?"

"She's doing what she's always done. This is just another escape for her."

"Eddie, let it go."

"Denise, don't you see? It's all connected! She knew about Uncle Ted. She didn't do anything about it."

"What was she supposed to do?"

"She was supposed to believe you! She was our mother! She was supposed to protect us."

"It's over now. You should let it go." Denise folded her arms and looked at me with big sister eyes. The breathing pillow filled with air then sank down onto brittle ribs.

"Denise, if none of it ever happened, it would have all turned out differently."

"No Eddie, everything would have been exactly the same. C'mon, it's time to stop hating her."

"I never hated her. I just . . . never liked her."

"Let it go," she said and the sun behind her head made cooler reds prevail. In the hallway a man yelled for Helen.

Her face turned sharp and finely focused, before she could strike I told her, "It was Uncle Ted who put the rosary on your casket. I removed it twice. But every time I turned my head he snuck it back."

"What was his problem?"

"I don't know. He was always religious." Denise let out an unexpected giggle, silver shards of sunlight burst inside her corneas.

"It's good to see you like this," I said. "The last time was . . . well, you know." She gave me a knowing grin.

"What do you want me to do about the guy in the pictures? It was him, wasn't it?"

"Don't do anything," she said. "Let it go."

She gazed out the chickenwire window, her mind flew off like birds set free from cages. The patient sucked life from squiggly lines on ugly paper. Yet I knew she was in there somehow, listening to it all.

"There isn't anything you want to say to her?" I asked.

Denise looked down and gently shook her head. "No, I have no bad feelings."

"Well . . . you were always more forgiving than I was. I guess I always did hate her. I didn't want to. I hated myself for hating her."

"You expected too much."

"I know . . . Denise, if I ask you something, will you tell me the truth?"

"What?"

"Are you in with the dog?"

"What dog?"

"The dog that's following me."

"I don't know about any dog."

"I thought I killed him but listen . . . Hear him on the floor? He's invisible now."

"I don't hear anything."

"He wants me to kill her."

"Don't listen to him. All this shit is in your head anyway."

"What about you? Are you in my head?"

"How many reds did you take before you came here?"

"Seven."

Denise let out a twisted laugh from twisted lips curled into a smile.

"Alright. But what about the guy in the pictures? What do you want me to do about him?"

"Don't do anything."

"Maybe I should go to the police?"

"Don't be crazy. They'll arrest you."

"So what should I do?"

"Are you listening to me? . . . Don't do anything. Let it go."

"Then what should I do about the dog?"

"Call the ASPCA!" she said, and giggled a laugh that tickled my ears.

12

YOU'RE GOING TO LET HIM just walk away scot-free?!"

"You don't understand."

"I understand perfectly!"

"It's what she wants."

"It's what she . . . What did you have, a fucking seance and ask her?!"

"I . . . I . . ."

"I . . . I . . . ," Kaval mocked. "Blackmail! Extortion! Murder! You never cease to amaze me."

"Why are you so fucking bent out of shape over this?! I was doing it to help her. She was in trouble."

"Now what is she in?!"

"That's not fair!" I snapped and popped four reds in spastic fashion.

"Good!" she spit out. "Now go into your coma. You talk about your mother escaping, what about you?"

"My escape is from the pain!"

"That's my point exactly!" Kaval fixed a glare with plenty of attitude to fix it with.

"So what do you want me to do?"

"Something! Anything!" she cried in blue exasperation. "I don't care what! Just do something!"

"If I go to the police they'll arrest me."

"Then do something else!"

I tried not to breathe as I tried to remember what we were talking about. Shaken when I realized what she wanted me to do.

"You're crazy, and I'm not doing it."

"I didn't ask you to do anything."

"I know what you're thinking. I can see it on your face."

"Why don't you grow up!"

"Why don't you leave me the fuck alone."

Kaval turned back on her way out of the room, freckles glowing red.

Later that night I couldn't sleep a wink, tossing like a salad with Kaval's face still churning in my mind. Out in the hall two voices fought like bumper cars on foreign highways, bullets from Spain ricocheting off the plaster. I listened to a woman cry and moan hoarsely, a man snarled and his footsteps ran up the stairs. I got up and peeked out the hole as a tired senorita in tee shirt and jeans came limping into view heaving up strings of gooey mucus, she stopped on the stairs and bent over choking, then continued on wiping her mouth with the back of her hand. I smoked two joints and popped four reds and held my fingers over the candle flame till dripping blood extinguished it.

Sat in the tub and stroked a razor gently fine across my veins, not enough to kill but just enough to chill, practice runs of cowardice, thinking thoughts so pleasantly Denise-like, when playing out in front of me on movie screens of infamy came politics and clergymen; with whips and chains and wet remains as anal sex and oral hygiene shared the Vaseline. Gaping holes and hatchet wounds revealed their inner secrets, moistened lips gave birth to my imaginightmares, my kaleidoscopics. Theater curtains crimson red behind the stage where Christians bled, Jesus Christ and wooden crosses Judas giving head to horses Mary whispered of her dark and Magdalene depravities. The light bulb flickered twice in her chamber with my tripod and mystery when she came into view waiting on tables for restaurant degenerates. His fat and sweaty face preparing for the deed with concentrate intensity and bloodshot cheeks. Denise in her little white communion dress with ribbons in her hair and trouble on her face, all those yellowed photographs unsmiling and defeated. The mark looked into my eyes with slimy snakes for grinning lips but Denise wasn't smiling this time her features blank and empty. The mark laughed an evil laugh and sister's face imploded for no reason, her cheek popped in with broken skullbone forehead bashed in dripping blood down into her eyes, her nose smashed flat on her face a leaking flap of skin, piece by piece her face changed into something not so human anymore. My hands squeezed tight in quivering balls as scraping laughter twisted in my ears. Ticking clocks and crying whimpers of Denise as a child gagging and gurgling and begging please stop made her face continue pounding into mushy red pulp like bleeding sores on eczema. Still he laughed. Tears of silver fell in droplets to my chest as mother's body floated past my face and disappeared into the faucet. I closed my eyes and laughed an evil laugh.

13

I DON'T KNOW HIS NAME, I don't know anything about him other than what he looks like."

"Well that's a start. How many lawyers could there be in New York?"

"How many rats are there in the dump?!"

Kaval gave me a twisted smirk but knew that I was right.

She folded her arms like sister used to do with eyes gone small and sharpened blue.

"There must be some kind of listing, maybe like a catalogue, or a college yearbook type of thing."

"You think so?"

"It's worth a shot. I have an uncle who's a lawyer for IBM. I could call him and ask how to locate a certain lawyer.

"And what do we do once we find this certain lawyer?"

We both stopped short uncertainty.

Kaval spoke to her Uncle Morris in San Francisco who asked about her father and his whereabouts and of the family and cousins and weather in New York and how's her career going and then he mentioned his daughter coming to New York in a few months and maybe she could stay with Kaval at her fine Park Avenue apartment. When Kaval finally got to the point of her phone call he told her she was crazy, that there were hundreds of law schools and thousands of firms and trying to find someone without a name or a number was like trying to find a haystack in a needle. Kaval hung up and crushed a bug on her knee with her thumb.

"I have an idea," I said.

14

B ARBARA SAT ON HER COUCH OF MOD DESIGN with puffed up cushions colored lime. I sank back into the rocking chair, lost in orbit for a moment. Barbara waited for me to land. Then said, "Eddie, I've talked to my lawyers about it. Denise didn't leave a will. Everything she owned and all her assets now goes to the surviving parent, which in this case is your mother, who's incapacitated, thus, her husband, your uncle, is in charge of her affairs and controls her money."

Barbara waited for my reaction but none to find as feelings fled like fleeing Nazis. "Do you understand what I'm saying?" she asked.

"You're basically saying that Uncle Ted has everything Denise owned or accumulated."

"Yes, that's right. We could take him to court but I really don't know on what grounds we'd have a case. He's still legally married to your mother. Even if we did have a case, the time and expense of bringing it to trial . . . As long as he keeps your mother in the hospital, maintains the same standard of living . . . If he stopped doing that then we could take him to court."

"How much did Denise have?"

"By my figuring . . . four hundred thousand dollars plus in cash and bonds."

"I see."

"I'm sorry . . . I know she would have wanted you to have it."

"I don't want her money."

Barbara sipped her wine as holograms of G.G. Allin danced inside her eyes. I took two reds to make them disappear.

"Are you okay?" she asked sitting up.

"I'm fine. Just a headache coming on."

"How are you doing with everything?"

"Fine."

"Do you need any money?"

"No."

"Let me give you something."

"No, really, I don't want it."

"At least take something."

"No."

She sank back into the soft green cushion. "Just like your sister. Stubborn to a fault."

"She was, wasn't she."

We both smiled. Barbara's eyes glazed over like French pastry.

"Barbara, can I ask you for a favor?"

"Sure, what is it?"

"Would you happen to have a key to Denise's apartment? I wanted to go through some of her personal things, to keep as mementos. I don't have anything to remember her by."

Her eyes dried up and sharpened. She said, "I gave her my key when I moved out."

"I see."

"But I have some things of hers that I could let you have. Things I took when I left, small gifts she gave me."

"No, I could never take those from you."

"I could let you have some of them."

"No."

Outside several sirens wailed through the streets and just as quickly disappeared. A dog barked twice. Barbara watched me with her lower lip swelling and quivering like a naughty girl in family court.

"Are you okay?" I asked.

"Yeah, I'm fine."

"You don't look so well."

A second later she clutched me to her breast and stroked my hair with burning tears on splotchy scalp and held me like a parachute. "God, I miss her so much," she sighed. I whispered vacant words from empty thoughts that drowned my heart in mercury.

We stood across the street from her building. Kaval fixed my collar, straightened my tie. Rolled up my sleeves and folded them inside the arms—Dezmond's jacket fit two sizes big. She took a step back and eyed me up and down.

"Alright, you'll pass," she said. "How do I look?"

In her black dress white blouse with high heels and hair

tied back in a bun, pink rose lips and cheekbones blush, she looked quite different. "Beautiful," I said.

"Don't get used to it," she snapped. I took a deep breath and we walked into the marble spattered lobby past the deskman and onward to the elevator. Kaval gave me an excited gleam—she loved this sort of thing. The doors opened and she stepped into the hall and walked along the numbered doors.

"Here it is," she said and motioned me over as the doors slid closed behind me. Barbara's newfound key slipped in and opened our adventure.

Denise's place was as it had been my last time here, nothing touched or rearranged. Kaval stood in the middle looking around and deciding where to begin. Scenes of Denise played in my head, her life in these rooms, on the couch and at the table with music and art and eating and laughing and loving just living as my stomach turned sour rubber balls into mushy red clay. Kaval was in the bedroom going through the dresser drawers.

"What are you doing?" I said somewhat angrily.

"What do you think I'm doing?! Looking for clues. C'mon, help me look!"

I took Barbara's picture from the night table and sat on the bed. Kaval went through the walk-in closet racks of clothes and suits and gowns and shoes and hats and belts accessories hung like convicts on death row. I stepped to her dresser makeup tray an altar of lipsticks and brushes and pads and lotions in tiny crystal bottles with rouge and creams and sweet perfume her scent like spirits guarding sacred tombs. I touched her things and tried to feel her through them. I went through a chest of bracelets anklets silver gold. Hidden in the bottom drawer were mother's antique brooches.

"This is a waste of time," I called out to her. "There's nothing here."

"How do you know if we don't look?" she said, holding up a sequined black gown with slits in the sides.

"We have to go to the dungeon, that's where her office was."

Kaval came peeking over my shoulder.

"What are those?" she asked.

Denise gazed out from the backyard swings her feet in the air and her hair flying off her back and her pretty blue dress puffed up off her thighs in days of laughing carelessness. The sandbox near the garage had castles and tunnels and cold wet secrets with plastic figure army men to protect them. I guarded the fort while Denise stood regal in her kingdom. Her crooked smile skinny legs in dresses pleated plaidly told the private story at her twelfth-year birthday party, hanging from her breast were ribbons trailing bubble gum like roses bleeding thorns. Then Denise with short cropped hair and her arm around my shoulder and a black eye on her face from that fight with Peter Jensen and how Peter had been picking on me for years and taking my lunch money and me not saying a word to anyone ashamed and helpless till Denise found out about it through Debbie McCormack, then she went up to Peter Jensen during recess and ripped a clump of hair out of his head and they went at it like junkyard dogs with Denise kicking and clawing and punching and biting and by the time Sister Grace came hobbling out Peter was sitting on the ground crying like a rainy day. Sister Grace grabbed Denise by her long red hair and slapped her face so hard everybody gasped like breathless debutantes. But Denise didn't utter a sound, she touched her cheek and gave Sister Grace a look with all the fire in the world funneled into it. Then as punishment mother dragged Denise to the barber shop and had her hair cut off like little-boys-who-like-to-fight and for two weeks Denise never left her room except to go to school. One day she proudly stormed into the kitchen and announced to the apron that she was keeping her hair this way for the rest of her life. And for three years she kept that vow.

"What's so funny?"

"Huh? What?" I said breaking my gaze.

"I said, what's so funny."

"Oh, just a memory."

"Would you care to share it?"

"No."

"Suit yourself . . . Where's this dungeon I've heard so much about?"

"Across the street."

I held up the key and flashing lights on tractor trailers shined inside her eyes.

Police tape rips so easily.

The dank smell of darkness, wet like a sewer, Kaval clung onto my shirt as I crept into sister's cryptic mausoleum. I turned on the overhead lights, seven bulbs spread out in a row and built into the ceiling, Kaval let out a gasp. The place had been torn apart with shelves and objects flung everywhere, all the tools of her trade scattered along the floor amongst the batteries and springs and wires and things. Half the floor was rusty brown in splotches making Pollock frown, while the drain was dry and the holes crusted over with coagulation. Kaval's nails dug deep into my forearm face scrunched up as we both stepped to the river's edge. Seven single silver studs sat sideways facing south as I stood flaccid fascination. Kaval let out a whimper and in the whistling breath from her nose came a sound like children having sex. Piercing pins and ampallangs and nipple clamps with leather binds were lying in the corner. Standing at the farthest wall was the wooden X but now bent sideways like a cross with no messiah.

Kaval let out a sniffle and I pulled her to the office which was ransacked even worse. The desk was overturned with drawers smashed to pieces, white papers covered the entire floor and the file cabinet stood with shelves open and the closet door ripped from its hinges. Kaval picked up a handful of blank papers.

"He was here already!" she announced. "Everything's gone! The police would've just taken it, they wouldn't have destroyed the place."

Kaval started kicking through papers and junk on the floor and with a purple sigh she asked, "How could they leave all the blood out there like that?"

"I don't know."

"It's . . . unbelievable! Did you know it was like that?"

"No, this is the first time I've been down here since."

Kaval took a swallow and her eyes clicked in with ferocity. "Show me where you did it," and I led her to the main room across from sister's ministry. The picture was slashed on the floor and the wall had been smashed in and Kaval examined the shredded wood around the hole touching the splintered shards with her fingertips and deciding it must have been a baseball bat. I stuck my hand in the hole and lifted off the panel then dropped it to the floor. Kaval looked over at the stain on the drain as I crept into Plato's little retreat. She followed in and stood where the tripod used to go. Looked out into the main room. "So this is it!" she proclaimed with her hands on her hips and a flame in her eye. "Very nice!"

"Please, don't start in today." She didn't say another word about it.

Kaval went back into the office digging through debris. I stood over the drain and crouched down and touched the milky red swirls and heard a child singing from within, a faint and tender singsong lost in wild afterthought. I removed my fingers and the voice trailed off. Came back upon my touch. A dog barked twice.

I took the garden hose from the nail on the wall and turned on the water and seconds later misty spray came spritzing from the pinholes in the side. I started hosing down Denise's life and washing it into the center of the room. Voices screamed in agony then echoed down the pipes.

Kaval came up beside me, holding something in her hand.

"What did you find?" I asked.

"A matchbook. It's got a number written on it."

"Let me see it."

It was black. On the cover: Cosmogony. On the inside flap written sloppily in green ink were the numbers 475-6002 but not in Denise's handwriting. Kaval took the booklet from my hands. "I want to call this number," she said, "see who answers."

"The phone's been ripped out." Kaval stepped back as the foamy mix of blood and body fluids swept across the floor and wept into the drain.

"There's no answer."

"Let it ring," I said as the tape recorder spun.

Fifteen rings later she said, "If there was a machine it would have come on by now." She slammed down the phone and examined the matchbook in her hand. "We have to find out what this Cosmogony is. It's not listed in the phone book or information. It sounds like it might be a night club, or an after-hours joint."

"It could be anything, or nothing. Anybody could have left it. I mean, if it was important he would have taken it."

"If he knew it was there! It was under a pile of papers. Besides, it's all we have. Maybe your sister's friend knows what it is."

"I doubt it."

"She might have overheard something, maybe a name. You should call and ask her."

"Barbara wasn't part of that life. And if I ask her for names she'll know exactly what's up . . . she already suspects."

A salamander crawled along my arm and bit into my

skin then burrowed into my vein and slithered up into my shoulder. Its throbbing lungs swelled and fought for air until it suffocated and died. Kaval grabbed the receiver and called the operator and tried to get a name or an address for the phone number but the operator said she couldn't give out that information. Kaval slammed the receiver.

"Dezmond might know," I said.

"Who? That jerk?!"

"He's a jerk, but he might know of this place."

"Anything's worth a shot. But just don't tell him too much."

"I'll tell him you got the hots for him."

"You do that and I'll cut your dick off in your sleep!"

Kaval gave me a hard smile with gleaming metal eyes that made me squirm with glee, white horses galloped in my gut as engines churned and automation spewed its icy cold insomnia.

Kaval chalked up her cue as Wally broke the balls. Dezmond sat next to me at the bar sneaking glances over his shoulder at her thighs covered by skintight black pull-ons.

"She looks fucking hot! How is she?"

"She's room temperature."

"C'mon, tell me about it."

"There's nothing to tell. We're friends."

"C'mon man! I tell you about Lucille and me."

"I'm telling you the truth, we're friends."

"You're not fucking her?"

"Why do you have to be so crude?"

"You are, aren't you?"

"We're just friends," I said. Then seeing the unsettling suspicions in his eye and the questions taking shape in his mind, I gave him a Dezmondesque grin which he returned immediately.

"Fuck! I knew it! Good for you, ya fuck! You got any weed?"

"A little."

"Let's step outside."

Outside I handed Dezmond the joint and the Cosmogony matchbook. He lit the end of the joint and put the matches in his pocket. "So, you're not going to tell me anything more?"

"There's nothing more to tell, we're friends."

"C'mon man, give me something to work with here!"

"What are you talking about?!"

"Lucille's got me down to once a week! Every Wednesday at 10:30. Her idea of kinky is to leave the light on."

"So what's your point?"

"I'm dying here and you're not giving me anything to work with. Details! At least let me know what I'm missing out on."

"Oh, you should have told me that. Me and Kaval fuck like ravenous dogs every night. I installed a trapeze over my bed and she suspends herself from it, we play 'tragedy at the circus.' My face is the net. How's that? Can you work with that?"

"Yeah. That's not bad. Tell me about the money."

"What makes you think she's got money?"

"I called you in Beverly Hills, that's no ghetto. Her parents are loaded, aren't they?"

"They're not poor."

"What's her old man do?"

"He's a farmer."

Dezmond let out a laugh and the smoke in his lungs stuttered out of his nose. "Alright, fuck with me. I'm only concerned for your well being, that's all. Watch yourself, she looks like she's been around."

"You're right, I might catch something."

Dezmond spit on the wall and picked a speck from his lip. The joint went out. "What did you do with those matches?" I asked.

"Oh," and he reached into his shirt pocket and handed them over. Reading the cover I asked him, "You ever hear of this place?"

"No, what is it?"

"I don't know. I found the matches somewhere and was curious."

"Who gives a shit? Say, when are you going to see Lizard Len again? I want to get some more reds."

I gave CandyBar my last two reds and she popped them in one loud gulp. Never heard of Cosmogony, she said. We stood against the wall while Zero Zero Minus One watched us from his Saab parked at the curb, as long as I wasn't scaring away customers Zero let me stay.

"Slow night, huh?"

"Pretty slow. My legs are killing me from standing. Zero doesn't let me sit in the car anymore. He says it looks like I'm not available."

"Do you like working for him?"

"Who? Zero? That depends on what you mean by 'like.' "

"Does the sight of his face make you want to puke?"

CandyBar scraped out a laugh and touched my chin with her fingertips. I checked to make sure Zero wasn't watching but he was.

15

KAVAL CHECKED THE VOICE AND NEW YORK and dozens of magazines and underground papers and porno rags and Screw magazine and the sight of Kaval poring through Screw gave me a rise. After two weeks we couldn't find out anything and lately my head seemed to be throbbing worse than before convinced that Denise was in there somehow trying to point the way until I couldn't take the pressure anymore so I went to turn myself in but Detective Webster was out on a case. I left my name and Kaval's phone number at the desk and walking past all that blue I remembered the reds in my pocket. Outside a homeless guy with twisted fingers palsy scabs and scars on his brow shook a paper coffee cup, watched me closely as I walked past and in his eyes were bloodshot veins from onion roots.

After a long pause Kaval buzzed me into her building. Up in her apartment was a skinny guy with lanky limbs and sunken face with red hair braided together like licorice sticks. His black skin clothes clung to his bones as if they were painted on. Kaval stepped out of the bathroom and introduced me to Chris who shook my hand with his zipper undone. Silence hung in the air like guilty verdicts as Chris looked around the room and picked up his canvas knapsack from the floor and flung it over his shoulder and stepped to the door. He said he had to go and Kaval gave him a peck on the cheek which made him kind of uncomfortable. When he left Kaval turned to me, her face a mask of corduroy.

"Well?" she asked.

"Well what?"

"Don't you have anything to say?"

"You fucked him. What is there to say?"

I turned and went into the bedroom and closed the door. Sat down on the bed and wondered if this was some kind of prison cell where the bars and walls were my ribs and flesh. Her voice came through the door as if it were liquid, her face poured in behind it. Into the room like soup.

"I want to talk to you." She kneeled down on the bed next to me and put her hands on her lap. Softly, with sincerity in her eyes she said, "Chris is an old friend . . ."

"Kaval, you don't owe me any explanations."

"But I want to explain. I don't want to hide things or lie to you."

"Then don't."

"I don't want to hurt you either."

"I'm not hurt."

Kaval noticed her record album lying in the corner. Skinny Puppy. "How did that get over there?"

"It must have crawled."

Her lips tightened into a smile, then she turned serious and looked into my eyes. "C'mon, don't be mad, please."

"I'm not mad."

"C'mon, let's talk about it."

"I don't see what there is to talk about. I don't own you, you're not my property. You can do whatever you want."

"And so can you."

"Then it's settled, there's nothing to talk about." But Kaval kept a smirk on her lips and mischief in her eyes and I wanted to hurt her because of it. I asked, "Does Chris know he was playing with a loaded gun?"

"He's kind of a loaded gun himself."

"So you shoot each other."

"I'd rather shoot you," she said and kissed me on the lips.

"I've been thinking about this Cosmogony place," I started. "I think it's going to be a dead end. Even if we do find it, it's not going to tell us anything. We need to find those pictures." Kaval licked me kitten-like and playful, her hair fell down on her breasts and the blue gleam of her eyes made volcanoes blow. I hated her for the way I loved her and I grabbed her shoulders pulled her close with hugs and licks and pixie sticks as anatomic astronauts landed on the moon. Her tongue became warm pudding in my mouth and her breath like dew melting under sunlight as I pressed my hands along her back and ass and halfway down her thighs with pulsing thrusts and hollowness, I fell flat on top of her with her legs wrapped around my waist and that pudding on my neck and my fingers pinching nipples getting hard as Kaval panted and squirmed like dolphins trapped in fishing nets. I knew in another second there'd be nothing left to fuck her with, so I ripped off her tights and panties and undid my pants and saw factories close and move away as workers died of mass starvation, their souls ripped out and stepped on by the government. I collapsed on the bed empty and asexual, lay on my side as she took a deep breath and adjusted her bra.

"I'm sorry," I said.

"For what?"

"For starting what I couldn't finish."

"You're not finished yet," she answered, and took my hand and put it between her legs. With her fingers she guided me around her and up and down her then gently flicked my thumb back and forth across the lips and sighed with every swipe. I went inside her and secret magic mysteries came flooding to my brain, she moaned and dripped like ripened nectarines.

"Go around," she said. "Move it around." I started circling my finger and Kaval grabbed the pillow and clenched her eyes. My left hand slid up under her bra and her hand on the back of my head guided me down as she told me to suck harder with teeth gently pinching and tongue poking my finger revolving faster and faster and Kaval holding her breath for a minute stiff as wood until she broke like glass and sprayed my palm with passion oil. Wondrous revelation, I raised my hand and licked it clean like dirty dogs with salty balls, looked around the room but he was nowhere to be found.

"Come here," she exhaled, and pulled me to her face and kissed me hard on the lips her skin like roasting chickens on a spit. "See, there's more than one way to skin a rat."

"I never saw anything like that before. I didn't know it could be done."

"There's a lot you can learn. Guys—you think all we want is a hard cock."

"It does seem to help."

"You're all idiots."

I let out a laugh and Kaval rolled onto her side. "Let's see what else you can learn," she said.

"No. Wait . . ."

"Shhhh," she whispered with a finger to my lips. "I don't want you to do anything but lie there. You don't have to have a hard-on. Just relax."

Kaval took me in hand and stroked me softly up and down just nice and slow her thumb encircling the head with kisses on my waist. I closed my eyes and tried to think sensation. Kaval took me into her mouth and I turned to sands of grain. Looked up at the paint chips on the ceiling and the hanging wire from where the light was supposed to be, a twisted bony finger pointing accusations. Kaval put her hand on my chest and told me to relax, not to think of anything, then took me back in her mouth as she cupped my balls in her palm like Parcheesi dice. I lay there trembling as someone crawled inside of me. Water dripped down the side of my face and Kaval sat up and grabbed my head and held me close and kissed away the tears. She thought I was crying over her.

I dreamed of green grass apple blossom orchid fields and myself as a young boy pure and undamaged sitting on a checkered cloth across from Raphaella, her wavy hair and olive skin shimmering from the sunlight coming through the leaves on swaying branches overhead. A picnic is spread and Raphaella's blue cotton dress lies fanned out around her with her black schoolgirl shoes with buckles and straps sticking out from underneath. Gray calico stallions danced softly in the distance their hooves on grass like fingers on my chest. I asked Raphaella to tell my future and she touched my head emptied of black ink landing at my knees. When the world stopped spinning I knew that I was cured. Raphaella opened her mouth and music came out; strings

and horns and Copland songs as the hair on my neck stood
up trombones.

I woke up racing inside with Kaval on top of me and something to race with. I clutched the sheets and squeezed her hair
and lost myself in blue despair. Kaval's hot breaths and pas-
sionate sighs fueled the flames of my acceptance. Evil as evil
can be, I enjoyed it now with the power and filth rigid like a piston rod as I pushed her away and rolled her down on the bed.

I got on top of her and she took me in hand and guided me
between her legs and rubbed me against her body, dry and
firm like sun-dried tomatoes. I slid along her stomach kissing
and licking with no sense of urgency not giving a shit if I
stayed hard or not, past her silky fine bush and into the valley
of delight as she blossomed rosebuds in spring. She grabbed
my hair and held me firm as pumping thighs and peanut butter sealed us into one, Kaval and I in love and harmony with
gender identities somewhat skewed like two fingers on a
mangled hand. I looked into her eyes and saw myself.

For joy.

Two days later me and Kaval were riding the train to
Forty-Second Street to look for underground clubs when at
Fourteenth Street this guy got on and immediately started
ranting that he was poor and hungry and that he had full-
blown AIDS and then he held up a folded piece of paper
from his back pocket saying it was a certificate from the government proving he had AIDS and me and Kaval stared at
him in fascination. Everybody else pretended not to see him.
He bawled out that if anybody had any questions about the
truth of his story he could prove it and then he pulled up his
shirt and showed his chest around the car all blistered and
bloated dripping puss-infected scabs. Kaval softly gasped
and gripped my arm, I couldn't look away, one of those
moments when I felt lucky. Somebody gave the guy some
change and he hobbled to the end of the car and waited for
the next stop. Disappeared once he reached it.

On East Seventh near the park I walked alone past the stores thinking things now forgotten, a young kid about ten years old in tattered jeans and grimy tee shirt came up the street holding his forearm snapped broken and bent like a boomerang. The kid was sobbing in pain but trying not to show it, dirty tears dripped down his cheeks like melted wax from wicca candles. On both sides of the street the homeless sold their belongings on the sidewalk and there were old clothes and socks and warped rock albums and doo-dads and jumper cables and a single crutch and silverware and broken earrings books and magazines and ripped shoes and just about anything you could borrow or steal.

I stood outside her building and looked for the kid with the broken arm but he was gone.

Kaval bit into my nipple soft at first but when I didn't respond she bit harder.

"Ow!"

"Just checking," she said.

"Checking for what?!"

"Signs of life."

"You're a sick bitch, you know that?"

"Yeah." She giggled and licked away the teeth marks imbedded in my skin. "My mother's been sending me less money. I called her yesterday."

"What did she say?"

"She said she has to cut back expenses, but she's full of shit. There's been no word from my father, the police are still looking. His girlfriend hasn't turned up either."

"They're probably out of the country by now."

"No. He didn't run away."

"Why do you say that?"

"Because he would have tried to contact me. He would've sent me a postcard, or tried to call. I know something's happened to him."

"What . . . what do you think happened?"

"Something bad."

"What about all that missing money from his job?"

"My father wouldn't take off for a couple hundred thousand dollars. That's peanuts to him! Besides, three years ago my mother inherited over seven million. There was a good reason for him to stay. And I don't like the way my mother just accepts him leaving so easily. I think she knows more than she's letting on."

"What do you think she knows?"

"I don't know. I just don't trust the situation."

"I'm sure he's fine. He'll turn up."

I put my hand between her legs but she moved it away.

"Don't. I'm not in the mood."

Outside a car came screeching up the street followed by a crash of metal and people screaming then the car squealed away as a siren roared up from the distance.

Me and Kaval were walking past the Knitting Factory on Houston when a group of people came out and a woman in ripped fishnet stockings and pleated black mini with rust-colored hair and dark makeup and black nun shoes with the laces undone was screaming at this normal-looking guy in a tee shirt. She called him an asshole and a disgrace to his sex but he seemed to be enjoying it and everybody around was laughing and the more the guy taunted her the angrier she became until the guy turned around and mooned her and then she kicked him full flush in the ass and the guy landed flat on his face. The crowd ooohed and stepped back as the guy got up with his eye bleeding badly while the woman stood her ground but looked a little scared about doing so. The guy grabbed her and slapped her face and when she tried to kick him again he started beating her with his fists. Kaval grabbed my arm and pulled me along.

"C'mon," she said. "She shouldn't have kicked him."

16

KAVAL CAME IN ALL EXCITED holding a mangled piece of paper and when she showed it to me it had the word Cosmogony written on it. I grabbed it from her hand and read the print telling me about the show at The Vault on June 7 which Kaval told me was in two days. I felt alive and excited in ways that gave me purpose. That night we made love by touching each other and I rubbed her back massaged her thighs and licked her feet like slaves in Roman movies, kissed her shoulders and armpits and sucked her inner forearm then squeezed her waist and breasts compressed against mine our tongues in choreography. Kaval's body like the keys on a piano with its hidden symphony waiting to sing when plucked just right.

We went to the Vault and Kaval paid the seventeen dollars they wanted to charge me at the door. I held her hand and she led me into the dungeon of despair toward the bar where the sound of dragging chains surrounded us as dogs and their masters performed their Pasolini. A guy at the bar told us that Cosmogony was a special event planned for the evening about the universe and the beginning of time and the first S & M slaves which he likened to Adam and Eve. In one corner two guys went down on two others and glancing at Kaval she was turned on by the whole thing. A fiftyish woman with long gray hair appeared next to me with her breasts exposed and black electrical tape covering her nipples, sparks shot from one to the other and I imagined myself the conduit. Kaval ordered two beers and then told me to wait at the bar as she disappeared into the crowd. I took a long gulp and lowered the bottle, a young blond stood in front of me with a stud in her nose and a dungaree dress with no blouse underneath. Her nipples pierced by safety

125

pins had beads connecting one to the other like photo-spreads in PFIQ. She didn't move and I thought she might have been a spirit until the speakers in the ceiling stopped and with battered child eyes looking into mine she said, "My Master ordered me to come over here and service you."

"What?"

"My Master—see him over there?" A big fat brute with balding head and goatee chin with leather vest gave a knowing nod. The blond continued, "He ordered me to do whatever you want."

"Oh."

"Would you like a blow job?"

"I don't think so."

"I'll swallow your cum," she added.

"I don't think that would be a good idea."

"You can do whatever you want to me. You can piss on me, fuck me up the ass, you can hurt me if you like."

"I don't want to hurt you."

"If you don't do something to me he'll be very angry." The brute glared at her, Neanderthal brow on cinder block skull.

I told her, "If he hurts you I'll stab his eyes out with a ballpoint pen." She smiled warmly at the thought, then Kaval appeared to my right.

"What's going on?" she asked but not as a question.

"She was ordered to come over here and give me a blow job."

"Ordered?! By who?"

"That guy over there." Kaval glanced over.

"The fuck she will! Go back to Frankenstein!" she snapped and gave the blond a push. Kaval gripped my arm and didn't say another word as she scanned through the crowd. I was tingling inside.

An hour later the lights went out and everyone turned to a platform stage where a spotlight struck a figure wearing white and standing still like a statue. One by one people in white jumpsuits came from all directions and appeared on the stage in vogueing pose mechanicals. Their faces painted with colored designs and one guy had flames igniting from his neck, they started circling the stage and mumbling about time and space and the universe and the absence of god and knowledge and scientific ramblings of Darwinian dogma and Kaval yelled in my ear that it was all a crock of shit. I looked through the crowd but faces unfamiliar. Onstage they were performing sex acts with their clothes on and one guy pulled down his pants and bent over and a woman whipped him with a metal wire and welts rose up like cherry tomatoes. Another guy was being fucked up the ass with a caulking gun and the crowd was cheering him on and soon the stage was alive with depraved sex acts and one guy forced a condom over his head and struggled for air till he fell to the floor and writhed in silent suffocation. An old-fashioned bathtub was wheeled out and a bride and groom sat inside it toasting their newlywedded life together. The group then shrieked in mockery and ripped away each other's jumpsuits revealing leather straps and bustiers and they started pissing in the tub and the groom and his bride were catching the spray in their champagne glasses. The crowd howled as Kaval watched it all with a disgusted scowl.

"This is the most pathetic thing I've ever seen," she said.

Next to me a guy started jerking off and I grabbed Kaval's arm and moved her a few feet away. "Do you want to go?" I asked.

"In a minute," she said. "Keep looking." I did and slipped a red and gulped my beer.

The group was dancing and chanting and forming a circle with their arms above their heads reaching for salvation when all together they fell to the floor and in the middle of the pile stood a man in leather panties and nothing else. He had rings through his nipples and long thin scars on his arms and chest and when Kaval took hold of my arm I knew that she knew him.

"His name's Steven Hopeless," she yelled in my ear and from his Auschwitz haircut skin and bones I knew it to be true. "We can talk to him after the show."

Steven Hopeless slithered like a serpent with his arms in geometric angles, commanding the stage and our attention. From behind him came a fluid-moving woman with her head completely shaved holding a pillow in her outstretched arms and sitting on top of it was a straight-edge razor and the sight of the razor made the crowd yell for Steven Hopeless to kill himself. Steven Hopeless lifted the razor and swung it around like chukka sticks in Chinese movies, the artful precision of his every move froze my eyes in admiration. Looking at Kaval I put my hand on the back of her neck and it was cold cadaver-like. The slaves around him bowed in humble servitude as Steven Hopeless swung the razor at their heads but missed by inches every time. The shaved-head woman held up a piece of white paper and Steven Hopeless sliced it down the middle and she fell away to the floor as if he'd sliced her soul. Steven Hopeless screamed out that he hated himself and the world and the audience and life and god and love and death and sex and AIDS and his own cock as his screams blended into one long primal belch of hatred. He ripped off his leather panties and piercing his cock were pins and rings and other things like fishing weights hanging from his balls. Steven Hopeless swung the blade at his cock and gripped it with his hand and stroked the metal along the head till he drew blood and everyone cheered in jubilation. A dog barked twice. I gulped two more reds and saw blood pour out of my sneakers, my legs warmed with liquid careening from my waist and into my socks. Steven Hopeless ran the razor across his shoulder over and over deep in skin and with every pass of the blade the crowd screamed out a number till they reached fourteen.

Steven Hopeless lowered his arm and waited as the worms of blood slimed down his ragged chest.

"Do you see anyone that you recognize?" she asked.

"No."

"Look at the faces in the crowd."

"I am, I don't see him."

"Are you okay?"

"Yeah, why?"

"Your pants are wet."

Steven Hopeless sliced himself again and held his arms out to his sides as blood dripped to the floor, his shoulders looked like raw cut up meat and the group at his feet started clawing at his body and two men and a question mark pretended to lick his bleeding cock. Steven Hopeless started swinging his arms in arctic circles and everybody rushed back as blood sprang from the cuts. Kaval got shoved by the crowd but after the wave had passed we were the only two left standing there. Steven Hopeless locked his eyes to hers and now I knew what kind of friends they had been. Steven Hopeless rubbed his arms on body smearing blood like native warpaint, around him the group was groping in slow-motion pentathol. Looking like a shaman from the grimy pits of hell Steven Hopeless screamed out more hatred and bile loud and distorted as my eardrums prayed for sound malfunctions. One by one the group disappeared off the stage and into blackness until Steven Hopeless was the only one left standing arms outstretched like Jesus Christ on grassy knolls. The lights popped out and everything went black. There was silence for a moment, then the crowd screamed and howled yet still in blackness. I couldn't see Kaval and wasn't sure I wanted to.

"Are you there?" she asked.

"I'm right beside you."

"Let's try and get backstage."

I took her arm and headed for the stage as the lights

came on and the music burst from the ceiling. Through a hallway leading to the back where modern primitives lined the walls showing off their fleshy mutilations, we stopped at the door and Kaval told the Cosmogonist guarding it who we wanted to see.

"You'll have to wait," he said smugly. "He's getting cleaned up. He may or may not come out when he's finished."

Five moments later the door opened and actors came pouring into the hall but no sign of Steven Hopeless.

"Maybe he's getting a transfusion," I offered. Kaval gave me a smirk and told me to be patient. The shaved-head woman came out in jeans and tee shirt with thin gold chains connecting earlobes to nose and I noticed a tattoo of a rat with a coiled tail on her arm. Kaval asked her to pass on a message and she kissed Kaval hard on the lips then went back into the dressing room.

"Do you know her?" I asked.

"No."

"She just kissed you."

"She was being friendly."

"Invite her back to your place."

"Forget it," she said, eyes like empty crab shells.

She finally came out and said, "He's in the back room off to the left. He's expecting you." Then she gave Kaval a sexy gleam and disappeared into the hall.

Steven Hopeless sat on a chair wearing baggy white pants and nothing else. A stick-shaped woman jet black hair like Olive Oyl stood behind him toweling off his bloody shoulders then dabbing the towel into a bowl of pinkish water on a table against the wall. She didn't look up or acknowledge our presence. Steven Hopeless let out a sly smile as Kaval folded her arms like scolding teachers at detention.

"I see you haven't lost your touch with a knife," she said.

"It's good to see you too, Zoe."

Steven Hopeless and Kaval-as-Zoe didn't say anything else as their eyes in battle soldiers army boot camps—history between them dynamic and mysterious. I stepped up jealous and unworthy.

"We're looking for somebody. Maybe you could help us."

Steven Hopeless broke his gaze and looked at me for the first time, Kaval-as-Zoe came out of her foxhole.

"Steven, this is Eddie. Eddie, this is Steven."

Steven Hopeless gave me a nod and Olive Oyl opened a bottle of peroxide and placed a towel under Steven Hopeless' armpit. She tried to speak but words fell out of her mouth like blocks of granite, she had no tongue. Steven Hopeless flashed his hands in circular sign language and she started pouring the liquid over the cuts in his shoulder and they bubbled white saliva dripping teardrops to his elbow. Without a reaction, Steven looked up and said, "So, you're looking for somebody, eh?"

"We're looking for a lawyer," she said. "We think he's a lawyer. We thought he might be connected to Cosmogony."

"We don't have any lawyers in the group. You know how I feel about lawyers, Zoe. You still dancing at that club?"

"No."

"What happened?"

"My tits began to sag."

Steven Hopeless let out a laugh like birds crushed under hammer blows.

"The guy we're looking for is about forty, forty-five," I said. "Short, about five feet tall. Husky. He's got a round, babyish face and short cropped black hair. Do you know anybody like that?"

"Yeah, my Uncle Herbert from Toledo. He's your man."

"No, I'm serious."

"That's what's so funny," he said and the sound of his laughter filled me with cement.

"The guy we're looking for likes to eat shit," Kaval-as-Zoe added. "Do you know anybody who likes to eat shit?"

"Yeah. Me. I've eaten my own shit. As a matter of fact, if you take one now I'll eat it for you."

The chair to my right called my name and I placed my hand on its back waiting for further instructions. Kaval-as-Zoe must have sensed my purpose, she stepped up and put her hand on my shoulder. "Show him the matchbook," she said and I took it from my pocket and held it out. Steven Hopeless read the cover and the numbers written inside it.

"Why is it wet?" he asked and I told him perspiration.

After a second he said, "Never saw it before. It's not ours. What's this guy's name that you're looking for?"

"We don't know."

"Too bad. I'd like to meet him."

Olive Oyl inspected some of the slices and pulled them apart with her fingertips but Steven Hopeless acted not aware.

"Doesn't that hurt?" I asked.

Steven Hopeless chuckled. "Any pain can be blocked out if you set your mind to it. It's a Zen thing."

"You're full of shit, Steven. You only do it to get attention."

"How's your pussy, Zoe? Remember how Troy used to shave it and carry the hair around in his pocket?"

"Fuck you."

Steven Hopeless motioned with his hands and Olive Oyl giggled out a trilling sound as Kaval-as-Zoe burned like tissue paper.

"Excuse me," I said with sulphur. "I know this must seem like one big joke to you, but we're looking for this guy because he murdered my sister. He beat her face in with a baseball bat until I could barely recognize her. We couldn't even open the casket at her wake. The only clue we have is this matchbook. If you can help us, please do. If you can't, we'll go. But if you say one more fucked up thing to Zoe, I swear I'll rip your fucking heart out and feed it to you."

Nobody spoke and nobody moved and Steven Hopeless looked at me with a face of uncertainty. Defiance then replaced it. "I'm sorry about your sister," he said. "But I don't know any lawyers, or where this matchbook came from. So it looks like I can't help you. Now, if you'd like, you can still rip my fucking heart out—if you can find it. If not, then get the fuck out of my dressing room! And take this with you." Steven Hopeless tossed the matchbook and Kaval ripped it from the air and put it in her pocket. Olive Oyl stood there with a look of discomfort on her face till Steven Hopeless waved his magic hands and she started bandaging up his wounds. Kaval and I stepped to the door and Steven Hopeless called out sharply, "It was good to see you again, Zoe. Drop by any time. Leave your friend home!"

On the street Kaval took my hand and we walked to the corner. We walked another two blocks before I remembered what I wanted to say. "Kaval, I don't know who the fuck you are sometimes."

"I'm the person you're with right now."

"Which is who? Kaval, Nancy, Caroline, or Zoe?"

"I'm myself. It doesn't matter what they call me."

"What about you and Steven Hopeless? You and he had a thing, didn't you?"

"No. we didn't."

"It looked to me like you did."

"I don't care how it looked. I'm telling you the truth, we didn't."

We walked across to Eighth Avenue, trash cans over-turned and bleeding into the street. Kaval squeezed my hand at the sight of the hookers and their pimps.

"How could you think I would have sex with him?" she said with a slight crack in her voice. "I don't find him the least bit attractive."

"I don't know. I guess I'm jealous. I'm sorry."

"That's okay," she said, let out a sniffle.

"What's the matter?" I asked.

"Nobody's ever stuck up for me like that before . . ." her voice trailed off and she touched my cheek. "I want to make love to you."

"Let's go home," I answered.

I rolled onto my back with my hands behind my head and beads of sweat rolling onto the bed. The reds kicked in with hydrogen.

"I want you to stop taking all these pills," she said. "It's not good, no matter how much you think it relieves the pain."

"You don't know what it feels like without them."

"Alright, I don't. But it's still not good. You black out for minutes at a time, you wet your pants and don't even know it. You haven't had an erection in weeks."

"That's not from the pills."

"You're losing your functions and it's all because of these pills, I'm convinced."

"You want me to live in agony?"

"No, I want you to get treatment. Real treatment."

"I've tried so-called treatment."

"When was the last time you saw a doctor?"

"Four days ago."

"I don't mean those quacks you get drugs from."

"They're *real* doctors."

"They're criminals! And you know it."

"Kaval, please, let it go. I've tried it their way . . . I'm not going back to the doctors."

Kaval looked into my eyes and saw a solid wall. "So stubborn," she said in resignation.

"I have to try and find some work. I'm two months behind on my rent."

"Two months?! Why didn't you tell me?"

"Because I don't want to take any more of your money."

"That's ridiculous. I have money in my trust, and you're in no condition to work."

"I'm not a fucking basket case. I can work."

"What are you gonna do? Hand out pamphlets for that titty bar?"

"It's honest work."

"You could . . . move in with me. It would be easier for the both of us. And save us money."

"We'd kill each other."

"No, we wouldn't."

"Yes, we would."

"I'd kill you long before you could kill me."

"Kaval, I could strangle you in your sleep and you wouldn't even know what hit you."

"The second you put your hands around my throat I'd kick you in the balls and you'd be history."

"I don't think so."

"Try me."

"Okay, pretend that you're sleeping." She closed her eyes and slept. I positioned myself and attacked.

She was right.

I woke up alone in bed to a whimpering in the bathroom. I sat up and called her name but no answer. Kaval was slumped against the bowl crying and holding her stomach eyes puffed red and face bloated like an old man's.

"Kaval, are you alright?"

"I'm sick. My stomach, my head. I hurt all over."

"Let me get you something."

"No, I've already taken it."

Jars and bottles marched along the sink, Pepto Bismol led the attack. My hand on her back and she was burning inside. I grabbed the thermometer and shook it clean but sticking it in her mouth she gagged it into the toilet. Floating on top of the water creamy foam and bile formed the word REPENT.

"Kaval, I want to take you to the hospital."

"No, I'm just sick. It'll pass."

"You're white as a ghost. You're always telling me to go to the hospital, now let me take you. Just to be sure."

"No!" Then she spit into the porcelain. I wiped the hair from her eyes and she looked at me helpless child. "Just let me sit here for a while," she said. "I'll be alright."

I sat against the wall and popped eleven aspirin chewing chalky talc.

"Take it easy with those, you'd think they were candy."

"I can see you're feeling better already."

She grabbed her stomach and let out a groan. "Fuck. Tell me a story," she said, leaning against the tub. "A secret story. Something you've never told me before. About yourself."

"I've pretty much told you everything there is to know."

"There must be something you left out. Tell me your deepest darkest secret."

"I have to think what it is."

"Tell me more about your childhood."

"Wait! there is something I have to tell you. But it's not about my childhood. It's not very good news."

"What is it?"

"Try not to get mad, okay?"

"What is it?"

"Well, remember when we were at your parents house in Los Angeles?"

"Yeah."

"I think I might have killed your father in the back yard. It was an accident."

"That's not funny."

"I'm not joking."

"Stop it!" she snapped. "Dammit! If you're going to make me upset then don't talk to me at all."

"Alright, a childhood story. A secret story. You're going to like this one. It's really fucked up."

"Go ahead."

"When I was about six years old, I was home alone one afternoon, it was me and Uncle Ted. Denise and my mother were out shopping. Uncle Ted called me into the kitchen, and when I went in he was standing at the stove jerking off. I didn't know what he was doing. I'd never seen that done before. His cock was hairy, and a lot darker than the rest of his skin. He told me to come closer but I didn't. Then he came over and took my hand and made me hold it. It was heavy, as if it were filled with rocks. He tried to put it in my mouth but I turned my head, wouldn't take it. He laughed and told me to go to my room. I backed into the doorway and watched him jerk off. He was moaning and his eyes were completely white, it was really weird. I went into my room and closed the door. Didn't come out till dinnertime."

Kaval looked at me, her face a little shaken. "Is this true?"

"Yes."

"Did he ever do anything else to you?"

"No. I think shortly after that he must have started in with Denise."

"And you never told your mother?"

"I never told anyone. Except you."

Kaval took a deep breath and sat up straight against the tub, blue eyes angry red. "It sounds to me like we're going after the wrong guy."

I leaned back and rested my eyes, counted to seven.

Sunlight blinding through the shades I sat up aching bones and saw Kaval curled up fetal on the tiles next to the tub. Raging at her beauty and her innocence and God almighty who let his son die on wooden crosses, I lifted her up and carried her into bed and under the covers. Put my head on her chest and listened to her heartbeat pumping stubbornly. His tail swept past the doorway and into the kitchen with his paws scratching on the tile floor.

Tick tock knock knock I closed the bedroom door behind me and went to see who it was.

"Yes?" I asked through the chain link holding the door.

"I've been trying to call you at this number you left me but it seems to be not working. I got your address through the phone company and decided to come over and make sure everything's okay."

"Oh, uh, everything's fine."

"You came by to see me last week?"

"Uh, oh yes, that's right."

"Well, can I come in for a minute? I'd like to talk to you."

"Oh, uh, sure, come in, Detective . . . uh . . . I'm sorry, I forgot your . . ."

"Webster. Detective Webster."

"Yes, that's right. It's a little early for me."

Detective Webster came in and immediately looked around at the boxes and things on the floor.

"You just move in?" he asked.

"Uh, no, actually this isn't my apartment. It's my girl-friend's."

"But you're staying here?"

"Yes, no, uh maybe, I don't know."

Webster let out a deep, trombone chuckle. "That wasn't a multiple choice question."

"Won't you have a seat, Detective?" I took the books from a folding chair and motioned him to sit down, his massive frame swallowed the chair into oblivion. I glanced into the kitchen but it was empty. Detective Webster followed my gaze then scanned the room again. I noticed my bag of pills on a cardboard box.

"Well," he began, "Is there anything you'd like to talk to me about?"

"I, um . . . I wanted to ask you if you found out anything about my sister's murder."

"Well, I've been working on it but it's hard without any

leads to go on. I was hoping that after you've had some time to think about it, you might be able to help me."

"I don't know how I could help."

"I went to see your mother at the hospital. I didn't realize she was fully incapacitated. I'm sorry."

"It's brain cancer. Terminal."

"A nurse at the hospital mentioned that you might have the same thing. I'm very sorry to hear that."

"Thank you."

"Edward, I want to find this person who murdered your sister. It was a brutal, horrible crime. One of the more shocking crimes I've ever seen. I think you knew what your sister was doing in that basement . . . I'm not here to investigate her, or you—I don't care what people do in their private lives. But whoever killed her might have been a client, an associate, whatever. Will you please tell me what you know?"

"What's going on?" she said from the doorway.

We both looked over at the same time, Kaval stood in shorts and tee shirt stained with last night's illness.

"What happened to her?" Detective Webster asked, his face in concern.

"Who's this?" Kaval demanded.

"She's sick," I answered.

"I'm Detective Webster, from Midtown West."

"What do you want?" on ice.

"I'm investigating the murder of Edward's sister, Denise."

I jumped in, "Remember Kaval, I told you about him?"

"Yes," she said dryly. "What have you found out, Detective?"

"I'm afraid not too much. That's why I'm here."

"I doubt very much the person you're looking for is in this apartment."

Webster let out another slide from his trombone. "No one here is a suspect."

"Eddie, would you get me my medicine, please. It's in the bathroom."

"Sure."

I listened from inside.

"He's not well. You shouldn't be bothering him."

"He called me last week. I'm just following up."

"That's very commendable, but I don't want you in my apartment."

Webster looked at the cardboard box and the pills on top of it. "If I were you I'd put those away before I see them. Then you'll know what being bothered really is."

Kaval shrunk with fear. She took the pills and put them in a box.

"Here," I said handing her the jar. When she turned to leave her eyes gave me winter. "I wish I could be of more help, Detective. But I really don't know anything to tell you."

"Alright, play it your way," he said and groaned as he stood up. "It just makes it harder for everyone."

"I'm sorry."

"Yeah, right."

Webster stood at the door. "If you decide to change your mind, call me. But don't wait too long, cause I've got a case-load the size of your friend's attitude."

Webster left and I stood in the room afraid to move.

"Is he gone?" she called from the bedroom.

"Yes."

"Get in here."

I did.

"You have some fucking nerve letting a cop into my apartment."

"He tried to call on the phone. Why do you leave it unplugged?"

"Because I don't want any calls! We could have both been arrested with those pills all over the place!"

"I know."

"How many times do I have to tell you about those fucking pills."

"I know. I'm sorry."

"You're always sorry but that doesn't solve anything."

"Alright, but I wasn't expecting . . ."

"You don't fucking use your head!"

"I know, but please, don't yell at . . ."

"And then you let him into my fucking apartment!"

"I said I was sorry. Please, don't yell at . . ."

"You make me yell at you! If you weren't so fucking careless . . ."

"DON'T FUCKING YELL AT ME!!!" I screamed with shredding lungs and Kaval jumped back. I collapsed to my knees clutching my head and trying to hold it together. Kaval stood still a moment, then she ran over and tried to calm me down but I couldn't hear her voice, silent movies had more synchronicity. She gripped my wrists and pulled them from my ears as freezing tingle dentist drills burrowed out through bone. Fumbling with reds she shoved some into my mouth with water but I couldn't swallow throat closed tight like flooded tunnels. She grabbed a joint next to the bed and lit it blowing sweet perfume and pungent pickles into my brain. Then everything went green.

Kaval stroked my forehead and whispered, "Please, let me take you to a doctor. Just this once."

"Kaval, let's stop with the doctors, okay?"

She curled her lips, amusement rides and cotton candy closed on rainy days, then she went into the kitchen. I shut my eyes and saw my kidneys weep.

I sat up to the fragrant smells of eggs and toast and Kaval stood in the kitchen at the stove cooking. A portable radio scratched out a tune of ripping cardboard. Her hand circled graceful in the pan and her lips sang words of vague familiarity. Sunlight through the window lit up her hair like sparklers in July and as she raised her voice in formless song, I tried to read her lips: "You make me feel . . . you make me feel . . . you make me feel like a natural woman." Fevers rose inside my clothes from watching old-time movie shows of tragic love with Romeo and Juliet holding hands yet no happy endings in act three. She glanced into the room and smiled shyly.

"I'm making you some eggs," she called and turned off the stove and came in with my plate.

"What's the matter?" she asked.

"I love you," I sniffled.

"I know. Now eat your eggs before they get cold. Later, we'll go over to your place and try and sneak your stuff out."

"Okay."

"I'm so fucking tired," she said and laid down. "Wake me up in a little while, okay?"

"Sure."

"Dezmond, can you get me a gun?"

"Going on a killing spree?"

"I wouldn't call it a spree."

"What's up? Why do you want a gun?"

"I just want one, for protection."

"If you want to protect yourself, use a condom!"

"C'mon, don't be a jerk! Can you get one or not?"

Jackie stood behind the bar yelling at Old Man Costello about his tab. "There's a guy at work who might be able to sell you a gun. I'll ask him when I see him."

"When will that be?"

"I don't know. Tomorrow, the next day, the day after that."

"Let me know, alright?"

"I'm not responsible for whoever gets shot."

"Why is Wally crying?"

"Oh shit. You don't know. Camille's dead."

"Dead?! How did that happen?"

"We don't know. They found her body dumped along the West Side Highway a few days ago, near the water."

"The police don't know who did it?"

"Not yet. Right now they've got all the suspects locked up in Shea Stadium." Dezmond laughed out proud and I joined him out of reflex—evil as evil can be.

"Look at him," I said, watching Wally wail like weeping women at a wake. "He always hated his sister. Now that she's dead he loves her. Don't forget about that gun, okay?"

"Chill, Killer."

Kaval was walking along Avenue A with a little girl maybe four years old holding her by the hand. She was looking up and down the block as I approached. "What are you doing?" I asked.

"I'm trying to find this little girl's mother. She's lost."

"Where did you find her?"

"Right out here, her name's Kinsasha."

"Who? The mother or the girl?"

She ignored that. "Why didn't you wake me up before you left?

"I didn't want to."

The little girl watched us both, her dirty face in a confused pout.

"What are we going to do?"

"We're going to try and find her mother."

"What if we can't? Maybe we should go to the police."

"Wrong! They'll take her away and put her who knows where."

"Well if the mother leaves her alone on the street maybe that's what should happen. There's a cop car around the corner."

"You call a cop and I'll never speak to you again!"

"Alright, forget I mentioned it. What do you have against cops anyway?"

"Everything."

"Well, did you ask her where her mother is?"

Kaval crouched down and put her hands on Kinsasha's shoulders. "Honey, are you sure you didn't see which way mommy went?"

Kinsasha pointed downtown toward the park and said, "Over there."

"Great!" I said. "You know what she's doing in the park."

"Don't jump to conclusions."

"Hey Kinsasha, you want to see a trick?" I crouched down and squeezed my hands together into a cup and made a quacking duck sound. Kinsasha seemed genuinely amused. "How do you do that?" she squeaked. I showed her and as we walked to the park she tried to quack and Kaval gave me a smirk out of the side of her face.

"We can't get my stuff."

"Why not?"

"My landlord changed the locks on my apartment."

"How do you know?"

"I was there earlier, while you were sleeping."

Her face sank into horror films. "He can't do that!" she snapped. "That's fucking illegal!"

"Well, he did it anyway."

"We're going over there with a fucking crowbar! We're breaking in and you're getting your stuff out. Fucking bull-shit . . ."

"Excuse me, there's a child present."

Kaval looked down at Kinsasha walking between us and trying unsuccessfully to quack. "And besides," I added, "I don't care about the stuff. It's garbage. What am I fighting to keep?!"

"Your clothes, for one thing."

"I have clothes at your place."

"It's the principle of the thing!"

"The guy's out two months rent, let him keep whatever's there."

Kaval reached back for Kinsasha's hand and pulled her along. I quacked and Kinsasha broke out a smile, crooked teeth like bent nails.

A woman about thirty years old came running up to us with a bandanna on her head and a tattered flowing dress and sandals on her feet with skinny legs on thin waist in between bony arms and an excited toothless grin on her face. Kinsasha pulled free and ran a few steps forward and into her mother's arms; as her mother reached out for the little girl I could see that she was using. Glazed and bloodshot eyes that hadn't slept in days only confirmed it. The woman thanked Kaval and said it was all an accident and that it would never happen again and then she scolded her little girl for not staying put. They walked away from the park and I stood there picturing the different scenarios of Kinsasha's life and what might happen to her and would she turn out like CandyBar.

17

ZERO CAN GET YOU ONE."

"Where is he?"

"He'll be around later."

"How's business today?"

"Slow. Just a couple of blow jobs."

"It's the recession."

"Yeah, right," she chuckled.

"Did you hear about Wally's sister Camille?"

"No. Who's Wally?"

"You know, the fat guy at Jackie's? Always shooting pool?"

"I don't think I know him. I only go to Jackie's to get in out of the rain."

"Oh, well this guy Wally's sister was killed."

"That's too bad."

"They don't know what happened. They're waiting on an autopsy."

"Do you have any blow?"

"No. I have some weed on me."

A blue Volvo with Jersey plates pulled up and CandyBar wrapped her arm around mine and pulled me close and the Volvo drove off with its tailpipe sputtering Swedish curses.

"Would you walk me home?" she asked. "I'm not feeling good."

"Sure. You look a little pale."

We walked two blocks to her building and reaching the stoop she asked me if I wanted to come up. "Please," she said, "I don't feel like being alone."

I followed her into the dark hall creepy fun like haunted mansions. I stopped on the third flight to catch my breath, CandyBar continued on until she realized she was alone.

"Are you alright?"

"I just have to rest for a minute."

"Let's take the elevator the rest of the way."

"Yeah, that's a good idea."

The doors opened on the ninth floor but CandyBar lived on the eighth. She went to the end of the hall and opened a metal door and sinking sunlight poured like orangeade. "You wanna get some air?" she asked, stepping out onto the roof before I could answer. I shielded my eyes as purple pigeons circled in my retinas. CandyBar stood near the ledge looking down at the street below.

"You ever wonder what the drop would feel like?" she asked.

"I imagine it's probably like a roller coaster."

"Except it's a one-way ride and you don't need a ticket,"

she said and broke out a smile. "I'll have some of that weed if you still want to."

I took it out and rolled a joint. Lit it and passed it to CandyBar who put her fingers on the end and toked without letting it touch her lips. Smoke filtered out of her nose and mouth and she toked again, passed the joint and said thanks. We gazed out over the city and at the buildings and to our right the Hudson held a bed of smog while up above pictures of Jesus hid in the clouds. Cowardly saviors like faces on coins. CandyBar let out a sigh and said, "The whole city in front of us, all these lives, imagine if you could see them all."

"Just seeing my own is bad enough," I said and CandyBar giggled.

"You're crazy sometimes."

"I'll take that as a compliment."

She faced me and her eyes seemed old, bags and lines and too much hardship underneath. "I really thought I would have a future," she said.

"What about that restaurant you want to open?"

She gave me a sad, tired smile. "Oh yeah. That's right."

"You're going to do just fine," I continued. "For a twelve-year-old you have more smarts and common sense than most people I know."

"I turned thirteen last month," she said, perking up. "On the fifteenth."

"See? Your future's already shaping up. Happy birthday."

"You're sweet," she said, and gazed far off visions into the clouds as lights popped on in cold metallic windows. "Sometimes I wonder what it all means. All these creeps I know."

"There's no shortage of creeps."

"That's the damn truth. You're the only decent person I know."

"That's not saying much," I said with a grin.

"You're crazy," she answered and gazed back down at the street.

18

VAMPIRELLA SAT IN HER LAIR BREASTS exposed like baker's dough with blood dripping from her teeth and black shiny boots up to her thighs and a whip in hand just a tiny little whip for naughty teenage boys. Kaval stood at the next table St. Marks Place browsing through pornography and misogyny with blue biology on folding tables lining the curb and the more she browsed the angrier she became as female parts and he-man fantasies killed her as a person.

"I'm going to buy this," I said, holding up a Tales of Terror.

"How old are you, six? Or twenty-six?" she asked.

"You're right. I'll take this one instead," and held up a copy of Snatch. Kaval puked out a laugh then ripped the Tales of Terror from my hand, paid for it and we left.

On the stairs leading up to the second floor a dirty used-up needle with a drop of blood underneath it sat in our path and Kaval grabbed my arm and froze. "Fucking junkies," she said and I scooped up the needle with my Tales of Terror and chucked the whole thing in the trash. Starting back up the stairs Kaval took my hand and said, "I'll buy you another one."

Kaval plugged in the phone and called that number on the matchbook over and over but there was no answer. She tried to trick the operator into giving her more information but it never worked. I told her finally to give it a break and she looked annoyed and slammed down the receiver and unplugged the phone. I didn't tell her about me trying to get a gun or what I was going to do once I got one. I wasn't exactly sure myself.

I helped Kaval make a salad at the sink and she was putting in all kinds of weird green leaves with red spots and funny veins and small tomatoes and fresh-grown oregano and flattened pea pods with chunks of tofu and when I told her to leave out the tofu she said that it was good for me. Standing next to her I noticed how much weight she had lost and her face was getting paler as the blood drained out of her head and every day she seemed to be taking more vitamins and herbs and juices teas with secret potions, some days she couldn't hold it all down, and while my condition seemed to be getting better hers was getting worse. Indifferent days of loneliness I wait for you.

19

DEZMOND STRUCK OUT on the gun.
"His brother got busted," he said. "Had you asked a few months ago . . ."

"Don't worry about it," I told him.

"Why don't you try Lizard Len? I'll bet he could get a gun."

"It's no big deal," I said and gulped my scotch. Dezmond motioned for Jackie to refill our glasses.

"What's up with you?" Jackie snapped at me.

"What do you mean?"

"Where the hell you been? You don't hardly come around no more."

"Can you blame me?"

Dezmond turned to the room. "He's living downtown in a lovenest with his little honey!"

Everybody broke into teasing laughter even Wally lifted his round tomato face from the bar and looked at the disturbance.

"Nine Ball!" Dezmond yelled across to him. "Ten dollars a game."

Wally just grumbled and sunk back into his arms, an overturned glass near his elbow.

"Hey Jackie, the fuckin' guy hasn't moved from that stool in two weeks. Maybe you should start chargin' rent."

"That's a good idea. Your stool rents for twenty bucks. Pay up!"

"Pay up on this," Dezmond shot back and grabbed his crotch.

"That ain't worth ten cents."

"That's not what your wife said last night!"

"Oh yeah . . ."

"Alright, give it a break," I jumped in. "I'm sick of it."

I got up to shoot some pool with Dezmond but before we reached the table Harper came running in excited news through panting words. "The ambulance just took her away!"

"Who?"

"You know that little whore, the one that stands on the corner, what's her name . . . CandyKane? She used to come in when it rained?"

I stood there disbelieving and numb as Dezmond sprang out the door followed by Harper and the others. Wally lifted himself up and flabbed out like his sister used to do. Jackie stayed behind the bar wiping it with a towel.

Two cop cars were blocking the street and a small crowd of people stood outside her building and at the curb sat a gray car with its hood caved in and its windshield smashed. A cop was talking to a strung-out junkie wench with short spiked hair and coke bottle eyes as people murmured around me and one guy described the body as being twisted like a chain. I listened to the words and phrases melded into patchwork facts of fiction. Shaken and responsible thinking one loss too many I tried to imagine that moment when she stood there looking down at the street lost and alone with despair like a straitjacket squeezing her guts but when my brain told my eyes to start crying my heart said why bother. Across the street and hiding in the alley he sat on hind legs watching me, now I knew why.

Kaval was still sleeping when I came in. I smoked two joints and drank half a bottle of cheap wine. Amazed at myself so calm and collected with no sense of feeling not even sadness. I stared at the holes in the wall and wondered if Kaval would jump and maybe we'd jump together. I snapped back to a tapping on the door. Ignored it until it grew inside my head.

I was surprised to see a woman with a feathered hat impeccably dressed with pearls and makeup strong perfume.

"Yes?" I said through the crack.

"I'm looking for Nancy," she answered with a scowl.

"For who?"

"You know who I want."

"She's asleep."

"Wake her."

"Who should I say is calling?"

"Get my daughter now before I call the police!" she barked with a slight shriek in her voice.

"Um . . . wait here." I went into the bedroom where Kaval had her head under the covers. "Kaval, wake up! Get up! Somebody's here for you. I think it's your mother."

"What?" she grumbled.

"Your mother's here."

"My mother?!" then sprang up as if jolted by a prong.

"That's right," we heard from the main room.

The bedroom door swung open and Lillian stood glaring at her sleepy little girl. "So this is the nice Park Avenue apartment we've been paying for all this time."

"What are you doing here?"

"I couldn't reach you by phone, all my letters were returned unopened. I had to hire an investigator to track you down."

"You what?!"

"Look at yourself! What's wrong with you? Are you sick? What has he done to you?!"

"Stop it, Mother."

"You look like death warmed over. What has he been doing to you?"

"Nothing."

Lillian looked around her face in twisted disbelief, eyes on rotted floorboards climbing up the cracked and peeling wall. "My God," she sighed, then snapped with a flourish, "Pack your things, you're coming home with me."

"No, Mother. *This* is my home."

"Nancy, I'm not going to argue with you. You're not staying another day in this pig sty."

"It may not be to your liking, but it is to mine."

"You're leaving with me if I have to drag you out by the hair."

"Try it," and the cold little smile on her lips made Lillian drop that thought. Lillian planted hands on hips and bellowed, "What have you been doing with all the money we've been sending you? Where has that gone?"

"You haven't sent a check in weeks."

"I wasn't going to continue sending checks to a post office box."

"Daddy would have."

"Your father is in no position to send checks anywhere."

"What does that mean?"

"I spoke to your father a week ago, he called and said he won't be coming back."

"You spoke to him?"

"Yes. He told me to tell you that he's fine and in good health."

"Where is he?"

"He wouldn't say. He's with his little tramp, I'm sure. It's now a civil matter as far as the police are concerned. The studio has declined to press charges."

"And you're the only one he talked to?"

"He also called your Uncle Clayton."

"Clayton is not my uncle."

"Regardless, they spoke for over an hour on Tuesday evening."

"Why would he call Clayton and not me?"

"Your father wanted some legal advice, statute of limitations, civil liabilities against the estate, that sort of thing."

"That's all very convenient. The police believed you two, of course."

"Why wouldn't they? What are you trying to say?"

I stood there invisible as Kaval and her mother froze in time and history, no one goes unscathed. The piercing pain and acid rain made me reappear again. "Would you like something to drink, Mrs. Erikson?"

Lillian acted as if a bug had talked.

"Nancy," she said and softened features honey-like not vinegar. "Please, I'm asking you to come home with me. Just for a little while. You can come back to New York once you get your life together. Your friend will understand, won't you?" She looked at me with shiver chills and bitter pills sucked deep from empty lobster shells. He was inside of her now.

"Mother, Eddie and I are engaged to be married. And I'm staying here with him."

Honey turned tabasco sauce. Even I was taken by the spice.

"You're just doing this to punish me!" she shrieked. "Your whole life has been spent defying me and trying to hurt me."

"This isn't about you. It's about me. This is my life we're talking about!"

"And I don't want to see you ruin it!" she barked, then turned her canine eyes with subtext so revealing. "You're giving her drugs, aren't you? I know that you are because she didn't look this way a few months ago."

"She's sick. She's got . . ."

"An upset stomach," Kaval cut in and gave me a look to shut my mouth. "He's not giving me drugs, I'm not taking any drugs. I'm into health and natural foods."

"Oh, you look very healthy and natural," Lillian said sarcastically, a slight scrape from battle fatigue.

"Mother, I'm living my own life now. Whatever happened between you and Daddy is over. You're free. You should be happy. Now let me have my own space."

"You blame me for your father. You've always blamed me for the way things were. It wasn't my fault. I tried. It wasn't easy."

As he worked his magic wonder tears, good as he was, this evil dog, the gun became imperative.

"Mother, please stop crying. It's not going to change anything. I'm staying where I am."

Lillian pulled out a lavender handkerchief and fluttered it open and dabbed it to her eyes, tried to compose herself. With measured words she said, "So, if this is the way you want to live, fine, I'm not going to stop you. But I want you to know that I can't allow myself to support this lifestyle. I will not. When you're ready to wise up, then everything I have will be at your disposal. Until then, you and Edward are on your own."

"His name is Eddie! Not Edward."

"Actually, it's Edmund," I broke in.

"Shut up!" and so I did.

"Very well," she sniffled and pulled out a compact and wiped her eyes using the handkerchief. "When you come to your senses, you know where I am." She turned to leave and gave a glare but underneath I saw him there. Laughing.

Kaval wiped her face with the sheets and once the door had closed she leaned back on her elbows and gave me a sunny smile.

"Why didn't you tell her about it?" I asked. "She would have given you all the money you wanted."

"Because she would have never left us alone, she would have had me committed when it got bad."

"What about that stuff about getting married?"

"I knew that would get rid of her."

"Oh."

"But lately I've been thinking about it."

Kaval then proceeded to tell me about our marriage and its convenience repeating how she hates the thought of marriage and that it wasn't about me but about marriage in general cause no one she's ever met who is married was happy and though I disagreed completely, I made believe I didn't. As her future husband she gave me the details of her funeral just a simple affair without Jesus or God or even her mother but with kind words and a few friends except for maybe Dezmond. I took my prize with sorry understanding then thought of the possibility of me going first and told her my wishes which were twosome. "Bury me in jeans and my white button-down shirt. I don't want to be buried in black, okay? And I want you to put something of yours into the coffin."

"What do you want me to put?"

"I don't know. Surprise me."

20

ZERO ZERO MINUS ONE stood near the glassless window facing out onto the Hudson.

"Close the door and put the beam through the arms," he said. I waited in the doorway for my eyes to adjust to the dark. Slurping water dying seagulls puking on pollution lapped up against the rafters lost in the huge expanse of the warehouse. Feathers floated down from blackened beams overhead as fluttering wings pinched the water's whisper. Zero turned his head and the circle-scar on each cheek burned from red hot cigarettes back when Zero was a boy put black eyes on his face which gave him four. Something was wrong, I'd never seen him so calm.

"Well?" he said and I proceeded in with sneakers scraping grimy pavement glass and cans and splintered wood on musty air as thick as fog. In the corner a burned out Volkswagen sat rusted and mangled with the word FUCK painted on the side. Zero watched me closely as I stopped at the window, the jittering whites of his eyes made me relax. The dog would've known what I was up to.

"You got the money?"

I pulled it out and Zero smiled greedy as money changing hands smoothed all misunderstandings. Zero had asked for 250 but I handed 270 to test his good intentions and he counted it out and slipped it into his pocket. Without missing a beat he said, "You sure you want this?"

"Where I live, I've been jumped twice. I need to protect myself."

"Where you at?"

"East Tenth and Avenue B."

"You think that's bad?!" he cackled voice rising high. "Shit! I been in fucking nursery schools that are badder than that. You should try living in fucking Bushwick, you wanna see a fucking sewer. Where I grew up we had to sleep on the floor cause of stray bullets coming through the windows."

"I guess it's a little different growing up on Staten Island."

"I hear that."

"How about the gun?"

Zero pulled out a tiny little piece no bigger than my hand, an ivory-handled cowboy gun from days of Hiyo-Silver.

"What's this? You said it would be a .38."

"This is better than a .38!" he squawked. "It's easier to conceal. You carry around a .38 and everybody knows you're packing. Cops'll pick you up ten minutes after you hit the street."

"It looks like a toy."

"It shoots bullets. What more do you want? . . . Look, you want the fucking thing or not?"

I held it in my hand and tried to open the chamber, Zero showed me how. I looked at him.

"What do you think," he said, "I'm gonna hand you a fucking loaded gun. You shoot me dead and take your money back."

"Oh, right. I didn't think of that."

I pointed it out the window and aimed at infinity, pulled the harmless click of trigger. "What about bullets?"

"Give me the gun." I did and Zero took out a cardboard box no bigger than a matchbox car. Very light. I shook it hollow jumping beans in empty cans. "Can I see them?" I asked and Zero shook his head with impatience. Eight toy bullets rolled into my palm with seven facing west and one straight at my eye.

"They look awfully small. How come there's only eight?"

"What are you a serial killer?!" he snapped. "They're .22s, like the gun. I split the tips so they burst on impact."

"They just slip into these holes?"

"Eddie man, why you breaking my balls?!"

"Zero, I'm from the suburbs, what the fuck do I know about guns?"

"Exactly! Leave the toys to the big boys."

"You know, I've been wanting to tell you, I'm really sorry about CandyBar. I know how you must have felt."

Zero's eyes dug deep at mine but frozen earth won't give so easily. "She really loved you, you know. She was always saying how good you were to her."

"She said that about me?" His guard untamed from flattery.

"All the time."

"Damn, who knew what was in that girl's head? If she was fucked up about something she could have come to me, I would have straightened it out."

"Well, you can't blame yourself. How can you know what people are thinking? Anyway, I wanted you to know how sorry I am."

With a wave of his hand he said, "Aaah, bitches . . . Leaves on a tree."

"So, these things just slip into the holes, huh?"

"You figure it out. I gotta go." Zero turned to leave and I clicked the chamber closed.

"Hey Zero, I think I got it!"

"What?" he said and turned around as microscopes and camera lenses shattered eyes and wire fences focused on New Jersey. Hatred and revulsion with its furniture scraping along the floor of my skull as her body fell past my eyes made my hand snap back as weasels popped and Zero gasped in shock. He didn't drop, just stood there stunned, trying to speak with nothing left to form the syllables. Clutching at his lips half of which were blown away and at the tiny hole under his nose where blood spilled out, he crumpled flat to the floor his arms and legs flopping fish-like out of water. Zero managed to roll himself onto his back and tried to sit up, gurbled out a clumsy curse before his mouth filled up with blood and bubbles. His face contorted rubber latex and he reached into his jacket with shaking hands and seizure tremors. A pool of liquid crawled from his ears and rancid air burst like steam from his nose. His hand came into view gripping a gun twice as big as mine and aiming at my chest I dropped my bullets scattered at my feet. Zero's barrel shook and his eyes glazed over but still that spigot poured. I reached for seven on the ground as he lowered his gun in my direction and hung on one last act of retribution. All the while lipless teeth kept chattering lame like talking skulls in horror movies, more angry than anything else. His plasma under feet and fishing for bullets in the red I felt his heart-beat pumping in the stream. Blast my ears as the wall behind me spit with fire. He quivered spewing bloody bile hammer cocked in readiness, this time pointing at my head. Fearful calm I clicked the chamber closed and finished vigilante. The pavement reached up and ripped him down his head slammed hard with ultrasound, half his face was gone with maggot larvae oozing from inside. I lowered my arm as his soul rose out of his chest and disappeared high into the rafters. Gray and evanescent like subway smoke in chilly winters. I tried to scrape the grime from sneakers wiping hands against my pants and waiting for eternal damnation. When I realized there was nothing, I rose to my feet and took my gun.

It was dark outside and Zero's body lay still on the ground, surrounded by a pool of serenity. I zippered my jacket and went downtown.

She stood at the sink and I snuck up behind and wrapped my arms around her and buried my mouth in her radiant hair.

"What's come over you?"

"I love you so fucking much I could puke!"

"Is that supposed to be a compliment?"

"You take what you can get."

"Where have you been?"

"I was on the West Side. Had to see somebody."

Looking into my face, "Are you alright?"

"I'm fine."

"You look a little strange."

I kissed her hard my tongue in crevices along her teeth.

"Are you sure you're alright?"

I answered, "You had ice cream for lunch."

"What flavor?"

I licked her teeth and proudly told her coffee.

"Maybe you can lick my ass and tell me what I ate for dinner last night."

"You're gross."

She grinned and the dimples appeared.

I remembered my pocket unempty and incriminating and carefully pulled off my jacket, eased it softly to the floor. Kaval went to her duffel bag in the corner and pulled out a purple piece of clothing. "Here," she said excitedly. "I picked up a shirt for you when I was out."

"Thanks, my favorite color. Hey, it's still got the shoplifting thing on it. Kaval, you stole this shirt! I thought you weren't going to do that anymore."

"I'm rebelling against a consumer society."

"One of these days you're going to be rebelling from prison and I'm not going to bail you out."

"What's the matter, don't you like it?"

"How am I going to wear it? It's got this plastic thing stuck to it."

Kaval went to the bedroom and came out with a brick, placed the shirt on the floor and smashed the plastic disk repeatedly until it cracked in seven pieces. "There," she said proudly pulling away the back plate. "Now what do you want for dinner?"

"Surprise me."

We ate on the floor with plates on our laps and I thought to myself, Kaval must never know.

21

I STOOD ACROSS THE STREET THE YARD overgrown with weeds and thorny hedges. Driveway clear, the tree was leaning over like a weary widow with arthritis, a frayed rope and tire hanging from her twisted arms. Peeling two-tone green and white garage doors sat crooked off rusted hinges. Walking around the back yard with broken swing set dried out sandbox and onto the patio where Denise once let the Playdoh sit to bake her rainbow cookies, I took the hidden key under flower pot and pulled back the ripped screen door, let myself in. Stepped into the rear hall leading to the kitchen, laundry to my left had the dryer open and a body of twisted clothes trying to escape out of the hatch. Past the musty smell of dirty linen floating in the air I entered Mother's chapel, shocked at the neglect with the sink overflowing of greasy soiled dishes silverware and mugs, crumbs on the counter and a piece of petrified bread; the tablecloth checkered red with ancient spices stacked along the edge, the cabinet doors were missing handles and opening the refrigerator rusted wire shelves held up ketchup mustard and a six of Bud, spoiled yellow cheese wrapped in orange cellophane tucked inside the door. Above the kitchen doorway pies of cleanliness from ornamental plates where Jesus Christ once hung.

Denise's room a faded pink was lined with boxes up against the wall her dressing mirror reflecting closet doors and metal hangers. I crept in tiny crawlspace knocking hangers tinkling laughter how could I have fit inside here twelve years old peeking out the crack as Denise and Audrey Ockerman sat on her bed with kissing lips and slurping tongues, my stomach jumping trampolines then finding out later Denise was aware of my presence. When she asked me not to tell Mommy and I swore that I wouldn't she gave me her lucky rock.

My room across the hall still had my bed and dresser and the cracked wall from baseball practice, the dresser drawers half-filled with tee shirts and underwear black socks and grandma's birthday handkerchiefs. I took one out and shoved it in my pocket.

Mother's bedroom once so clean with dressers shined and kept pristine, now tornado sights would look no harsher. Her bed undone and deranged a thousand raging nightmares with soiled sheets pulled in clumps into the middle. Her silk beige spread was draped to the floor with shoes and socks on top. Over the headboard hung her goldframed portrait of some long-deceased cardinal from upstate New York, statuettes of cherub angels in priestly robes and chipped faces holding golden globes with crosses on top watched me from the dresser. Over the closet Jesus cried in agony from his crucifix, blood dripping from his wrists and feet, his crown of thorns and pained conceit. The world's most famous masochist. On the top shelf were mother's flowered housecoat and slippers and hidden underneath was Denise's yellowed wedding album thick white leather with silver leaf print. Pictures inside of people who never could or did exist. Posing in my tux that day and watching sister tethered like a raging beast in Africa, I prayed for her, yet fed the furnace of mother's blind estrangement. The jealous little scowl on Uncle Ted's face made it all the more pathetic.

In the living room the windows were open, the faded blue curtains breathing in the outside air. There was a new wall unit with a Sony large-screen tv. The worn out couch had two lumpy pillows and a sheet on top from Uncle Ted's most recent slumber. The coffee table stained from dripping glasses had overflowing ashtray on top of boating magazines, an empty can of Bud lay on its side its middle dented in from clumsy callused fingers. The end tables covered with a sheet of dust and a lamp on top of each, under the right one sat the massive ancient bible with its full-color reproductions of death and despair and serpents eating fruit, I cried when Adam lost his kingdom. The upright piano warped with decay stood behind the front door, it used to be in the middle of the wall. Chipped yellowed keys smiled like beggar's teeth unmelodic and dull. Fingers splayed across the keys in dissonant C-minor with flatted fifth but held in apprehension for what might be heard or not heard. Plunking on the hammers dust rose up and nothing else.

Behind the desk in front of the window a computer sat dark and powerless on a metal stand. Reading names and numbers seeped into the faded green blotter on the desktop; his airplane ashtray sat off to the side, its propeller cracked from accidents on Labor Day; underneath his writing pad my initials still scraped into the wood and immediate thoughts of the beating that followed. His drawers were filled with bills and forms and purchase orders, all the bullshit boredom shipping clerks adore. The bottom drawer with built-in lock wouldn't open and I turned to search the wall unit when a bumblebee flashed through the open window. It buzzed the room with whispering wings then hovered near the ceiling, its vaporous voice like stale air in a bottle: Beware of the man with the soviet plan . . . the soviet plan—that code again. A pencil rolled off the desktop and landed at my feet . . . !

I tugged and jerked on the drawer sweat bleeding into my eyes after all these years to see that plan revealed, but it fought to keep its mystery. I ran into the basement past the monster closet where the lizard-man had lived until Denise killed him with a long-handled gardening spade. Pulling assorted tools from the shelves built into the wall I headed back upstairs.

The drawer started cracking under the weight of the screwdriver and I wedged it deeper but the lock refused to budge. I pried until the tool broke weakly in my hands. The gun in my pocket whispered my name and I touched it and told it to be quiet. I took the saw and started friction back and forth and metal shavings sparked with every strident stroke. My clothes became soaked and my muscles ached anticipation as I struggled to keep the air in my lungs and the pounding out of my head no time for reds, hysterical now as I grunted and panted wild boars in captivity for perhaps it contained his signed confession or maybe it held her diary or hid the cure to my condition and Kaval's recovery. Maybe locked inside was my soul ripped out in the dark of night and all these years of ominous doom and depression were what manifested in its place.

"It's not in there," he said and I looked up to see him filling the doorway. Unshaven and disheveled as if he hadn't slept in days, his skull pressed tight against the jagged veins in his scalp. He wore a white denim shirt with the sleeves rolled up and faded jeans with rubber boat shoes on sockless feet.

"Maybe I should change the locks on the house," he added.

He stepped into the room and I backed against the window, kept my cool as cool can keep. I told him, "I was on the Island to visit Mom and thought I'd drop by and see the house."

"You're wasting your time. It's not here."

Uncle Ted took a step behind the desk and I strolled to the piano. There was something catlike in his movements, smooth and fluid, so unlike him.

"I was just curious," I said to fill the gap.

"You were always curious about this drawer." He sat on his chair and opened the top drawer reaching underneath and taking a key that was taped inside. Holding it up he then bent over and after a moment of fighting the damaged lock the drawer was opened. Uncle Ted sat upright and put his hand on the desk, a thin black gun lay underneath it.

"This is why the drawer was always locked. I couldn't have you kids playing with guns, now, could I?"

"I was just curious," I repeated, mellow mantras taught by maharajas. Uncle Ted gave me a sideways glance and a fox-like, cartoonish grin. "What you're looking for is put away where you will never find it."

"I don't know what you're talking about."

"Maybe your friend Henry would know what I'm talking about."

"I don't have any friends named Henry." Uncle Ted sat back and held his pregnant gut, the gun alone in front of him, a satisfied smile creased his lips.

"I knew you were involved somehow. She could get you to do anything, couldn't she?"

An obscenity whenever he mentioned her by name or not.

"I still have no idea what you're talking about."

"Remember in high school when you took that photography course? Set up a darkroom in the basement. You still taking pictures?" he smiled.

Playing cards and poker faces kept the stakes intense. But the secret in my pocket like an ace up my sleeve, royal flushes dealt from dirty dealers. "It was a nice little setup you and your sister had. What happened? She got a little too greedy?"

"Why don't you ask Henry?"

"I have." He paused for my reaction but none to find. "He's quite terrified over the whole thing. He's terrified of you, in fact. Though I didn't mention you by name."

"Why isn't he afraid of you?" I asked but not as a question.

Uncle Ted sat back, his gold tooth barely visible through smirking lips. Forehead shining under the thin strands of his remaining blond hair. He pulled a cigarette from its pack and lit it in his mouth. Lucky Strike. After a moment I said, "So, what's with the gun?" and found it with my eyes.

"It's not hurting anybody."

"It's not helping anybody either."

"That remains to be seen," he said and again, that smirk. I asked him, "What are you going to do?"

"I don't know yet. But I have enough material to put you and Henry away for a long time."

"Then why don't you?"

He looked across the desk with eyes sincere and probing. "Because you don't have a long time," he answered softly. "And I don't have any grudge against you. You should be making the best of the time you have left, not snooping through my house for things that don't belong to you."

He lazily stretched out his legs in front of him, and with crab eyes small, continued, "As for Henry, I'll handle that in my own way." Greed like cancer spreading oily peanut butter, but the sham of his scam, so obvious now, gave me a better idea.

"I didn't come here to look for things."

"I know. You just came by to see the house."

"Truthfully, I came here to settle up with you."

Uncle Ted raised his brow and asked, "What do we have to settle? The estate is quite clearly settled." And his victory gaze with green flake sparkle sent through my legs a chill of recognition. I glanced into the kitchen but it was empty. Back to my cards.

"Someday, somehow, you're going to have to pay for what you've done. It's called justice."

"I've got nothing to pay for. I've lived a good life. I've

been a good husband to your mother, tried to be a good father to you and your sister."

I had to laugh. "I think you got your signals crossed."

"What is that supposed to mean?"

"Uncle Ted, you may have been able to fool Mom, but I knew from the beginning what you were doing to her."

"Doing to who?"

Blackened bile burped up from Bermuda, I cracked, "Don't play stupid! You're as responsible as if you had killed her yourself!"

Uncle Ted bolted upright in his chair, the lamp toppled over and he bellowed through tan cheeks, "Who the hell do you think you're talking to! Sick or not, I'll still give you a good beating!" He snubbed out his butt and I let the trail of his words melt into harmless silence, then leaned back on the piano.

"I'm not afraid of you anymore. So if you're going to beat me, then do it. If not, fuck off."

A jousting match of eyes took place until Uncle Ted sat back and let out a sigh. "You make me so damn angry some-times. Why do you do that? I've never had any beef with you, why do you always provoke a confrontation?"

"I guess it's just my nature."

"You should try to change it."

Silence and its roller coaster ripped around the room. The drop in my stomach and the sense of falling endless, I tried to hold my balance. "You don't know this, but I saw you, from outside her window. I was peeking over the sill. I saw what you were doing."

Uncle Ted sat up stiff as wood and leaned over the desk.

"You were mistaken," he said firmly, his finger pointing like a bayonet. "Whatever you thought you saw, it never happened."

"But it did happen. I saw it."

"Remember the time you saw the statues in church come

to life? You came home hysterical, swearing they were alive and moving."

"I was six years old."

"Remember when you saw the faces in the trees, all the saints and the spirits floating in the trees?"

"All the kids in the neighborhood saw them too."

"In your mind! All of it. The statues, the faces. Monsters. And now this. It was you who planted the idea into your sister's head until she believed it herself. You poisoned the whole house. And that's all there was to it. I never held it against you, you were a mixed-up kid."

Uncle Ted sat back and folded his arms as if that settled it.

After a pause, I said, "You know, I thought maybe we could talk about it; after all this time if you explained it to me I might understand, find some thread of logic that I never thought of before. But you can't admit it, even in private, can you?"

He answered, "You're a very sick kid. You need to be hospitalized. I'm going to see if there's anything legally I can do."

"And now it doesn't matter anymore, because she's dead. Right?"

Uncle Ted went flush at those words; the color drained from his face and he didn't move, troubled eyes growing moist with bloodshot veins. He said in a quiet puff of voice, "I never mistreated your sister. I loved her as a daughter. And she loved me as a father. That's the God's honest truth. And for you to come here and make these accusations now, after all that's happened . . ." A look of supreme discomfort played across his face. He took hold of his gun with trigger finger wrapped around it and I waited impending doom. After a moment he bent over and put the gun back in its drawer, sat back exhausted. Impotent murderers wilting under movie lights. "I never laid a hand on her," he said as if to himself. "Never."

Blood back to my head I thought of scenic routes that sometimes led to short cuts.

"I noticed McGarrity's is gone. When did he sell his shop?"

Uncle Ted snapped back as if pulled on a string. "McGarrity? He died over a year ago. Some Koreans bought the place and turned it into an all-night deli. They charge a dollar and a half for a quart of milk."

"That's about what I pay in the city."

"That's outrageous. I go to the A & P. Seventy-nine cents."

"How about Dino's Tavern, is that still open?"

"Dino's retired and moved to Florida. But his sons run the place. It's still the best pizza on the Island. They make this thing called a white pie, there's no sauce on it, just cheese and ricotta, throw in a little bacon, it's pretty good."

"That's progress for you."

He shook his head. "God, Eddie, it's all so different now. Everything has changed. You can't recognize the neighborhood anymore. All the old stores are closing up, going out of business. Strangers coming in. They knock down one house and build five townhouses in its place, you can't drive on the streets they're so congested. It's a shame, a damn shame. Remember how it used to be before that stinking bridge went up?"

Blossoms filled the window curtains breezy cool with inspiration and serenity. Thoughts reflected off my skin like placid lakes in Canada.

"One time I did tell somebody about you," I said and his gaze caught mine. "I went to confession one Saturday afternoon, it was during the feast; I was twelve years old. I told Father Michael what I saw. I told him about the bingo nights."

"Bingo nights?"

"Every Wednesday when Mom went to bingo, and you

locked yourself in Denise's room. I used to listen outside the door."

"I was helping her with her homework. If I spent more time with her than I did with you, I'm sorry. But you're wrong about everything else . . . Are you sure it was Father Michael you spoke to?"

"As soon as the screen slid open I could smell his after-shave."

"That's Father Michael, alright. Did he know it was you?"

"I caught him peeking out the curtain as I went to the altar. He knew who I was."

"He did the right thing. It would have served no purpose to destroy the family."

From the kitchen came my bumblebee buzzing near the shelves to Uncle Ted's right. Rainbow color LSD trails swirling in its flight. Uncle Ted rolled up a sheaf of papers and followed the bee with his eyes. I told him, "It's only a bee. It'll be out the window in a second."

But when the bee landed on the edge of the shelf Uncle Ted swatted it away and it fluttered awkwardly in a spiral onto his desk, its battered wings buzzing spastically but unable to fly. Uncle Ted wound the papers tighter and the bee tried to crawl along the wood. I sat up tension gripping stomach muscles, "Let it go, Uncle Ted. It's not going to hurt anybody." But Uncle Ted crushed it into a gooey yellow mass. "I hate bees," he said with a shudder, then scooped it up in his papers and tossed it out the window.

Kill or be killed shot through my mind as a bus roared by with grumbling guts and vacuum-packaged cowardice. Uncle Ted turned around to find a new chamber in his heart. He frantically ripped at his shirt clutching the hole and the bullet inside it with spastic fingers and terror in his eyes. He dropped clumsy to the floor and twitched for a moment, legs hooked up to live electrical current, jiggling like a go-go dancer. I glanced around the room and out the windows at summer breeze and chirping birds as everything stopped moving. Uncle Ted wheezed softly on the floor, dilated pupils oozing water down the sides of his face. I leaned over straight in his line of sight but he couldn't see me, searching instead for answers and for reasons why. I put my gun on the desk and sat on the edge, noticed the hammer damaged, bent into the chamber it would fire no more. Information screamed my name and I grabbed him by the shirt and pulled him into a sitting position. Yelled into his face, "Where's Henry? Where can I find this Henry?! Tell me!" His marble eyes locked open and no sound escaped from his lips, just pink soap spittle. I dropped him to the floor and his head bounced "no" even in death defiant devious. I waited for the joy I expected to feel but nothing but absence flowed through my veins.

I lifted the body by the arms and dragged it over to the basement and pulled it down the rotted wooden stairs, its legs plopping on each one with a simple Ted-like thud. At the bottom I looked around for its final resting place. I opened the padlock hanging key and pulled the squeaking aluminum door. The boiler let out a faint vibrating sigh. Crouching down to fit under the five-foot ceiling I pulled him in and laid him next to the big machine, heard the insects scatter for the corners; pulled apart a spider web and wiped it from my hair. The overhead light bulb outside the closet shone darkly on the bottom of his upturned soles as the rest of him disappeared into the void. I noticed a pile of ten-pound peat moss bags against the basement doors. Started burying the body under the black flaky grains beginning at the head. Five bags later a mound had been set and I thought of resting the crucifix on top like he had done to sister.

Upstairs I closed the windows when through the curtains buzzed my bee alive with reincarnation, past my face and onto my hand its stinger shooting sodium pentathol. I plucked it out and felt its secret karma pulsing through my arm. Visions of detective shows with dumb Columbo finding clues, I started cleaning the floor wiping the trail of blood with paper towels and dishwater liquid, arranging the desktop and closing the drawers, took Uncle Ted's gun from the bottom and exchanged it for my own, locked the bottom drawer and hid the key. I wiped the desk and windowsills piano keys and bedroom doorknobs with precision and a rag. Stepping back into the living room the bee was gone and I took one last look around. With his gun in my pocket and the clip in my sock, I went out the back door wiping my trail as I did. Nobody saw me leave, all new neighbors none would know me anyway.

Parked in the driveway it stood out of place in this world of secondhand Fords, I tried the driver's door but it was locked. Going back inside I tracked his trail, checked the counters in the kitchen and the table and the desk but no keys anywhere. I wrapped a towel around my hand and went back down into the cellar unlocking the monster closet and pulling aside the door. The mound had come to life with arms reaching up and whimpering sobs of moss and pain from underneath. He was trying to sit up but unsuccessfully so. Frozen for a moment in panic and despair, I felt my knees go limp as the cement inhaled and sucked me down.

I opened my eyes and the mound was gone, a sound near the stairs became a slithering charcoal snake shedding its skin. I pulled the gun from pocket and took aim before remembering the clip was in my sock. The snake stopped moving its middle rose and fell with pulsing bursts of lava dust. I searched around the room and found the long-handled gardening spade that sister used in childhood, stood over the snake weakly groaning on its stomach. Evil as evil can be I raised the spade above my head and brought it down with all my might. Black spray rose up from the impact and a final wheezing sob fought to be heard and then there was silence. Mixed with the smell of earth. I sat on the stairs and balanced the spade across my lap, lost in complexity nothing was clear to me anymore. Wretchedly sobbing deeper into Judas' tightening noose I cried out her name, begging her please to appear and tell me what to do. Finally I dragged the body back into the closet but this time the head was where the feet had been, was about to pile more peat moss on top when I remembered my reason for returning. Checking his pockets the keys were still on their original dealer's keychain. There were no other keys on him. I left the money and wallet untouched. Then started piling another three bags of moss on top. When I was finished I rammed the spade down through the middle and it stood tilted to the left. Taking a step I kicked a metal object hidden partial underneath the boiler. I reached down and pulled a metal tackle box with a padlock through the loop—Uncle Ted was fond of locks. A hammer did the trick.

Negatives and magazines and stacks of rubber-banded Polaroids, a small red phone book but opening it up the print was too small and the light too dark to read it in. Photo after photo of nude young girls no older than puberty posing in motel rooms, one wore a green plaid school dress from St. Adalbert's and I wondered if the dress was real or just a costume for the camera. Another stack of Polaroids hidden under kiddie mags were of Denise naked in her room; yellowed and ragged with use. Her matted hair and drunken smile with barely the slightest growth of breasts, while beside me the peaceful mound of moss, its mast leaning over from the weight of its hellish journey, made no violent act too cruel or catastrophic. I took the pictures from the box and systematically laid them out one by one on top of him, his gravetop markers, except for Denise's pictures which I put in my pocket. I sealed his tomb and swept the floor of moss.

Upstairs I did the towel thing and heading through the

kitchen the phone began to ring. After the fourth ring the machine clicked on, his voice like nuclear fallout over Japan. After the beep a young female with fear in her throat said, "Ted, if you're there pick up. Ted? . . . I guess you're not home yet. Call me the second you get in." I waited for the machine to beep off, ripped out the tape once it did and put it in my side pocket with the red phone book.

Once the Mercedes was inside the garage I shoved the padlock through the loop and felt that missing joy from before. Sex and food had nothing on revenge.

I walked four blocks away and stood at the curb. Fumes rose up from the sewer mixing human waste with chemicals. I took two reds and dry gulped them, the second capsule stuck to my tonsil. As it dissolved in burning grains of pain-lessness cars came screeching down the street, red peppers hanging from the mirrors and macho men screaming out threats. Sun pressed down on baking skin underneath black clothes, lines of sweat rolling down my sides and simmering blood inside my skull. A pretty young woman about thirty years old wearing a flowing flower dress came walking toward me carrying two shopping bags until her eyes caught mine and she crossed the street. As she passed staring straight ahead I wanted to apologize for frightening her. A bus growled by and kept on going, tailpipe spewing harsh black dust as two young models kissed in lust—I thought of Audrey Ockerman. Approaching from the corner a pack of happy dogs with hanging tongues and mischief eyes snooped through trash cans on the sides of houses. They paid me no mind and trotted past on my right but when I turned to my left they were nowhere to be seen. I waited and still no sign of the pack, the smell of soiled fur and dread. I glanced behind me as an audience of k-nines sat on hind legs panting in unison. A minute later no one moved or made a sound. Finally, the rust-coated mutt with a Lassie face tilted his head and spoke.

"What's up, Eddie." There was nothing threatening about his voice or demeanor, and his three friends just sat there quietly, so I decided to play along.

"Nothing much. Just going home."

"So soon? You just arrived."

"Well, I really should be getting back."

"What about Uncle Ted?"

"What about him?"

"Is he nice and dead?"

"I don't know. You'll have to ask him."

The dogs snickered at that, they were enjoying themselves.

"Where's your girlfriend?"

"Who?"

"You know, the blond. She's the next one. Can't run."

"I . . . I don't have a girlfriend." The dog and his friends snickered again, but this time through bared teeth saliva hanging from their snouts. Out of the gust of humid wind the ticking of a clock grew up in my ears. The street was deserted, not a car in sight, waves of swirling heat climbed up from the pavement restrictive and unsustaining. My legs trembled rubber bands stretched across two pencils and plucked.

"Why don't you leave me alone?" I pleaded. "I didn't do anything to you."

"It's what you've done to yourself," he snapped, his voice now a terrible groan. "What's that in your pocket?"

"Nothing."

"Evil as evil can be, is he?" And the dog and his others laughed like poker playing puppy dogs. Faking brave I turned to confront them. "Don't you think it's getting a little old? This stupid game you're playing. Why don't you guys grow up and go to the pound?"

Confusion slapped across their noses like a soggy newspaper.

"Here comes my bus," I said. "Gotta go." The driver wore a funny little cap down on his eyes, but when he rested his paws straight out on the wheel I knew it was Him, their master. He looked up evil laughter all at once the pounding clock had piercing needles cracking bone and gristle. The dogs behind me growled and the bus stopped short with a hazardous shriek and when the doors opened and the dog met my eyes with his bee buzzing corneas, asking with a smile, "Going my way?" I bolted with his raucous howl echoing in my ears. Immediately snapping teeth chomped out bits of pants and leg, the bullet clip bitten free and sent tumbling down a sewer grating metal reverb into water. Feet striking pavement friction rubber soles and stinging burns from blood washing down into my socks, the dogs kept with me every step. I ran through busy Decker Avenue burst in front of a car with blaring horn on impact and looking back one of the dogs was crushed under the tires yelping with its legs snapped broken, its snout sticking out from under the passenger door shooting misty sprays of blood. The others rallied around their dying comrade and I tore down Beekman Place through Newman Alley which brought me onto Seymour Street, the corner where Nancy Juliardi had her thirteenth birthday party, playing spin the bottle first time ever kissing pretty girls. I jogged along the rows of one-house families nicely done with lawns and lovely flowers. Bees hovered over yellow petal sunflower beds and I called to them but they didn't seem to hear me. Glancing over my shoulder there was no sign of dogs. I checked my pockets for the pictures still intact but the red book and phone tape were missing. I reached the corner of quiet Orange Avenue where the haunted Pee Lady house stood her ghost its only guest. I ran to the side of the house adult and unafraid and sat on the steps, checked my soaking pants and the deep scratches underneath them. Too hyped up adrenaline to feel the pain I went to the door and pulled on the knob, carefully jabbed my elbow through the window and picked away the broken glass. The smell of urine spoiled food and salty flesh came up with flies upon my face, I swatted them away. Entering the kitchen covered with powdered oatmeal Quaker boxes rolled out on the floor, the tiles groaned under my weight. Dried out insect shells hung trapped on webs that covered every corner and every window frame. The back door nailed shut with two-by-fours and plywood, I stepped into the hallway leading to the living room. Quiet but for wind through whistling crevices. Fifteen years ago hiding silent in this room as teenage homos gave each other head until my presence found then chased like hunted rabbits through streets of Norman Rockwell, remembering the tall kid red hair dungaree jacket as he chased me terror shame and vengeance in his eyes. The couch was ripped apart with foam scattered everywhere chairs overturned and table broken newspapers and magazines flung across the floor, rancid odors rose up from the radiator where sticking out from underneath a decomposed cat had a million flies and maggots working Mother Nature's food chain. The room behind the living room had swords of sunlight holding dust and plaster, antique dresser drawers sat splintered on the floor. At the foot of the dresser a loose plank of floorboard jutted up. "What's that in your pocket?" echoed in mind with that terrible groan.

When I was finished I covered the floorboard with a stack of newspapers and pushed the dresser over it, felt a lot lighter in my step. Now to cab it to the ferry but first to quench my thirst. The sink was dry as paper towels but underneath the spout a droplet crawled into my palm. I looked around and insects watched me from their prison bars. The refrigerator door swung back and forth like cowboy doors in dark saloons, putrid empty except for germs. My heart began to struggle-pump as piston rods in ceasing engines made this liquid urgent. I raced up the stairs and the

bathroom sink lay on the floor the toilet just a pile of shattered pieces no pipes in shower nothing wet not even
mildew. Back down in the kitchen holding my throat I
searched in panic yellow desperation. The cabinet under the
sink where the water valves were hidden, I fell to my knees
and reached for the handle but it wouldn't budge; struggling
to pull it free when sudden earthquake tremors shook it from
inside. I leaned back as the doors blasted open with rabid
dogs attacking at my face. The force of their thrusts pro-
pelled me into the hallway fighting to hold them off kicking
and thrashing I gripped one by the throat. With fatal blasts
adrenaline I rolled on top squeezing till my fingers ached
and arms went numb. The eating others seemed to disappear
as I banged his head awkward against the floor again and
again with oatmeal flakes flying into my eyes, looking down
Uncle Ted alive and bleeding laughed a priestly laugh. Still I
kept my grip. Cursing God his rules so vastly broken when
reality rips its own report card, a tear fell from my eye and
landed on my tongue, felt its healing fingers. Uncle Ted and
the dog were gone. Alone with myself in the living room, my
sweaty palms wrapped around rubber foam cushion from
the couch, I listened to the ringing in my ears. Rose to my
feet with knee joints cracking frozen ice cube blocks, and
stepped into the kitchen where everything was back as it had
been except that sitting at the table was poor and pitiful Pee
Lady smoking from a long-stemmed cigarette holder; a black
veil covered her eyes and silk gloves up to her elbows, white
exhaust scrolled out of her mouth in ancient druid lan-
guages. She didn't turn or speak and I watched her thinking
years ago the laughter and taunting whenever she walked
the street in her soiled dress and ripped stockings talking to
herself and squatting over the curb to urinate. Watching her
now a lump grew in my throat.

    "I'm sorry, Mrs. . . . I . . . I don't even know your name.
I'm sorry."

She didn't respond just kept smoking her cigarette. I turned and went down the stairs and out the side door. Exhausted and trailing bloody sneaker prints I stumbled along the street on constant lookout for dogs. I fell into a phone booth and dug for a quarter then dropped it in the slot and it tinkled out the bottom, repeated the whole thing until it stayed put. I pulled a paper out of my pocket hoping the numbers would cooperate and Kaval had left the phone plugged in. Cars drove past with laughing skulls and mucus eyes inside them, looking into my hand the receiver began to throb. I threw it down as the wire tried to whip around my head. Back on the street running and coughing for air nothing looked familiar anymore, the houses and stores and people and cars and Uncle Ted was right-as-rain as clouds and lightning bolts rumbled in my brain. Hatfield Place came up in a field of weeds the sign pointing west to Stevie McCormack's house where his brother Alvie fell off the roof retrieving the frisbee Stevie threw up there and as Alvie died in a heap on the side of the house Stevie and his parents cried for him to live. Soon after they moved away and I never had another friend like Stevie again.

A dog barked twice.

Losing my balance and vision I tripped up the porch of her house and banged on the door checking behind me then up at the dark gray clouds. I puked up living beans of coffee scattered roaches under light. Hobbled around to the back yard my calves a shredded mass of tuna steak. The yard was my own and I'd been traveling in a circle, rats in a maze would fare no better.

I fell back against the door and landed in a checkerboard kitchen, unable to lift myself. Her navy-blue slipper-shoes stopped near my face and she leaned down her eyes through black-frame glasses smiled warmly.

She held a cup of cool water to my lips and I choked from swallowing hard. "Go easy," she said, her voice was soothing oil. "Take it slow. You're going to be fine now."

"My legs," I coughed between gulps, and she looked back at my feet and smiled. Safe security in Elizabeth's loving gaze. She sat me back against the cabinets and went to the oven peeking inside as a wave of heat and sugar cinnamon swept along the floor. I heard children playing outside and Elizabeth called out the window and told them to be careful.

"Yours?" I asked.

"Cathy and Anthony," she said with maternal pride. "Cathy's four and Anthony's seven."

"Seven? . . . How could that be?" I said. "We were together five years ago. You didn't have any kids then."

She seemed flustered, confused. "Oh? Did I say seven? I meant five."

Betrayal cries infinity when no one pays the butcher. I clamped my eyes and cried for Kaval, all around me Turkish voices spoke in broken English. The smell of jasmine mixed with turpentine. Gravely, the voices grew silent and I stopped iconoclastic.

2 2

A BED OF FOG DRIFTED AROUND MY BODY, cool like autumn clouds. I didn't move afraid to harm tranquillity. The clouds stirred roughly as seasoned thunder blew from southern winds and through it walked an angel with a tray. Squinting from the white of her body I tried to sit up but she put her hand on my shoulder and told me not to resist. Took a large hypodermic and measured its contents against the light and pulled up my sleeve and injected the point into my eye. A thousand silver pigeons dispersed into the air like confetti, a blazing light eased out of the sky and I shielded my eyes and tried to see its face the heat a mild afterthought. The presence felt there tasted resurrection and I asked it, "Am I dead? Is this death?" The Light didn't answer, pulsing in refractory beams like sun spots on a camera lens.

I pleaded, "Who are you? Why won't you speak? Do you really exist? I have to know!"

The Light grew hot, intense white energy Moses on his mountaintop. In basso ostinado it spoke. "If everything is a fact, where is your faith?"

"I've tried to have faith. But it's not enough. There has to be more than faith, there has to be some proof!"

The Light laughed heartily. "And you don't see proof of my existence? Is your life so truly empty?"

"Yes."

"Evil as evil can be."

"Yes, exactly."

"The choice is yours. It's always been your choice."

"No, it's not a choice at all. We do what we're forced to do."

He laughed Santa Claus on Macy's Day. "Nobody forces you to do anything. You *choose* how to act."

"No, that's not true."

"More true than you choose to believe." And the Light's intensity softened slightly, his presence weakening as if spilled through a drain—I realized then his trick. Angry at my foolishness I told him, "It's not going to work. I know who you are."

The light dissolved instantly into golden strands of cottony hair. Kaval leaned in close to my face her crooked smile and the blue in her eyes brought me back to clarity. "How do you feel?"

"I had a dream. I was flying."

"You've been flying alright, but not in your dreams. They found you unconscious. At Elizabeth's house."

"Elizabeth's house?

"On Staten Island."

"How . . . how did I wind up there? Where was Elizabeth?"

"She was in Virginia Beach, on vacation with her family. A neighbor saw you lying out on the steps and called the police. An ambulance took you to a hospital and they found my number in your pocket. I had you brought here."

I sat up with head light as helium. Waited for Newton's law. "What hospital is this?"

"St. Vincent's."

"In the city?"

She nodded her head.

"What happened to me?"

"You had a seizure, too much pressure on the brain. They've been trying to relieve it with drugs and treatment."

"How long have I been here?"

"A day and a half. It's Tuesday afternoon."

Panic came with target practice. "They haven't cut me open, have they? Don't let them do that! Whatever you do, don't let them operate on me!"

"Relax. They can't do that without your permission, or mine. I told them I was your wife." And she held up her hand to show her gold-plated wedding band.

"Where did you get that?"

"I used to wear it so creeps would leave me alone."

"When can I get out of here?"

"I don't know. I don't think you're strong enough, maybe you should continue with the treatments."

"What are they giving me? Radiation? Chemo?"

"I think both."

"I'm gonna lose my hair, my head is gonna bloat up like a basketball."

"It was either that or let you die. I had no choice."

"That's my point exactly."

"What?"

"No choice. That's what I was telling him."

"Telling who?"

"It . . . It was part of the dream."

Kaval took my hand and gently squeezed. "You're going to be alright now, just relax and get better. Then I'll take you home."

"Tell them to give me some morphine for the pain."

"Are you in pain?"

"No. But I will be. My legs were bitten pretty badly." Kaval pulled the sheet off my feet but shins and calves to my knees and thighs were unmarked and clean. "The dogs . . . I . . . I couldn't have imagined it all!"

"With all the drugs you've been taking it's a wonder you're not insane. But that's going to stop now. No more reds, or acid or weed or anything."

"No more weed? That gets rid of the nausea. If I'm on chemo . . . Kaval, even the doctors will tell you that weed relieves the nausea."

Her face softened and a smile eased out. "Alright, some weed, but only for medicinal reasons. What were you doing on Staten Island anyway?"

Caught off guard with nothing but the truth I told her of Uncle Ted and the pack of dogs and old houses mentioning Zero and the gun and the money I took from her purse to buy it and about CandyBar jumping off the roof and the pictures of Denise hidden under floorboards and Kaval watched me with a look of dark surprise. Before she could speak I pleaded, "But Kaval, I know who did it now! I have a name." In a hushed voice, "Henry."

She stood a moment without a sound, something going on inside her head. "This is all true, what you just told me?"

I nodded my head.

A second later she exploded. "You're fucked!" her face in raging tumult. "You're a fucking murderer!"

"But Kaval . . ."

"But Kaval nothing! You . . . You've killed people!"

"They both . . . the both of them were . . ."

"I don't care what *they* were. I care what *you* are! Eddie, how could you do this!? Don't you see what you've done?! Who the hell do you think you are?!"

"Kaval, please, let me explain . . ."

"I don't want to hear it! Eddie, you lied to me, you betrayed me!"

"Kaval, I never lied to you."

"You didn't tell me what you were doing. That's a lie, a betrayal!"

"I didn't want to involve you. I didn't want you to get into trouble."

She stopped for a moment, blue eyes red and leaking water. Her voice cracked slightly as she said, "How could you be so fucking stupid!? This is beyond just you and me. This is . . ." She steeled herself tin can tuna and glared coldly at the stranger in front of her.

"I don't know if I ever want to see you again," she said and stormed out the door. I sat on the bed confused, wished I were somehow else.

23

MAYBE YESTERDAY WAS JUST A DREAM. Maybe it had all been a dream and Kaval and my life were nothing more than nightmares dreamt by naughty little boys. The morning light gave me an airy feeling in my head, I sat up feeling dizzy, noticed the things in the room for the very first time. A feather tickled my palm and I opened my fingers and a crunched-up scrap of paper took shape. Written in red felt pen it said:

"Pleese com see me. Im in room 374."

Nothing else just those words.

Intrigued I carefully removed the tubes and needles from my arm and crept softly out of bed and waited for the floor to stop tilting, the sight to come back to my eyes; found a thin blue robe in the closet and put it on. Peeked out into the hall and started for the elevators. The pungent fumes of flowers mixed with alcohol burned through aching sinuses; passing the nuclear medicine I followed a young couple heading for the elevator. The wife sobbed and leaned on her husband's shoulder, he stroked her head and held her up with love and concern and dug his face into her wavy auburn hair. As we waited for the car he softly wept.

I got off at number three and started down the corridor through swinging gray doors where wheeled tables lined the wall and a huge guy in a green scrub suit and hair net was taking out trays of food and disappearing into rooms. I passed a station busy nurses reading charts and calling doctors answer phones and no one noticed as I followed the numbers to the end of the corridor. Turning the corner I stopped: a cop sat on a bench drinking coffee and reading a newspaper. He didn't look up and I proceeded cautiously passing rooms 374 and 376. I went to the end by the bulletin board, snuck a glance behind me and the cop turned a page of his cup and sipped from his paper. I read the notices of job openings and pizza parties and the bake sale for God's Love We Deliver, words started sliding along the paper with the vowels raping consonants. I turned and the cop was walking toward the nurse's station. I approached the room checking the note in my hand, now blank, and reaching the door I quietly pushed it open.

Inside a mummy lay still with tv monitors overhead playing squiggly graphs and techno-beeps, I crept to the bedside and waited for my eyes to adjust to the white. It stirred and groaned in pain, "You got my note."

"There was no name on it."

"I'm supposed to be a secret."

"Is it really you? Or is this all in my mind?"

She let out a weak giggle. "Pinch yourself if you don't believe it."

"How did you know I was here?"

"When you were brought in, PeggyTail saw you on the elevator. I had her slip you the note. She's the only one who's allowed to visit me; no one else knows I'm alive. Why are you here?"

"I had a headache."

"You're on a cancer floor."

"It was a migraine." CandyBar let out another giggle. I noticed the bareness of the room, no flowers or cards; nothing to show that a person lived here. I told her, "I thought you were dead. How could you have survived such a fall?"

"I didn't do a very good job of it. Every bone in my body is broken. The doctors say I'll never walk again."

"Well, don't go by what they say. I was supposed to be dead six months ago and look at me!"

CandyBar smiled warmly then just as quickly replaced it with a grimace.

"What's with the cop outside?"

"They want me to testify against Zero and some of his friends. They're afraid someone's going to try and kill me if they know I'm alive."

"I was there the day you jumped. You smashed in the top of a Buick."

"Did anybody get hurt?"

"No. Just you."

"I can't remember it. I only remember the sound at the end . . . it was like an explosion."

"Why did you do it?"

CandyBar closed her eyes and smiled angry. "I told Zero I wasn't gonna work no more. I found out I'm sick, and I wasn't gonna do it no more. Zero flipped out and threw me off the roof. I mean, I would have jumped sooner or later. Zero made it sooner."

Her look told me it was true. "Does he know you're still alive?"

"Zero?" she asked with a light in her eye. "I don't think it matters now . . . Take my hand," and I took in my palm the only three fingers not bandaged. CandyBar closed her eyes and seemed pleased. I squeezed her fingers and swallowed hard. The pain marched across her face like soldiers in Berlin.

I asked, "How long will you be here?"

"Forever, I guess."

"Maybe you'll be able to walk again. I'll help you."

CandyBar dismissed it with a scrunch of her nose. I held her hand and watched her nostrils expand and recede with each puff of the machine to her left. Soon she was asleep and I let her fingers drop on the sheet.

Stepping into the corridor the cop was down the hall talking with a heavy-set man in a suit that I recognized as Detective Webster. I started in the other direction, glanced over my shoulder and Webster caught my eyes as I turned the corner.

Back in my room I was surprised by Kaval standing at the bed with a scowl on her face. "Where have you been?! You shouldn't be out of bed."

"We have to get out of here! Now!"

"What's wrong?"

"That cop Webster's here! CandyBar is alive and he's downstairs outside her room. I think he saw me." I ripped open the closet door looking for my clothes but none to find.

"Wait a minute. Run this by me again."

Kaval sat me down and made me start at the beginning. When I finished she gathered up my clothes from a compartment built into the wall and I quickly got dressed. She grabbed her bag and filled it with the bible a pack of tissues and a crucifix until stopping at the water bucket. "Wait a minute! If we run that's the same as admitting guilt. Besides, you're here for treatment, you may die without it."

"If Webster finds me he's going to arrest me."

"On what evidence? You said there were no witnesses. I'll say that I was with you the whole time."

"That makes you an accomplice!"

"I don't care. I want you to stay for these treatments. It's important to me that you stay." And deep in her eyes lay the crossroads in all relationships, the points and moments silver forks where love is tested crystalline. I sat on the bed and started unbuttoning my shirt when the door opened and Webster stepped in. Faking polite, he said, "Oh, I'm sorry. Hope I didn't interrupt . . . Are you going somewhere?"

"No," Kaval said and folded her arms, her face pressed into a boxer's smile. "We were just discussing Eddie's treatment, and as much as he hates the hospital, he's agreed to finish them out."

"Oh, well that's good news. I hope it all goes well," he said, then turned to me. "I saw you downstairs on the third floor and thought I'd drop in and say hello."

Kaval took a step forward, "That's very nice of you, Detective," and the tone of her voice—Kaval and authority like mice in tiny boxes. Webster went on undeterred. "Eddie, do you mind if I ask you a few questions?"

"Is it about my sister's murder?"

"It might shed some light on that, yes."

"I'm really not feeling well, Detective. Maybe it can wait until another time."

"It would only take a minute. Do you know a young woman named Agnes DeMillow, she's also known as CandyBar?"

"Um . . . CandyBar?"

Kaval jumped in on somersaults. "He told you he's not

feeling well. He needs to rest. Would you please leave him alone so he can get better?"

Webster took pause, attack or retreat played across his face. "I'm sorry if I disturbed you," he said gently. "I'll come back another time." But through the cool civility his eyes burned white suspicion. Webster went out the door and I turned to Kaval.

"What was that about!?"

"What?"

"That attitude! Why do you always provoke him? That's only going to make him more suspicious."

"He's got no right to come in and ask you questions and he knows it. I'm not going to let him walk all over our civil rights."

"Since when did you became so patriotic?"

"Since it suits my needs." And the fire proud smile in her eyes gave me bunsen burner ecstasy, so angry hot Kaval. But just as quick she froze me out.

Later Dr. Kolver came in the specialist Kaval hired to replace the quack they gave me originally. With scruffy beard and grayish hair a flowered tie beneath his smock he pinched my spine and read my chart and jabbed a needle into my arm. "You're responding well to the treatments," he said. "You have a growth on the tip of your spine that was pressing against the brain stem. Have you noticed any numbness or loss of motor functions in your limbs?"

"No more than usual."

"What's usual?" he asked, one eye perched.

"Sometimes my arms and legs lose their feeling. I can move them but they feel dead, like I'm shot up with Novocaine."

"How about eyesight? Has that ever left you?"

"No. Actually, one time it did. Everything went dark. But it was during an eclipse."

Dr. Kolver was not amused. Instead he said, "The

growths seem to be shrinking, albeit minimally. But I think you'll notice a big difference overall."

"When can I get out of here?"

"Whenever you want. I can see you on an outpatient basis. Just come in for your chemo once a month."

"Okay. I want to go home now."

"You're scheduled for a cobalt this afternoon. Why don't you stay one more day and go home tomorrow? Besides, I just gave you a strong sedative."

"Doctor, who's paying for all this treatment? I don't have any coverage."

"Don't worry about that, let's just get you functioning again. You realize there's little we can do over the long term. You're in a highly advanced state."

"Yes, I know. My mother has the same thing."

"Yes, I saw that in your chart. It appears to be a genetic susceptibility."

"I guess I can't say my mother never gave me anything, huh?"

"Well, that's an interesting way to look at it," he said with a puzzled smile. He seemed unaware of his stethoscope closing around his neck like a python until the ends sealed together and squeezed too late to stop as Kolver fought to break free writhing on the edge of the bed his face red and choking saliva bulging eyes flew out of their sockets he fell dead to the floor where his chest opened up and faceless fiends from Saturday afternoon crawled out. I watched it all with an air of boredom.

Very nice, I said to myself. Take two enemas and call me in the morning.

My arms were trembling body hard in places long ago unfeeling, heart racing with sweat seeped into the pillow and my neck slimy from the chill. Shaking like a branch in winter's freezing night I felt my ears unclog and the wind sweep through. Tears welled in my eyes and I couldn't understand why . . .

"Is the radio too loud?"

A stout middle-aged man with curly gray hair and large boyish eyes was looking at me from the next bed. A small radio sat on the table to his right. "I can turn it down if you like."

"No, please don't."

"You sure?"

"Please." I sniffled as the song ended and the DJ came on with gibberish.

"Yeah, that song always gets me too. They don't write them like that anymore."

"I've hated that song my whole life."

"Songs just kind of creep up on you sometimes. When I was a kid I used to hate Kenny Rogers. Now I like him. Go figure. Hi. My name's Pat."

"I'm Eddie."

"Glad to meet you Eddie, though not under these circumstances. I'm in for a biopsy. What brings you here?"

"Advanced chemotherapy."

"Oh." And Pat grew ominously silent. "Well, if the radio bothers you just let me know." He closed his eyes and tried to sleep as contagious tumors impaled themselves on his barbed unfriendly wire.

24

THE SUNLIGHT HURT MY EYES and for the first time in three years I didn't shield it out. We walked down First Avenue and Kaval pulled my sleeve left on St. Marks Place.

She hadn't spoken the whole ride down not even over music and it's glorious return. She walked three feet ahead of me past the cafes and folk clubs and people hanging out on the stoops the crisp scent of pot tickling my nose like fingers made of crepe. I stepped over homeless children poor and filthy matted neon hair with metal studs through lips and noses all tattooed and begging for change a small brown bird lay crushed and dead on the curb. Kaval crossed Avenue A and went straight into the park. I followed on the path leading to the dog run—my punishment as she now knew about the dog. Kaval sat on a bench near the gate of Avenue B and I sat next to her but not too close.

"Now," she said and turned to face me with her leg up under her rump. "I want to know everything. Why you did it. What you were thinking about. Were you insane at the time, did you have rational thought? I want to know every detail. And if you keep *anything* from me I swear I'll never speak to you again."

"Okay, fine. But first I want to ask you something . . . What did you think was going to happen if we ever found Henry? Did you think we were going to invite him out to dinner? Wasn't the plan to punish him for what he's done? To stop him from doing it again?"

"The plan wasn't to kill him."

"What were we going to do?"

"I don't know. I thought we'd figure it out if it ever came to that."

"You never thought we would really find him, did you?" She didn't answer. "I didn't go into that warehouse intending to shoot that pimp. It just happened."

With that I began the details and when I was finished Kaval sat still with diamond eyes boring strange holes into my mind. She took a deep breath and spoke. "Eddie, I can accept the fact that you were high on drugs, that you have a terminal condition and it's affecting your mind, but fuck! It's still murder."

"Do you want me to turn myself in?"

"No."

"Then what do you want me to do?"

"I don't know."

She gazed off at the monkey bars. I held closed the collar of my shirt, the wind snuck in through buttons. I thought of telling her about her father—maybe now she'd believe me.

"I need some time with this," she said. "I have to decide what I'm going to do."

"I love you, you know."

"I wish right now I could say the same for you." And the coldness in her eyes made dirty slates wiped clean still carry residue.

"How much time do you need?" I asked.

"I don't know. A lot."

She got up from the bench and suppressed a cough. "I gotta go," she said and walked off toward Eleventh Street. The dogs were laughing at me. I sat there chilled inside.

I came in after 1:15 and the room was dark. The bedroom empty mattress lying unmade on the floor gave me stomach cramps. I got undressed and went into the bathroom and turned on the light and Kaval was lying on the floor curled up around the bowl fetus-like. She had a pillow under her head and was deep in sleep. Heaving midnight nauseousness. I clicked off the light and went to bed.

Jackie was wiping the bar when I stepped in. The look of fear on his face told me he didn't recognize me at first.

"Shit! For Chrissakes! What are you doin' to yourself?! You look like the morning after doomsday."

"It's good to see you too, Jackie. Where's Dezmond?"

"As if you care! Your good friend! The fuckin' guy was laid off from his job last month and he's been mopin' around like a dog with no tail ever since. It's been like a fuckin' wake around here. Don't anybody know how to have a good time anymore?!"

"Where is he, home?"

"No, he's at Trump Tower havin' cocktails!"

Dezmond buzzed me in and waited outside his door on the fifth floor. I had to stop to catch my breath on the fourth. He met me in the stairwell and I went in behind him. Asked for a glass of water. Ben was crying in his crib in the kitchen, which was a disaster with dirty dishes in the sink and laundry piled in the corner and toys scattered on the floor. Dezmond looked frazzled at his wit's end.

"Jackie said you got laid off."

"That's a diplo-fuckin'-matic way of puttin' it. I'm on suspension. They're thinkin' of bringin' me up on charges."

"What for?"

"Disability fraud, perjury, who the fuck knows what else. Some fuckin' clerk in the department caught me playin' pool at Jackie's. I ain't supposed to be able to move and the fuckin' guy comes in while I'm bent over the table makin' a bank shot. I don't even know the guy, he's some geek they send around from time to time checkin' up. That's what one of my buddies in the office said. So, I'm suspended."

"Maybe that's not so bad. You hated the job."

"Yeah, but now what the fuck am I gonna do? I put almost ten stinkin' years in that department. Where do I go from here? And what am I gonna do for money?!"

Dezmond picked up a rattle and tossed it to Ben still screaming like a rusty train.

"Where's Lucille?"

"She's workin'."

"Working?! I didn't think you allowed her out of the house."

"Don't be a wiseguy. She got a job sellin' cosmetics with her sister."

"Cosmetics?"

"Yeah. She goes door to door, like an Avon lady."

"That can be dangerous, sending your wife out to strangers' doors."

"Don't you think I know it! What else can I do? I can't collect unemployment and I can't get a fuckin' job with this fuckin' suspension hanging over my fuckin' head."

"Fuck."

"Fuck is right!"

"Fucking fuck."

"Hey fuck you! It's not funny!"

"Alright, I'm sorry. But I told you this would happen long ago and you just laughed in my face."

"What I need right now ain't an 'I told you so.' And what the fuck are you doing to yourself? You look like the bottom of a trash bin!"

"I'm back on the treatments."

"See! Everybody's got problems . . . You got any reds?"

"No. I stopped taking them."

"How about weed?"

I nodded.

"Light up."

Ben let out a squeal while Dezmond tried to soothe him with a toy and a threat. I lit a joint and blew the smoke into the bathroom. Dezmond toked withdrawal fevers, held his breath till turning red then released a floating veil across his face. The lock unclicked and Lucille stepped in carrying a large attache case and dressed in a navy blue skirt with matching jacket. Her face made up pretty like I'd never seen before told me Dezmond was in trouble of losing her. Lucille plopped her case down on the table and waved the smoke from her eyes.

"This is just great! Getting stoned at twelve in the afternoon! Absolutely wonderful!"

Dezmond cried, "Eddie lit the joint!"

"Don't blame Eddie!" she snapped without looking in

my direction. "Look at this place! It's in the same condition as when I left this morning."

"Lucille, I'm doing the best I can." Ben wailed in his crib. "The kid doesn't let up for a second! Every time I turn my back he needs attention. And I'm depressed, take that into account."

Lucille stood with folded arms but she could never stay mad for long. "Alright, but there's no excuse for the pot smoking. We can't afford . . ."

"It's Eddie's weed! Honest! Ask him."

"It is mine, Lucille. I'm sorry for lighting up in your home."

"It's not you, Eddie, he should know better. Do you have my lunch?"

Dezmond ran to the fridge and took out a small plate with a sandwich on top, milky tuna fish oozed out from soggy bread.

"What am I supposed to do with this?"

"Well, you might try takin' it and . . ."

"So, how do you like working, Lucille?"

Lucille bit deep into the sandwich and Dezmond took another toke on the joint. I sat at the table across from her.

"It's okay. It's good to get out of the house. I'm glad that the *king* now knows what it's like to stay home and take care of the house."

"I knew what it was like."

"Well it's not easy, is it?"

"No, it sure as hell ain't. Makes me appreciate my beautiful wife a lot more."

Dezmond snickered and passed me the joint. Ben lay silent on his back shaking a rattle and watching the swirls of smoke hover over his crib. Lucille watched him suck on the rattle, smiled as it shook in his hand. "He's a little angel," she said. "I don't see what you're always complaining about."

"Wait till you leave. He starts goin' off like a siren."

"What kind of stuff are you selling, Lucille?"

"It's a portable makeup station. You can carry it on business trips, or on vacation, wherever you want."

"I'm sure he wants to hear all about it."

"Mind your own business!" she snapped. "He asked me and I'm telling him! Would you like to see it?"

"Yes."

Lucille opened the case and it grew into shelves of make-up around a lighted mirror with rows of tubes and bottles and brushes and perfumes and pads and tissues and lashes and dozens of colors of eye stuff and flash and glitz and hairspray spritzers. I'd seen it before but I couldn't place where.

"It's like a James Bond movie!" I remarked and Lucille smiled proudly. "Dezmond, remember on James Bond when he had that attache case?"

Dezmond exhaled and jumped in, "Goldfinger! Odd Job with the fuckin' hat that cuts off people's heads."

While Dezmond went on about different Bond movies Lucille touched up her lips when something caught my eye. The logo trademark name inscripted everywhere on every tube and every bottle printed fancy script: Cosmogony!

25

I SAT NEAR THE WINDOW FACING Avenue B watching dealers exchanging needles for cash. Wealthy NYU nerds walked smugly past the needle hawkers onward to the druggists where snorting made them chic. A decrepit old man wearing a policeman's cap with long green weeds hanging down like hair from underneath it begged meekly in the gutter. Kaval had been out all day and I hadn't seen her the night before and questions of her whereabouts fought like ninjas in my mind. Checking the cardboard boxes her clothes were still intact. I pictured myself dying and bleeding in the street and wondered if she would cry over my body or would she watch like a stranger with callous eyes. The pain crept in the cracks of skull and before I could will it out my fingers tingled violet. I popped six Tylenol with codeine when a frightening thought occurred. Ripping an album from the stack I forced it on the plate and threw the needle down. Sat in the middle of the floor as the life-force drained out of my ears and out of my soul.

It was dark outside when she finally appeared standing in the doorway. The needle skipped repeatedly on the end of the vinyl. She stepped into the room and saw my face. "What's the matter? Why are you crying?"

"I'm not crying!"

"Then what are you doing?"

"I'm sad!"

"Why?! What's wrong?"

"It's gone. I don't think it's coming back this time."

"What's gone?"

"The music! Melody!" in blind exasperation. "It's all scraping!"

Kaval went over to the turntable and wriggled her lips into a crooked smile. "Look at what you were listening to," she said and lifted the needle. Took the Foetus from the turntable and put it on the chair. She went through her stack of albums and took one out; the fuzzy sounds of velvet chords from underground ignited in my ears. She asked, "Can you hear that?"

Releasing my breath I sniffled, "Yes."

She crossed to the kitchen and asked over her shoulder, "Did you eat yet?"

Over dinner of brown rice and steamed vegetables she didn't speak the only sound were clinking forks on plastic plates while low in the background Mott the Hoople sang of dudes. The hair on the back of my neck stood up with every weeping chorus. Kaval left her plate half full and put it on the floor to her right.

"What did you do today?" she asked.

"I sat at the window and watched the crackheads."

"That sounds like a productive day."

"You can learn a lot by watching crackheads."

"What did you learn?"

"Not to do crack."

"See, you're thinking more clearly already."

"I guess."

I wanted badly to tell her about the new Cosmogony and show her the brochure I got from Lucille with the address on Third Avenue but was afraid to bring it up and start her steaming all over again. Instead I tried a different route. "It's just a matter of time before that detective tracks me down. What am I going to do when he does?"

"Nothing. Deny everything. No matter what he says, deny it. We should probably get married now as soon as possible too."

"What? Why?"

"So I can't testify against you in a court of law."

Pangs of joy no matter what the reasons, a roach crawled across her plate and dug into the rice and disappeared.

In bed her leg touched mine and in my thoughts I made love to her. Tired breaths whistled my name while down in the street a dog howled love songs. Through the quiet wind and distant traffic her thoughts churned rapidly in the air above my face. Tension plays the saxophone.

Finally she spoke. "I've been thinking maybe we should get the hell out of this neighborhood. Away from all the shit."

"Where do you want to go?"

"I've never lived uptown. We could move to the Upper

West Side. We'll leave no forwarding address, this way the
cops won't know where you live."

"If you're worried about the cops maybe I should move
out and you can stay."

"No, I want to leave. It's not just the cops, it's everything.
The drugs and the lowlifes, the filth. I'm sick of it. It's not fun
anymore."

The room grew silent as Kaval put her hands behind her
head. Without looking from the ceiling she asked, "This guy
Henry you told me about in the hospital, how did you find
out about him?"

"Uncle Ted mentioned him by name. He knew all about
the pictures. He must have found them in Denise's apartment before we searched it. He said he talked to Henry, and
I'm sure he was going to blackmail him as well."

"How do you know?"

"The way he smiled when he said it. Uncle Ted had the
subtlety of a hammer."

"All you have is his first name?"

"Yes."

"What would you do if you could find him?"

"I don't know. But I know what I wouldn't do."

"What's that?"

"Anything that would cause me to lose you again."

Kaval avoided my gaze and rolled onto her side. I closed
my eyes and saw Marlon Brando feeding kittens.

Sirens rattled the morning windows and sitting up I sat
alone. People ran yelling in the streets with screeching tires
broken glass and crunching metal as official words tinny and
transistorized ordered them away. A second later firecrack-
ers popped and Kaval stepped in from the bathroom.

"Get down!" I yelled and threw her on the bed as anarchy hit the ground outside. I covered her body and squeezed
her tight. "Stay down, don't move," I said and buried my
mouth in her dripping hair. Seconds later the bullets stopped

and I peeked out the window, couldn't see a thing as all the action had moved onto Ninth Street.

She called out, "Get away from the window! They might not be finished yet."

"No, it's okay. Look." And she stood next to me watching the flow of oglers get up from the ground and move through aging arteries. I put my arm around her shoulder and she hugged me close her forehead burrowed into my chest. When we released she kissed my lips and I was cured for an instant.

I helped her wash the dishes in the sink, a week's worth of dried food using two brillo pads for scrubbing.

"What are you going to do today?" she asked.

"What day is it?"

"It's Saturday."

"I don't know. What's this brown stuff? I can't get it off."

"It looks like soy sauce."

"It's too thick for soy sauce."

"Just scrub it harder."

"Give me the spatula."

The record skipped off and I dried my hands and went to play another. Returning into the kitchen the first strums of "Thick as a Brick" tickled out of the speakers and Kaval turned to me and pointed with the spatula. "You have the worst taste in music."

"This was Elizabeth's favorite song."

"That says a lot."

"From now on I'm going to play every record I can get my hands on. I don't care what it is. I want to memorize every song so that when they're gone I can play them in my mind."

She gave me a sideways glance and continued scraping the plate and I knew it was all unwinding soon.

Four in the morning sitting in the Yaffa Cafe I traced my finger along the naked breasts of the Venus on the tabletop. Kaval took my hand and moved it away.

"Don't be a pervert," she said.

I tried to relax yet the haunting paper in my pocket playing how and when and why like bishops chasing pawns. Our waiter sat at a back table with a pretty Yoko Ono massaging his shoulders. Kaval glared over ice cubes melting hunger and he quickly brought her food and refilled my empty glass with water.

She asked me if I was tired and I answered no and then she added, "Because there's a club I'd like to go to."

"But it's after four in the morning."

"This place doesn't open till four in the morning. I haven't been there in a long time. I'm going to go."

"Where is it?"

"Avenue B and Second Street."

"Can I come?"

Kaval held my hand along Avenue B just like old times with her the engine and me the caboose. Reaching Fourth Street people hung on the corner asking if we wanted "Godfather Godfather" or "New Jack Pump," a pregnant little Spanish wench whispering out of the side of her mouth "works works" made way for a teen on a bike dealing something called "Rejuvenator." Kaval brushed past them eyes firm ahead while children stood in lighted windows watching parents work. At Second Street a group of people milled at the curb as a strung-out junkie held his scabby forearm and cried about a broken needle stuck inside his veins; one young whore turned to the crowd and begged for an ambulance but nobody moved indifferent. Kaval stopped at a big blue door and a slick Puerto Rican with a skull tattoo put his hand on her shoulder.

"Wait a minute," he said.

"I'm a friend of Laylah's."

"Laylah?"

"Yeah. Tell her Shelly's here."

"Shelly?" he asked then turned to the door as Kaval-as-

Shelly gave me a look that said to drop it. The skull tattoo pulled the door revealing a narrow corridor purple lighted and sitting on a stool was Kaval's double, the brilliant strands of finely woven sunshine hair glowing neon from the black light overhead. She saw Kaval and let out a howl and the skull tattoo let us in and Laylah gave Kaval a great big hug and a peck on the lips. Kaval turned and introduced me but when I went to shake Laylah's hand it was filled with grimy wrinkled bills. Laylah and Kaval then talked about old times and boyfriends and that place they had on East Seventh and wasn't Craig an asshole and now he's working as a stockbroker and married to a wife who used to be a man. I noticed a small door buzzer on the wall beside Laylah's head. She told us to go on inside and Kaval said we'd see her on the way out. We proceeded through a red-lit hallway with a room to the left and a stairway to the right and we took the stairs and on the way down I tapped Kaval on the shoulder and yelled over the rumble, "She seems very nice."

We landed in a basement room of cement and pipes with colored lights and music blasting from the speakers lining the floor. People danced sardine cans with the thumping sex of music primitive thrusting in my groin. Kaval stopped near the wall and the crowd gyrated in front of us. A tiny blond in sheer black dress danced with a B & T from Jersey City dungaree jacket tied around his waist and they were all over each other rubbing and grinding and the guy was slipping his hand down the back of her dress and she was flicking her tongue along his neck and his eyes would close and spit would dribble from his chin. He worked his hand around to the front of her crotch and I thought of Kaval and myself. Eyes slit white as she melted in his arms. Kaval tugged at my sleeve and yelled in my ear, "Don't stare!" I nodded and looked through the crowd. Epileptic androgyny in miniskirts and flimsy halters doing X and riding horses, sweaty meat and muscled thighs, the blue one in the sparkle dress hiked it up through crotchless panties pussy on display. A curly crimson head came bopping through the smoke, the slope of her shoulders slinking to her waist in tight black jeans and leather boots gave acceleration. I took a step forward surrounded by languid limbs when she turned her head and I caught her from the side. Behind me Kaval was talking to some nosering punk against the wall. I took another step forward bumped by early nightlife crawlers when she headed for the stairs. I followed shoving bodies out of my way excited and out of breath. She was halfway up the stairs as I bolted after using the banister to pull myself up; someone punched me from behind. In the doorway I was flung hard against the wall, a GQ bodybuilder-type put his fists in my chest and ordered me to "Chill!" Pushing through the corridor I dashed into the side room covered with sand and debris and people sitting against the walls. Smoldering incense and candlelight burned my eyes. Something brushed my leg and I jerked around as the dog's tail flashed by. Catching sight of the faces talking behind me as the sound faded softly into heartbeat pumping ticks of that clock knock knock, I stood there naked as a child cold and abandoned when out of the smoke she touched my cheek with her palm. I held in a sigh.

"Hi, Eddie," she said and her voice floated in the air like soapy bubbles.

"Denise, I've been wanting to talk to you. Are you angry with me?"

"No . . . well, yes, I am." Then her forehead creased and she moistened her lips. "Eddie, I thought I told you in the hospital to let it go. Why didn't you listen to me?"

"I don't know. I'm sorry."

She let out a smile and my older sister sixteen years old taught me about girls and what they liked and didn't like in boys.

"Alright," she said and tugged on her sweater Maryanne

from Gilligan's Island. "I want you to promise me that it's over now. I want you to forget about it."

"I don't think I can do that."

"You're not listening to me! There's nothing to be gained, and you have everything to lose."

"Denise, I'm not doing it for you. I'm doing it for me. For the first time in my life I'm going to actually do something. Finish what I've started. And nobody's going to stop me."

"From what I've seen you've done quite enough already," she said sharply. "Listen to me, I want you to pay attention," then she took my arm and spoke slowly. "It's not worth it. Think about it. Is it worth losing your girlfriend? Maybe your life?" Her words dropped heavy shovels filled with loneliness. "I guess you didn't think of that."

After a pause, I asked, "Tell me something, have you seen anybody we know? Daddy? Or Grandma? Aunt Louise?"

"No, I haven't seen anyone."

"What about God? Have you seen him?"

"I've seen no one. There's nothing."

"Damn, I thought so."

Denise gazed longing through the shifting smoke of the crowd and said, "I'm going to miss it here." Then her eyes burned hot like charcoal embers. "What do you think of that one over there? In the black mini?"

"She's okay, but she's with that guy."

"That can be corrected," she said as lions watched young pelicans. She gave me a look and we both laughed. Her face turned sad and serious. "I don't think you're going to see me again," she said.

"Wait a minute, can't you stay just a little while longer?"

"I can't. The cops are coming. You better get out of here."

In that instant the crowd exploded back to life with screaming bodies running all directions colors flashed before my eyes, Denise a wisp of fleeting smoke. Pandemonium I fought the crowd toward the stairs and grabbed Kaval's arm but Laylah turned instead and ripped herself free. A huge brute cop in pigface blue shoved me aside and tackled Laylah at the bottom of the stairs as people ran for doors that didn't exist. The brute was trying to cuff Laylah's hands behind her back when a banshee from hell jumped on his neck and pulled at his hair and scratched at his face and wiping the smoke from my eyes it was Kaval. I tried to pull her off but she grabbed my collar and told me to help. The brute threw her in a heap near the door and I kicked his ribs as he crouched on the floor. Some guy stepped on Kaval's leg and I went to help her up as Laylah's hands were cuffed with blood cascading down her face and a knee planted firmly on her neck.

Laylah was led outside with the other employees while everyone else was ordered to stay put. Down at our feet fell white bags and glass pipes and newly purchased needles from the corner. Kaval folded her arms across her chest, angry fire in her eye she spoke into my ear. "Are you carrying anything?"

"Just some weed."

"Get rid of it."

"It's only a lid."

"I don't care, they're gonna search everybody. Sneak it out of your pocket and drop it to the floor."

I slowly dropped the packet to the floor when a young cop grabbed me from behind and ordered, "What's this!? You some sort of wiseguy!?"

Kaval jumped in, "He didn't do anything! Leave him alone."

"What are you, his lawyer!?"

"I'm his wife and you keep your fucking hands off him, creep!"

"Kaval!"

"Alright! The two of you come with me!"

"Fuck you!"

The cops were on us in an instant, shoving us through the corridor and onto the sidewalk where a crowd of people stood around Laylah and her friends; lined up against the wall her face was masked in red. Kaval burst off like steamboat horns.

"You fucking fascist pigs! So tough beating up women. Get her to a hospital!"

The huge brute pigface blue who Kaval had scratched earlier stepped up swinging hard the crisp sound of her flesh made the crowd gasp in unison, several guys asked for the brute's name and number but he covered his shield and went back inside. I was thrown over the hood of a car with my hands cuffed tight as Kaval stood crying with a cop poking his finger in her chest telling her to move along before she gets arrested too. I struggled to stand upright.

"Quit touching her, you fuck! Kaval, go home and I'll meet you there later." Before she could protest I was forced into the car head banged against the roof. Kaval came to the window her tear-filled eyes pleading sorrow.

At the station I was seated on a bench next to Laylah who refused the hospital but took a bandage instead, the sight of her hair in matted ropes of pulpy red, frightened familiar. She rubbed her wrists.

"You been with Shelly a long time?"

"Who? Oh, no. But it's the quality of time, don't you think?"

She let out a snicker. "If they charge you with possession you're going to be here longer than us. We'll be out in another hour or two."

"You've been through this before."

"Twice. The community board is trying to close us down. Fuck 'em! We've been there for seven years, now all of a sudden they want us out so they can gentrify the fuckin' neighborhood. We keep people off the streets, they should be thanking us. Did you see that bastard that arrested me? He was feeling up my tits. Fuckin' hardup cops. Hey Neil, we should file a complaint."

To my left the skeleton in leather pants and shirt told her in a proper English accent, "I've got to take a wicked piss. If we aren't out of here soon I'm going to pee on the floor."

A mohawk mutant studs across her lower lip jumped in with vigor, "Let's all piss right here on the floor!"

"Long live the revolution," I said and Laylah broke into a grin. So did Neil.

"So, how long have you and Shelly been living together?" she asked.

"I moved in about—how did you know we were living together?"

"Oh, Shelly told me. She's real special, ain't she?"

"Yes, she is."

"You fucking her?"

"What?"

A cop with a clipboard stood next to a plainclothes detective going over a list of names as Laylah and her friends started yelling for their lawyers. The cop pointed over with a pencil and the detective came up his shadow casting darkness and authority. "You," he said to me, "come on."

Laylah snarled, "What do you want him for?!"

"Shut your mouth and you'll get out of here quicker!"

I took a step when Laylah blurted out, "Cathy's four and Anthony's seven."

"What?" I said, and her face went blank like Linda Blair's and devil worship. "Oh? Did I say seven?" she added, "I meant five." Laughing eyeballs blossomed open, tiger-colored bumblebees flew from petals dripping urine from their stingers. My knees buckled and the detective grabbed my arm and lifted me up. "Whoa! Are you alright?"

"Uh, yes. Just lost my footing." Laylah's rolling laughter washed on shore as bloody tendons trailed from my legs, I

watched her till we turned the corner. Led past the desk and
through a hall where frosted glass doors lined each side the
gray suit talked.

"You're entitled to have a lawyer present but you really
don't need one because we're not charging you with
anything. We just want to ask you a few questions. Is that
okay?"

"What do you want to ask me?"

"I'll tell you in a minute."

He opened a door and ushered me in where Detective
Webster sat behind a wooden table reading Guns and
Ammo. He told me to have a seat. The creaking metal rattled
in my bones.

"I saw your name on the arrest report and thought it
might be a good time to talk to you. I think now you have the
time. How are you feeling?"

"Not too good."

"Can I get you something to drink?"

"No, thank you."

"Your girlfriend doesn't seem too fond of cops."

"Don't take it personally. She doesn't like anyone."

Webster burped out a laugh and looked to his partner
standing by the door. "The arresting officer says you were
trying to ditch some marijuana. What were you doing in that
club anyway?"

"Nothing. He's mistaken. It must have been someone
else."

"Alright, let's get down to business. If you cooperate
with me you'll be out of here in no time. Marijuana is a mis-
demeanor, a desk appearance. Who knows, maybe it'll get
lost in all the confusion." Human gods and power ball, now
I knew the deal.

"I want to ask you about Agnes Demillow—CandyBar.
You were visiting her in the hospital, so I'll assume that you
know her."

"Uh, I know who she is. I used to see her on the street. We lived in the same neighborhood."

"So you know where she lives."

"No, not really."

"But you were friends?"

"That depends what you mean by 'friends.' I'm not her enemy."

Webster's expression melted downward while his voice began to rise. "She seems to know you rather well! How did you know she was in the hospital? Do you know a man by the name of Reginald Harris?"

"No, I don't."

"He's a pimp also known as Zero Zero Minus One."

"No, I've never heard of him."

"I find that hard to believe. Did your sister know him? When was the last time you saw this pimp?"

Pecking ravens chipped my skull like poems from Edgar Allan Poe, pawsteps scratched along the floor as hot breathe pulsed K-nine down my neck but I didn't turn around instead creating scenes in my mind of peace and pleasure German leisure picture postcard countrysides from when Denise was eighteen years old. Her foreign friend with lanky arms and legs like wine her Cheshire grin and rigid spine, Gisela's eyes blue as summer sky with milky skin and rubber lips made more expressive with every spoken word. Sexy confrontation in her smile as she slid her wire rim glasses on her nose and took my hand. Asked if I'd marry her. I moved forward to kiss her lips and dropped tumbling out of the sky.

Webster's mouth was moving madly sound from Outer Limits, horizontal anarchy and blurry crystal clear, strapped into a loveseat nearly naked underwear. Strands of fur came up from the floor as my left hand fused into a paw, numbing foreign matter I covered with my right and felt the inner parasite. Webster's face grew round and pink.

"Alright, have it your way," he snapped and tossed his

pad down on the desk. Barked to his partner, "Get him out
of here!"

"What about the weed?" the partner asked.

Webster looked up tired and disgusted. "What weed?"
he spit. I got up and took a step to the door when he added,
"Don't let me catch you doing anymore illegal drugs. You're
on medication now, you don't need that other shit."

Kaval was waiting for me at the front desk. Laylah and
her friends had been released and Kaval asked if I was
alright and I told her yes and then the cop behind the desk
emptied out a large yellow envelope and a wallet and coins
and four tokens some bills and a red rubber skull came tumbling onto his blotter. He checked inside the envelope and
patted out the Cosmogony brochure. Kaval was on it in an
instant. I signed for my stuff as she read.

"When were you going to tell me about this?" she asked
and not as a question. We walked past the junkyard art.

"Tonight."

"It's now morning."

"I guess I'm running late."

"How long have you had it?"

"Yesterday. I got it from Dezmond's wife, Lucille. She's
selling cosmetics for this company and I got the brochure."

Kaval gave me a look of churning wheels in rapid formula, a homeless drunk stood pissing onto Seventh Street.

26

K AVAL AND I WENT INTO THE SPACIOUS ROOM with our license
and a witness. Dezmond kept his mouth shut the whole
ride down. We gave them our forms and signed the book,

waited at the holding pen on rows of plastic folding chairs
next to green-card seeking immigrants.

Dezmond fidgeted in his seat checking his watch and
snapping his fingers nervously. "How long do you think this
will take?"

"A few minutes."

Kaval leaned forward annoyed. "If you have someplace
to be then you should leave."

"I have to get back to the kid. I left him with the wino
across the hall. By the time I get back the kid will be sold in
Mexico."

Thirteen people ahead of us were moving in and
strolling out, assembly lines in factories would move no
faster. After each two-minute ceremony wives and husbands
holding hands took pictures against the flag tacked up on the
wall. We were called into the chapel and Dezmond whispered out of the side of his mouth, "It's not too late," and I
chuckled back, "It's always too late."

"What is?" she asked.

"Nothing."

Two minutes later we were married and I kissed her
much harder than was called for and we left the room and
before Dezmond could flee I had him take our picture
against the flag. I whispered in her ear that I loved her and
she pursed her lips and gave my hand a squeeze. "I love you
too," she said and not as a whisper.

27

THE EASE WITH WHICH IT HAPPENED made me think it was a
trap. Henry came out at 6:15 and started south along
Third Avenue.

"You sure that's him?" she asked.

"Positive."

Kaval clutched my arm and we followed keeping half a block behind. Henry walked a briskly step no sign of guilt or worry, carefree kids at summer camp. We hid behind a mailbox as he bought a paper from the Arab on the corner. Halfway down the block he started running and I grabbed Kaval's hand surprised that he could have known we were following. He was melting into the crowd until Kaval pulled me into the street where we could see him waving the paper over his head and calling to an unseen friend. The bus stopped short with a squeal of its brakes and Henry hopped inside. Me and Kaval stepped back onto the sidewalk as the dog roared away with his passengers.

"That's the Hampton Jitney," she said, folding her arms and creasing her brow. "Could he possibly commute back and forth to the Hamptons every day?"

"Maybe he's got a place he goes to on the weekends."

"But today's Tuesday."

"We've got to follow him," I said.

"Just remember the game plan!" And the warning in her frozen eyes made cracking ice release.

Henry didn't show up to his office the next day and when Kaval called up asking for him they said he was out till Friday. We stood across from the entrance until the building was dark just to make sure.

That night Kaval sat on a pillow with a notebook in front of her writing out financial holdings and assets and bank accounts and credit cards and then she said that I owned half of it but I told her not to bother.

"Look, tomorrow I'm putting your name on the accounts and you'll get your own credit cards and you'll have access to everything that I have, in case of emergency. We're married now and that's how it's going to be."

At midnight she called her mother and told her of the

wedding and how happy she was and asked if there was any word from her father but there wasn't. Her mother said she'd be sending along a gift with her misgivings and it all ended somewhat pleasantly.

I watched myself for an hour in the mirror, the shape of my head bloating up with sunken eyes deep into my brow and strands of brittle hair falling out past splotchy yellow skin. How could she stand to look at me? Self-repulsion knits its own disclaimer, but makeup men made Peter Boyle.

28

K AVAL WAS COUGHING IN HER SLEEP. Wheezing and clutching a pillow to her stomach she let out a whimper then grew silent. I sat up morning darkness near her face a stain of vomit settled in the sheet. I got dressed quietly and slipped on my jacket in the main room and snuck out the door.

I entered through the side as the sun was coming up; the stench had gotten stronger. I went right to the floorboard and started pushing away the dresser and pulling up the carpet. I put the gun in pocket and held onto the pictures; her only living scandal maybe if I pulverized it she would smile. I searched through the kitchen for matches and found a mildewed set in the corner of the drawer, struck the matchhead against the fraction of flint not yet moist. Starting on the newspapers I lit a torch and walked throughout the rooms, cushions books and cardboard cartons ignited like straw in a barn. I lit the stack of pictures and held them till they burned my fingers, tossed them onto the fiery couch and watched them scream and die.

Ten blocks away I saw the hellish plume of smoke rise

up, smelt the charring spirits fizzle into space. Maybe Denise would meet up with the Pee Lady. Sirens broke the silence minus dogs and evil insects.

I smoked two joints and went to Jackie's for a drink, no more treatments now that food and liquid lost its taste. Perpetual nausea spoiled eggs and orange juice mixed with radium pulsing through my tubes. I called Cosmogony twice and hung up when Henry got on. I called again and asked the receptionist what time the office closed and when she asked why I wanted to know that I told her I was a messenger and had a delivery. She told me five o'clock. I sat at the bar and Jackie treated me like a stranger which was an improvement. Wally slobbered out of the men's room and went to his stool at the end of the bar and then took his glass half-empty and came and sat next to me. Drooping off the sides of the stool like rotten legs of liverwurst, he slurred with saliva forming at the corners of his mouth, "Hey Eddie, tell me something, you lost a sister . . . how the hell you deal with that? I mean, how the hell you ever get over that? You know, my mother died last year, my father ten years ago. Me and Camille were the only ones left. Now that she's gone I'm not connected to anything. It's like I have no past, there's no connection to the past! You know what I mean?"

"Sure. You feel alone and abandoned. But that's how you're supposed to feel so just get used to it."

Jackie dried a glass and quipped over his shoulder, "Just cause you're miserable don't wish it on everybody else!"

Wally looked at me with a drunken gaze.

I waited across the street in full view of the entranceway. My legs were tingling charges to my fingers. Bodies fled out of the building commuting into the sunset when something poked me from behind and turning around Kaval was smoldering barbecue.

"So, this is more of your love and loyalty!"

Her coughing fit through mucus lungs made the whole thing moot. We stood facing the entrance silent hunters using slingshots. A cop car blew past with lights and siren wailing followed by an ambulance, a row of taxi cabs came speeding in their wake. Kaval leaned against the No Parking sign and pulled her hair into a ponytail. Freckles and the Bobbsey Twins.

"I'm sorry," I said.

"You're always sorry," she spit. "It doesn't mean anything. That's what this is all about . . . You're sorry."

Five minutes later Henry came out and Kaval stood straight.

"Okay, let's be careful," she said and we followed this time close behind. Kaval let out a cough and then covered her mouth. Henry played as if he wasn't aware. Kaval said we'd need something to hide behind on the bus so she bought some papers at the newsstand while Henry stood behind four people waiting at the stop. We leaned against the building reading papers. The line was growing by twos and threes and when the striped green luxury bus pulled up there were fourteen people waiting to board. I peered into the cabin and the driver was a human being with beeless eyes and stumpy fingers, nothing even dog-like. Kaval and I got on the end of the line and she opened her bag and whispered, "How much money do you have on you?"

"Fifteen dollars."

"How were you going to pay for this trip without me?"

"I have tokens."

She let out a derisive laugh. "This ride costs over twenty bucks."

"Twenty bucks?!"

We got inside and Kaval paid the driver, turned and started down the aisle. There was no sign of him until halfway down the bus he sat gazing out the window. I tried with all my might to not look him in the face. Kaval sat two rows behind him window seat and I sank in next to her, peeked into the aisle. The bus pulled away and Henry didn't stir for a long time until he slumped down with his head against the window. Kaval opened the paper and began to read. Then she reached into her pocket and pulled out a small black box with wires attached.

"Here, I got this for you. I bought it."

"Thank you." I put the earplugs in and tuned a scratchy sour station, knew it would be gone soon.

A few hours later we arrived at a church. Kaval and I waited till the bus emptied out then we got off. Henry walked toward a blue sedan Mercedes parked near a small firehouse. I looked around but was lost. If not for gibbous moon it would be pitch.

"I think this is Amagansett, or East Hampton," she said. "My father used to take us here when I was young."

"There he goes," I said as Henry pulled away down the lightless blackened highway. People were getting into cars picked up by wives and husbands, the bus drove off and Kaval ran over to a dark green van as a woman climbed out of the back seat.

"C'mon," she called. "This is a cab."

We got out of the cab on a dirt road where tire grooves and muddy puddles formed two crooked lines. Far off the road the blue Mercedes sat in the driveway next to a luxurious house painted white with grass and trees and a child's swing set in the front yard. The air seemed thinner here, harder breathing helium. All around darkness and its insects taunted us to leave. Kaval started coughing deep wheezing phlegm bent over I patted her back until she stopped.

"Are you okay?"

"Yeah," she said with edge.

"Wait here. I'm going to check out the house."

"No, I'm going with you."

"Kaval, don't argue with me. You'd give us away in a

second. Now I'm not going to do anything but look around. I'll be right back."

I started toward the house on cool moist grass, crickets chirping under moonlight. Looking back Kaval's hair shined beacons on the shoreline and I wondered if maybe Denise wasn't right, was it worth it? The front windows were dark and I walked along the side past the swing set stepping on a broken Bart Simpson doll. A trunk of wood with lumber logs and wood chips at the back of the house where voices giggled into the night and I peeked in through the sheer white curtains. The family sat at a dining table with Henry next to his wife their two young daughters opposite, maybe eight and ten years old. The smaller one had a ribbon corsage trailing bubble gum pinned on her pink flowered dress. His wife attractive early thirties wire glasses blond hair tied up in a bun wearing jeans and a plaid shirt got up from the table and stepped into the kitchen. Henry spooned sugar into his coffee while his daughters talked and sipped milk through twisted straws. The lights went out and Henry's wife stood in the doorway holding a birthday cake with lighted candles reflecting off her lenses; the girls sat up and the cake was placed on the table and all together they sang Happy Birthday as the younger one counted the candles. "How come there's ten?"

"The extra one's for good luck," said her mother. "Now make a wish and blow them out before they melt."

Her older sister helped her snuff out the last one and Henry applauded and the lights were turned on and his wife removed the smoldering candles and put them on a napkin. Henry stuck his finger in the icing and the daughters yelled and his wife swatted his hand. I crept around to the other side of the house and came upon two large old-fashioned glass pane doors, tried the knob and gently forced it open. I stepped into a wooden den with mahogany desk and chairs some bookcases along the wall lined with framed pictures of country landscapes. I searched through desk drawers filled with pens and paper envelopes a ledger notebook and trying to open the bottom drawer it was locked. Leafing through the datebook on the blotter the phone cracked brittle eardrums. I held my chest and caught my breath, heard footsteps cross the wooden floor. I cupped the receiver in my hand as his wife asked, "Hello?"

"Hello Natalie, can I speak to Henry? This is Robert."

"Oh, Robert, it's Dawn's birthday and he just sat down at the table."

"It'll only take a minute, promise."

"I'll get him."

A moment later Henry got on. "Hello, Robert."

"Henry, I won't keep you long. Is something wrong with your phone? The connection isn't very good."

"I'm on the cordless."

"Well, I wanted you to know that I spoke to my friend in the D.A.'s office. He tells me the complaint will be turned over as a civil matter and not a criminal one. So it looks like for now you're off the hook."

Henry let out a wild sigh. "Thank God! That's great news! If it's a civil matter we can settle out of court."

"That's my feeling exactly. Well anyway, I thought you'd want to know, so . . . get back to that birthday."

"Thank you so much, Robert. I owe you a big one."

"You sure do. I'll talk to you on Monday. Take care."

The phone went dead and the receiver in hand gave me an idea. I dialed the operator. "Hello operator, I just put a new line in and I'd like to check it out. Can you ring me back at this number?"

"Surely, what's the number?" I quickly scanned the phone plate but it was blank. "Uh . . . my wife wrote it down for me but I can't seem to find it."

"Stay by the phone, I'll ring you back."

I hung up and a second later it rang. Heavy footsteps

went for the phone and I picked up at the same time he did.

"Your line seems to be working fine, sir," she said.

"Thank you operator." Click.

"What?"

"Stay on the line, Henry."

"Who is this?"

"I'm someone you're about to meet. I want you to hang up the phone and come into the den."

"What? Who is this? Where are you?"

"I'm in the next room. I don't want to disrupt your daughter's birthday so just hang up and come inside. Do it or I'll be forced to do something I don't want to do. You're not in any danger, I only want to talk to you. Please, come inside and don't say a word to your wife."

Henry hung up and I went behind the door. Outside I heard, "Henry, where are you going?"

"I have to make a call. It's business and it'll only take a minute. Go on without me."

"Oh, Henry! Can't it wait?"

"I'll just be a minute."

I crept behind the door with hand on gun in pocket. Henry took a cautious step inside. "Close the door," I whispered. "Leave the light off." Henry stepped into the middle of the room, the moonlight caused a glimmer in my hand and he slowly raised his arms.

"What do you want? Who . . . who are you?"

"Please, keep your voice low."

Up close he seemed shorter than on the street and in the dark I could see him tremble, sweat forming on his face and in his palms. My stomach knotted self-reflexive hatred.

"Please . . . take whatever you want. Just don't hurt me or my family."

"I don't want your things, and I'm not going to hurt anyone, unless you make me."

"Then . . . what do you want?"

"I want you to make a phone call."

Henry raised his voice in urgency and confusion. "Phone call?! What is this about?"

"Keep your voice down. You don't want your wife to come in. I'd have to tell her about the pictures."

A slap on face he stiffened up and peered into my eyes. His, burning through the dark, gave me a chill. He lowered his arms and angry calm began, "I told you it's over with. I won't pay you another cent. I have nothing left to give. Do what you're going to do, I don't care anymore."

"You and I have never talked before."

"Then your partner . . . whoever's been calling me!"

"No, I'm with no one else."

"What's this phone call you want me to make?"

Before I could take out Webster's card footsteps approached from the dining room. I backed against the wall with pointed gun at Henry's chest and told him to be smart. Henry went to his desk and picked up the phone as the door was opened and Dawn stepped in. Visible through the doorway crack her tiger-stripe glasses big on her cheeks with innocent eyes protected and immune, she asked, "Daddy, why are you in the dark? We're waiting for you."

"Tell Mommy I'll be right in as soon as I'm off the phone."

"C'mon, Daddy. It's my birthday!"

"I know, Pumpkin. I'll be there as soon as I can. Now close the door behind you and don't wait for me. Go on. Leave the light off."

Dawn left the room and I lowered the gun, empty and clipless I couldn't play the terror game anymore. Henry went over and locked the door, then went behind his desk and tried to open the bottom drawer. I stepped up and told him not to. Helpless eyes like children trapped in poverty. "Who the hell are you anyway?!"

"I'm Denise's brother."

"Denise? Denise who?" He truly didn't know.

"Your ex-mistress. Denise."

As the images took shape in his mind replaced with self-survival, I expected him to plead for his life. Instead he let out a pained smile. "You're here to kill me, aren't you? Honor. That's what this is about."

"No. This is about justice."

Henry started laughing gleeful darkly.

"Maybe you could tell me what's so funny."

"Justice! That's funny. Justice. What about my justice? Justice for the way your sister terrorized my family?!"

"*You* terrorized them! You're the one with problems."

"Yes, I've got problems. Deep-rooted, serious problems. But tell me, what kind of problems does a woman have who would pick up an eight-year-old girl from her school, take her into the city, then call me threatening her life if I didn't pay more money?"

Henry wiped his forehead clean and continued. "I got a call one afternoon from my youngest daughter, telling me she was with Aunt Doris. Funny thing is, she doesn't have an Aunt Doris. I remained calm, asked if she was alright and where she was. She said that Aunt Doris had taken her for a ride in a car, that Aunt Doris let her drive. Then she said Aunt Doris was going to take her to a movie. I asked her again where she was but your sister got on. Told me if I didn't meet my obligations that Aunt Doris would be angry, that Aunt Doris was capable of anything when she got angry."

Henry stopped speaking, and I knew what he said to be frightfully true as Fatal Attraction was Denise's favorite movie. His face sagged as he added, "She said she was going to take some pictures, that she had some clients who would . . . Christ! We're talking about an eight-year-old girl!"

Movie screens and midnight madness set the table dinnertime with Denise across from me a look of mangled metal on her face. Uncle Ted sat to her left and told her to eat her steak. Mother weaved her fuzzy warm cocoon.

"That's an expensive cut of meat," he said. "Don't waste it."

"I'm not hungry."

"You were hungry an hour ago."

"I'm not hungry now."

Mother's eyes played Polish ping pong. "Denise, please," she said, "just eat your food."

"I'm not hungry!"

Uncle Ted barked, "You better get hungry real fast!" Then he glared over at my plate. "Don't tell me you're not eating too!" I shoved another piece of tasteless trauma in my mouth.

"There, why can't you be like your brother!"

"Because he's a worm!" she snapped and threw me a look that told me it was true.

Uncle Ted turned to mother under crucifix and holy plates. "You know what this is about, don't you? The piano lessons! She's upset because I won't allow her to be with that pervert!"

Denise jumped in. "He's not a pervert!"

"He had his hands around you! What kind of lesson was he giving you?!"

"He was showing me how to do something!"

"I'll bet he was! If I ever catch him near you again . . ."

"Look who's talking! The human octopus!"

Uncle Ted backhanded Denise off her chair and onto the floor, she landed in a heap at the refrigerator. Mother dropped her fork tinkling on the plate but kept her tongue. I eyed the steak knife on my napkin, the sound of punctured flesh and bursting bladders boiling in my ears. Denise crawled along the floor against the cabinets holding her red and puffy cheek. Tearless and defiant she cried, "The only pervert around here is you! Tiny little penis!"

Uncle Ted exploded from the table knocking his plate broken to the floor grabbing Denise and demanding that she apologize but she fought back with kicking flailing scratching limbs like wildcats and boogie men. Uncle Ted pulled her by the ankle across the floor but Denise clutched a leg of the table tugging it away until Uncle Ted stomped on her wrist and she let go. Mother hysterical pleaded mercy as Uncle Ted dragged sister through the hall and into her room where the door slammed shut and the beating began. Denise refused to apologize and if anything she said even worse. Mother sealed herself and told me to finish my dinner. To the sounds of sister's Catholic anarchy I cleaned my plate and threw up into the sandbox.

Henry weeped into his arms with trilling gulps of hurt and harm that slowly morphed to laughter. When he raised his head a snout had formed, syrup saliva dripped from his teeth and the room grew ominously quiet just the chirping bugs outside. I gripped the gun but kept it at my side.

"Where's Henry?"

A narrow grin on wormy lips, he answered. "He's near. Hear the tick of the clock? Knock knock." And the clock on the wall ticked loudly. Still wearing Henry's clothes he put his paws flat out on the desk and the tips of his claws took flight like hungry gray mosquitoes. I wiped them from my face and something scratched the tip of spine. A troubling pain inside my brain I raised the gun and asked again, "Where's Henry?"

With pungent breath like rat-infested pancake mix, he snickered air through stuffy nostrils and it occurred to me I'd seen him before but long ago the world changed worse.

"Remember that mutt you had when you were seven years old?" he asked. "Gray, with the black stripe across the head?"

"Shamby . . . He ran away."

"He was left abandoned on the side of the road. Released

from the car and told to go far, Shamby like Bambi was left on his own."

"No. He ran away. Uncle Ted told us that he—" and the words and their meaning stuck in my throat. "Are . . . are you saying you were Shamby?"

The dog closed his eyes and hummed a secret lullaby. Got up from the chair and walked unnaturally on hind legs over to the coat rack. His expression sly and challenging, he goaded, "Well, what are you waiting for? There's a round in the chamber, it's been there the whole time."

"That's not what I came to do. And the gun is empty." But it quivered in my hand, a lifeforce emanating from inside.

"You're a mouse," he said with laser pupils glowing red Nosferatu. "Did the police tell you that her face was bashed in with an ax handle? It wasn't a baseball bat. The wounds had squared edges. I clocked her from behind when she wasn't looking. She slammed to the floor and I pounded some more until her face like chili brains and beans. I poked out her eyes and crushed them under paw. Two cherry splotches near the drain, that's all that remained. Then I fucked the bloody sockets."

Suspicious disbelief he wanted me to shoot him and that's what held me back.

"Remember that cabinet in the dungeon," he sneered, and like magic it appeared on the wall behind the desk. The doors glided open and rows of plastic penis weapons stood at stiff attention.

"I took the biggest one and forced it deep inside her. Twisted and ripped till she looked like the Lincoln Tunnel. That's what those lumps were when you identified the body."

Cobras danced inside my spleen, a feast of snakes from Aberdeen.

"Did the cops tell you what I did next?" he asked, words

like sharpened butcher knives; a puddle of crimson bled from my pants and seeped into the rug. Smiling, he answered, "The autopsy showed piss in her mouth and nostrils. Some in her eye sockets too."

"Alright!" I yelled and clenched my eyes, tried to stop the pictures. "I'm not going to do what you want me to do! So save it!"

Henry's wife was tapping on the door and calling his name, jiggling the knob.

"Now you've done it," said the dog as Father Michael. "Now you have to kill them all! The wife and kids both big and small."

"Fuck you!" I cried, then tried to throw the gun from hand but steel had fused to bone. The door shook on its hinges as she kicked it from outside. The dog willed handgun pointing her intrusion, dead aim at her heart. Unable to move with suffocate intensity filling in my lungs, the pressure inside with nowhere to hide, my skull like fragile Christmas balls, I begged him not to do it.

"But you're the one doing it," he laughed. "It's what you *choose* to do."

"Then I choose this!" I choked and tried to point it his way but elbow locked and index finger cocked and squeezing trigger, I couldn't move an inch. A key inserted in the lock any moment swinging open. The dog let out a sinister grin. "Happy hunting," he said. My fingers metastatical, with all my might and all my mind I forced them to my head.

The dog shrieked horror, scrunched up nose as lightning bolts and sharpened teeth attacked me from below. He shot out through the glass doors and into the yard like sprinting wild horses. Watched him disappear and felt release, like poker bluffs and blackjack dealers; until the lemonade started pouring from my waist; neutered numbness dear salvation gone forever, taking my soul with it, and any chance virility, but empty holes from dripping clothes made one less victim play his role. I tore through the yard raging past his shedding fur and humid breath on sticky leaves. Flies and branches scratched my ears as paws crunched dried-out brittle weeds. A clearing up ahead where moonlight shone on flower beds, the dog's coat glistened under sweat and moist velocity. A babbling stream in Crystal Lake where teenage boys caught frogs and snakes, the dog splashed through clear blue water kicking tadpoles out of his way, I followed hopping over Zero's bloated body. Closing on his tip of tail, he sprouted wings and set to sail; I lunged for his legs and landed in a hall: outside Mother's morning bedroom where Uncle Ted and cousin Helen played in fornication. I hid there watching Helen squirm her face in pleasure pain and firm and I never said a word to my mother or Denise or to anyone else not even priests. I prayed myself to sleep that night with Ted and mother fighting over frequency. Two years later teenage Helen hit by car and died unconscious as once again he got away unknown. The dog hovered in the corner of the room with batwings spread in crucifixion and my lifeblood dangling from his teeth. Helen sat beside me on the bed and put her hand on my back, the smell of Uncle Ted's cologne faintly in her clothing. In soft soprano she whispered in my ear, "I knew you were watching me that day. It really turned me on. I fantasized about having sex with you many times." She glanced down at my leaking waist and said, "It's a shame, I guess now we'll never know . . ."

The dog let out a yelp of laughter that snapped a bone in my neck. I jumped from the bed and the walls exploded particles shattering eyes and I freefell blind with vertigo. An infant cried nearby and the dog's presence gave me edge. The guttural growl of his voice taunting from the netherworld. "Do you know your girlfriend's pregnant? She's been fucking her friend again. Didn't she tell you? Or just dispel you?"

Earth grew up underfoot cracked and parched with

bloodshot veins, tents and shacks scattered along a path
but no dog or living creature. I jogged along a row of burning fire campsights past the grapes of wrath and rusted
tractor trailer parts. Barren dirt and mountainous rock as
far as eye could see until reaching the top of a hill a group
of ragged working men beckoned me to join. I skidded
down into the center as the tallest one in tattered slacks
and smoking jacket skin in oily boils came over to greet
me. But it was the warm smile sunny on his face that gave
me chill.

"I've been waiting for you," he said. "God, you've certainly grown."

The others around him, pathetic sad and surreal murmured nervously as my father raised a webbed hand melted
fingers fused together and they all grew silent. "This is my
son and he's going to live with us now."

"No, Dad, I have to get out of here! Where's the dog! I
should have killed him when I had the chance."

"There aren't any dogs here. We do have worms, though.
Millions of worms. I'll get you some. But first, I'll show you
to your home."

"Home? Yes! Take me home."

The lepers turned and followed my father toward a
smoky plume in the distance. The stench from their bodies
fogged my eyes and clogged my nose as we passed a small
pool of clear water where the soulless eyes of a mouse looking up at me sent a tremor down my legs. We came upon a
settlement of cardboard boxes and my father looked back
and saw me crying. His smiling lips gave me insulin.

"It's okay, Eddie," he said with an arm around my shoulder. "You're home now. Everything's going to be fine."

"But Dad, this isn't our home! And nothing's fine. What
happened to you? Why are you like this?"

"You haven't seen me in a long time. You were just a
young boy when it happened."

Led by the hand I can't remember who into the living room where mother and grandma sat crying on the couch with handkerchiefs entangled in arthritic fingers. Four years old the house was black with endless phone calls priests and prayers. That night Denise took me aside and told me Daddy was sleeping with baby Jesus and that we should be happy. But for all that happiness the house was sad with Satan.

"I hear your mother remarried," he said with no sense of longing not even jealousy.

"Dad, Denise is dead. She was killed by the dog."

As if he hadn't heard, he said, "Remember how we used to put on those shows in the living room, you and your sister would sing and dance to records. Denise would hold a shoehorn and pretend it was a microphone. Then she put a bowl of fruit on her head and danced like Carmen Miranda. Remember that song I used to sing to you? It always cheered you up when you were sad. I still remember it." Father started warbling out a sour sound unmusical except for words of sad remembrance. "Smile, though your heart is aching, smile, even though it's breaking . . ."

He lifted his hands beseeching me to smile.

"Dad, please! This is all in my mind! I'm not here and neither are you. I'm in somebody's home."

My father stopped as if jolted back aware. "That's right. Home," he said, and stepped over to a large rectangular box. "Here, Eddie, this is your home. You can fix it up anyway you like."

The cardboard box with Kelvinator painted on the side barely big enough to sit up in; I turned to the group gun still in hand overcome with primal hatred as these creatures once men but now the lowest of low worse than junkies accepted their fate with no hope of redemption. Dragged my father down with them.

I screamed, "Tell me where the dog is?! Tell me where he is or I'll kill you all!"

My father seemed confused. "Eddie, how many will you kill with only one bullet?" And with those words the others pleaded one by one fighting each other to be killed. Begging me please to fire into their brains as father stood back and watched it with a resigned grin.

"This is madness!" I cried. "Where's Henry! And Kaval! DAD! HELP ME PLEASE!!!"

A scream broke out above our heads the lepers cried in fear and dread then scattered into boxes while my father stood his ground. A shadow swept the land as bat-winged serpent harpy dog my lifeblood still in tow soared above us pissing down like snow. Each glittering flake burned my skin with sizzling flesh my father's face in happiness as the dog cackled over his shoulder gliding into the distance. I took aim but he was too far away to hit. My father unbuttoned his wrinkled office postal shirt revealing a fist-sized crater where his heart should've been, bloody tubes and ligaments twisted out of the hole. "It's gone," he said without looking up. "He took it when I was only thirty-nine years old."

"Dad, if I get it back will you be alive again? Will you come back with me?"

He looked up crinkled ridges from his caustic eyes and sniffled, "You'd better hurry, he's getting away."

The dog was barely in sight on the horizon, I took one last look at my father then ran off through the mud and rain never to return again with one last bullet for myself if need be.

I chased him over gullies of trash in a junkyard stash past faceless men at flaming barrels warming hands on candlesticks. Until finally, he was gone and there was no one else to chase. I stopped in the midst of debris with nothing left to do or see; tried to catch my breath wheezing for oxygen, looked around and saw the reason why: the Staten Island landfill piled high with miles-long contamination where seagulls spiraled down haphazard weeping silent death. No outlet

save for self-immolation, I continued on through the waste-
land with no one in sight not even spirits.

Days later I stopped to rest on a mound of soft green
moss where thirty million red ants appeared and converged
on a slithering snake, ate it alive as its body became a moving red sea. When the flesh was gone save for scaly flattened
skin the ants disappeared back into their moss thanking me
for alerting them to the snake. I took the skin and put it on
my tender wound to stop the leaking.

I heard the cheers from behind the stairs sitting on
bleachers facing rigid goalposts silhouette against the moon.
The cool air brought gnats and the coming morning's dew.
Drunken laughter primate wails as one by one the train set
sail, sinking deep like German U-boats hit by submarines.
The springtime dance of football players taking turns from
mother's little tirade of take off that dress and wear the blue
one and the stubborn fight that followed as mother scrubbed
her face clean of any makeup. Then mother's final warning
with Uncle Ted in the doorway as no young daughter looks
that way as sluts and whores will surely pay. But Denise had
been paying for quite some time. The dancing crowd on
fancy booze and candy pills with Denise barely able to stand
up tumbling on the gymnasium floor till Harvey Wilburton
carried her out and told Mrs. Stumpman she was sick. I followed them outside and when I tried to take her home she
pushed me away with whiskey regal on her breath and told
me to keep a running count. I didn't know what she meant.
Harvey helped her to the field where Craig McGurney and
his no-neck teammates stood drinking beers and pissing on
cement. Denise fell into Craig's arms sticking her tongue in
his mouth and Craig mauled her breasts and under dress
Denise then asked him who was best. Craig yelled she'd find
out and all together they led her back behind the locker room
doors I came up running grabbed her hand as taunts and
threats and unpaid debts came down like dying seagulls.

Denise turned to me and sobered up with fire in her eye and told me not to stop what Mommy wanted. The cavemen cheered and scanning the crowd I saw Johnny Langelosi with a beer in hand and begged him with my eyes not to do it. Again I tried to pull her away and Craig came up with a fist on chest Denise unzipped her party dress, then disappeared in darkness. Through the raucous laughter I heard her counting numbers and rating each one better than the next and when it was finally over and they left her like a dirty used-up needle, Craig walked past me gloating like a junkie. When Johnny Langelosi came out a minute later roasting almond rage threw me off the bleachers knocking him to the ground and punching like a maniac. Johnny rolled me over and started beating my face and a crowd appeared someone poured beer on my head and the harder I struggled to get up the more they kicked me down. Johnny finally stopped hitting me and lifted himself up and grabbed a beer. Bloody but willing for more I jumped to my feet and waited for Johnny to make a move but he gave me a look that told me it was over. As they left everyone laughed cruel baboons except for Johnny. I found Denise under the bleachers straightening out her dress.

We walked along the trestle next to the football field. I held a tissue against my lip. "You look worse than I do," she said. "What are you going to tell Mommy about your cheek?"

"Nothing. She's asleep by now."

"You should know better than to start a fight with a football player."

"He's the kicker! I thought he was my friend. Why did you do that tonight? Now they're all going to call you a whore."

"What do you care what they call me. I did what I wanted to do. I was in control."

"That's not the point!"

"Are you ashamed of me?"

"I don't know what the fuck I am. Are you okay?"

She nodded her head and looked up at the streetlight. When we got home she showered for two hours and I never spoke to Johnny Langelosi again.

My mother stood in the kitchen at the counter cutting onions into tiny bits and sliding them into the sauce. The smell of beef and sausage filled the house with spicy warmth. I watched from the end of the counter, amazing skill with sharpened knives that never cut her finger.

"We won't be eating for another few hours. Why don't you go outside and play."

"I'd rather watch you do that," I answered. "Can I help?"

"You want to help me cook?" she seemed surprised.

"Sure."

"See those peppers? You can wash them off and then cut out the heart."

"The heart?"

"Yes, the inside stem. Remove all the seeds and throw them in the garbage. Wash your hands first."

Mother watched me do the peppers without a word between us. When I finished she said, "Okay, now you can peel those cloves of garlic, just remove the skin and leave them on the board."

Doing tasks with nothing to distract us I heard a sound at the table and turned to find myself as an adult watching casual, our meeting eyes exchanging places growing old on Jupiter. I got up from the table and stood beside her, her hands worn and wrinkled from scores of chores and chopping countless cloves of garlic. With many words and endless questions running through my mind I stepped into a different house with king-size bed and future time. The light clicked off and she stepped out of the bathroom in tee shirt panties easing under the covers and putting her glasses on the table next to the bed.

"Aren't you coming to bed?"

I started removing my shirt and laying it on the chair when I noticed our wedding picture framed and facing the door. Stomach pumped anxiety as I slid my pants to the floor the viscous lemon juice dripping from the wound. I carefully slipped under the covers and laid on my side. A second later Elizabeth touched my shoulder her breath on neck and tongue right after. We kissed our mouths in love and syrup. Her large breasts firm nipples pressed against my body with sizzling skin and panties moving gently to her ankles when sudden realizations delivered me angina. Elizabeth rubbed pubic against my thigh then started licking my neck and snuggling her nose in my ear and reaching for something that wasn't there. I trembled sweating Novocaine.

"What's wrong?" she asked.

"I don't know. I guess I'm not feeling well."

"Don't you find me attractive?"

"Of course I do. I love you. I don't know what's wrong with me."

"Am I doing anything wrong? I'll do whatever you want. What would you like me to do?"

"You do everything perfectly. I love the way you lick me and touch me. It's just . . . I'm the problem, not you. I'm sorry."

"There's nothing to apologize for. I just wish I knew what to do. It's been a long time now, and I need to be with you."

"You are with me, we love each other."

"I know." But huge brown eyes with hard desire and soft misunderstanding slit my wrists and dirt poured in. I put my hand between her thighs and tried to work my magic fingers but Elizabeth jerked herself closed. "Ow, that hurts. Your hand is so cold."

I removed the gun and Elizabeth kissed my cheek and told me she was tired. Stared at the ceiling as traffic shadows drove her heart off with them.

I got up from bed and walked through the house dark and unfamiliar except for the cellar door. I crept downstairs and heard the boiler vibrate, Uncle Ted was groaning under moss and shame. The outside doors were green ajar I slowly pushed them open.

Houston Street came into view where Norfolk and the playground grew. I stood outside the gates watching children play kickball when something froze esophagus. Their Catholic clothes and springtime shows familiar faces indigo as Sister Mary Gregory threatened detention after school and fifth grade repeated itself all over again! A husky voice like velvet in a cuisinart called my name and pretty Nikki Neiderman looked up pigtails and a smile. Pushed the red-framed glasses up the bridge of her nose.

"What are you doing out there?" she asked, green eyes sparkling emeralds. "If Sister Antoinette sees you you're in trouble."

"I'm too old to be with you now."

"Too old? How'd that happen?"

"It just did. I'm looking for a dog. Have you seen any dogs around here? Maybe he's inside of you."

"No. Recess is almost over. You'd better get back in."

"I can't. I have something to do."

"What is it?"

"A secret."

"You like secrets, don't you? Is that why you never told me?"

"Told you what?"

"You had a crush on me for years and never let on. Not a word. You never sent me secret love letters; you never told a friend, or wrote my name on the wall when nobody was looking. Nothing on Valentines Day. Why?"

"I was afraid. You were . . . are, so pretty."

"What were you afraid of?"

"I don't know. Rejection. Something like that. Looking

back it seems kind of foolish. But at the time . . . well . . . I was just a kid."

"It's not too late. We can do it over here," she said, and I followed her along the gate past the fire hydrant and over to the entrance, Nikki's eyes held me firm the whole walk over. Nikki undid her bleached white blouse and dropped it with her blazer to the ground. Flat breasts pink like babies riding snowmobiles. She unclasped her skirt with peach string bikinis and let them drop as tapeworms ate my spine.

"Is anything wrong? You seem like something's bothering you."

"We're in public. Everyone can see us."

"They won't mind. If we're quiet they won't even know we're here."

Nikki took my belt and undid my pants and I kept my hand hidden behind thigh as she sank hydraulic to her knees, imagined a bullseye on her forehead. She lowered jeans and peeking past my shirt tails squeaked out a sigh. Before I could fire she melted butter to the ground and seeped into the concrete.

Walking along Avenue A hoping to see familiar sights on the way to our apartment, thinking fuck the dog if Kaval is alright and I would be really home, I reached the park and pathways lined with needle-jabbing derelicts acting diabetic. The trees wept as I walked past. Our front door open walking in heard shoveling from the bedroom. Kaval and Chris going at it again and I stood there conscious gun more hurt than angry confrontation. The look on her face like cherub angels watching miracles. Chris had ancient tribal tattoos dancing on his back their keys unlocking doors that I could only dream about. A man called me into the kitchen and I stepped in white fluorescent light.

"Yes, right over here," he said. "Step in and have a seat," but I stood. Dr. Kolver sat at his desk perpendicular to the sink on a high-back leather chair with a serpent loose around his neck.

"I've been watching you," he said. "There's no need to put yourself through this agony. I think I can fix this little problem you seem to be having. If you like I can also remove that gun from your hand."

"I'll keep the gun for the time being."

"As you wish. Now, if you'll just sign this form I'll make all the arrangements and we can get started right away." I tried to sign his scrolling parchment but his pen tipped over on the page.

A table wheeled in and I laid down under cool silk sheets with operating lights above. I looked to my right and CandyBar lay on a table with tubes connecting her body to mine. She gave me a smile. The beeping sounds and chemo smells brought me back to jingle bells, Christmas in my mother's home the tree and lights with electric trains chugging through Jerusalem. Santa laughing pagan from wreaths and hanging mobiles mocking baby Jesus lying in his manger. Denise helped mother in the kitchen baking sugar cookies while I sat at the table cutting Christmas pictures out of magazines and pasting them onto cardboard.

"Do you know that *Santa* is an anagram for *Satan*," she said lifting a tray from the oven and breathing in the warm cinnamon spice.

"Oh, it is not!" mother said annoyed.

"Yes it is. Just move the *n* to the end and it spells *Satan*."

I thought it out and it did. She went on, "You know what else? *Live* spelled backwards is *evil*."

Mother angry and frustrated answered, "Where do you learn these things?! I send you to school to learn an education and this is what you come back with?!"

"Do you know that *God* spelled backwards is *dog!*"

"That's enough! If you want to be smart you can go to your room and stay there."

Denise gave me a happy wink and brought a tray o[f]
cookies to the table. "Don't eat them they're still soft," sh[e]
said and I poked my finger in the middle. "Ma! He's playing
with the cookies!" Then she flicked my ear.

"Hey! Denise flicked my ear!"

"Alright behave yourselves! The both of you! Denise,
grease these trays so we can do another batch."

As mother turned to knead more dough Uncle Ted came
in and snubbed his Lucky Strike in an ashtray. "What's going
on?" he asked then looked at Denise, the walls closed in
around her.

"Nothing," I said.

"They're teasing each other," mother added. Denise
stood trapped at the counter as Uncle Ted reached into the
cabinet over her head. He filled his glass at the faucet and
leaned against the counter with smiling eyes unholy.

As the anesthetic wore off I became sharply aware of her
panting moans of painful pleasure. Kaval buried her teeth in
my neck and her nails in my back so tightly stiff holding her
breath for two full minutes not making a sound until she
opened her eyes and coughed out a gasp. Started pecking
my neck like starving hens on chicken farms, telling me she
loved me over and over softness blue as summer skies I glided through. Elizabeth asked me where I'd been hiding all
this time and I told her Kansas City. She giggled low and
started purring like a kitten, wrapped her legs around my
waist and drew me into her hips moving in and out pumping fire engines cut to trains through speeding tunnels. One
by one the women from my life appeared their jewels buffed
to shiny orgasm. Some I'd seen for seconds in crowded stores
while others loved for years in secret chambers never been
revealed. But every blast of castor oil changed their faces violent; hideous and distorted they fell away like rotted bark
from withered trees. My stomach churned regurgitate and I
jumped up from the bed tossing their shells aside. Pointing

straight out from my waist was Dr. Kolver's monstrosity; holding firm with stitches made from fishing twine. The dog sat gloating in the window his batwings bunched around his shoulders as I picked through the balsam bodies searching for Kaval.

"Don't you like the new you?" he asked, dangling a brown paper bag out the window.

"Where's Kaval?" I demanded and she appeared on the bed with Chris having sex again. Uncle Ted sat in the corner jerking off his own red serpent's tail. Above him father's feet dangled gently in the breeze, the noose tight around his stretched-out neck a bloated tongue drooping from his teeth. I cried out, "Why do you have to bring him into it?!"

"Because you want to know the truth. And the truth is all-consuming. The more you learn, the more you burn! Stop now, while you can still return."

"But my father had a heart attack!"

"Like the tick of the clock knock knock!"

"Fuck the clock!"

"Didn't you think it odd there was no church service? . . . Father went to work one day and left forever after, they found him in a storage closet hanging from the rafter. I guess you could say he was a real swinger!" The dog cackled shrill and rolled back his head and I lunged for his cavernous throat; caught him this time unaware. We tumbled out the window down an endless drop of seashore cliffs with crashing foam slit by jagged rocks, Wolfman catching Dracula. The dog's wings ripped paper kites on windy days jolted by the shock of freezing water, still I kept hold as he struggled to get free. The dog spit the bag into the current and I watched it sink under surface but kept my fingers squeezing. "It's getting away," he groaned. "Don't be a fool! For once, think of yourself!"

A second later released my grip and dove down into

nature's swirling anarchy; tricked again as his laughter trailed me underwater. Blinded by salt I came up choking air, treading in the East River where the FDR went up on concrete pillars. The city and its denizens, Brooklyn Bridge and New York Post, I dove back down into the muddy green water, disappeared into an inky shroud where silent screams were heard in dark Atlantis. I burst to the surface in the midst of an endless ocean. Scoping miles of turbulent waves, the dog paddled off in the distance. Boiling sea erupted Krakatoa I grabbed the fin of a shark moving dorsal through the water and he let me ride for free. I woke up very late one night from nightmares chasing innocents. A lamp was on in the living room and father sat in cushion chair crying continental. "Daddy, what's wrong?"

"Nothing."

"Why are you crying?"

"I'm sad."

"Why are you sad?"

"I don't know." He sealed himself tightened upper lip and forced it into a smile. "What are you doing up so late?"

"I couldn't sleep. A monster was chasing me."

"A monster?" he was amused. "There are no such things as monsters, at least not in dreams. You should try and go back to sleep. Think of happy things. You have a birthday coming up, think of that. We'll have a nice party for you, with a great big chocolate cake. I'll have them put some spacemen on it like I did last year. You liked that, remember?" then he patted my head. "Now go back to bed. It's very late."

"I'm thirsty."

He got me a glass of water and sat down while I drank it fever. "Go easy," he said, his voice was soothing oil. "Take it slow. You're going to be fine now."

I finished and he took the glass from hand and put it on the table. "Okay, now off to bed." I took a step when father blurted out, "Cathy's four and Anthony's seven."

I lay in bed awake another hour till the lamp went out and I fell asleep. The next morning Denise appeared on the couch holding a tear-soaked tissue, the broken remnants on the table and the gold band twisted into a pretzel. I asked her what was wrong and she told me the ring was fake and worth just thirty dollars, all this after Jerry made a splash of spending thousands.

"Good riddance!" I announced. "You're better off without him."

"But we've made so many arrangements, the hall is booked, Mommy ordered the invitations. Aunt Louise already started the dress . . ."

"So what! Those aren't reasons to marry somebody. You don't love him anyway."

"I don't know. I might."

"Denise, if you're not sure then don't do it. What does he say about the ring?"

"He said it was a mistake, that they gave him the wrong one by accident."

"You don't believe that, do you? How did you find out it was fake?"

"I had it appraised. Elizabeth noticed a crack in the stone and so I took it to a jeweler. I was so embarrassed. It's not even zirconia, it's something he probably picked up at a pawn shop."

"Jerry always had style."

"Mom is going to blame me for this. Somehow she's going to say it was my fault. I don't know what to do."

"Don't do anything. Tell mom you've had second thoughts, that Jerry lied and is a stupid jerk, and that you don't love him. You're too young to get married anyway."

She gave it a thought and sat back on the couch.

Two days later Jerry came over apologetic on his knee presenting a real engagement ring in the living room in front of mother and Uncle Ted. For a week I couldn't look her in

the eye and when Elizabeth asked me what was wrong I told
her I was sad.

It was cold and dark my knees on wet cement. The secret
wall was ripped open and table overturned with clothes on
the floor. Denise's body lay eyeless near the drain and the
puddle of water was a pool of her blood. Blind insane I
scoped the room for the dog but nowhere to be found. There
was a knock on the door and Denise came out of her office,
cowboy boots with jeans and cut-off tee shirt wavy hair in
ponytail. She checked the hole then opened the door. "What
are you doing here?"

"I was in the neighborhood and thought I'd drop by."
Denise turned and walked into the center of the room. Henry
stayed in darkness but his clothes and height were finger-
prints. I looked at my feet and the blood and the body were
gone; everything neatly in its place; Denise seemed too
relaxed for this to be true. She took a broom from against the
wall and swept the floor of feathers near the cross beams. An
ax handle appeared against the garden hose and I called out,
"Denise! Don't turn your back on him!" But the fourth wall
never wavered. I checked my weapon still in hand as Henry
and Denise talked softly; confusion danced the foxtrot.
Denise laughed from something said then bent over with a
dustpan picking up the feathers. Henry leaned over gripped
the handle firm and stood with shadow casting mystery. I
tried to raise my arm but something held it dystrophy.
Denise looked up to see the handle poised above her head
but didn't cry or seem afraid her eyes were empty craters.
Frozen stiff I screamed a blast like kicks in kung fu movies
and Henry teetered for a second, tried to catch his balance
but with nothing there to catch he tumbled backward crash
of glass his shattered body tiny crystal slivers. A silent
shroud of powder hovered over the ashes. Stunned for a
moment I was alone in the room with no sounds but for distant midtown traffic. The light overhead pulsed hot and cold

beating neon heartthrob, I stood at his upturned shoes and leaned over, peered into his fractured face of diamonds.

My own looked back at me!

Twinkling eyes and caramel. Tiny squeals from furry rats chewing tissue underneath a sheet of red ants flowing silk across her body down into the drain. I started laughing darkly as the room became four walls minus doors. Tried to rip the gun from hand then searched for knives or sharpened objects. Finally I raised it to my head and closed my eyes, saw Adam killing Eve for maiden sins in paradise; knew it wouldn't matter soon. I whispered into the void, "Evil as evil can be." Then squeezed the trigger.

I opened my eyes and Henry sat behind his desk. The dog was gone. I pulled the trigger six more times to make sure, then lay the gun flat on the desk and slowly removed my fingers. Henry looked at me with bulging eyes of white, sweat poured off his face and his hair was soaking wet; fumes from soiled clothing. He reached for the phone.

"You . . . you're insane! I'm going to call the police."

I pulled up a chair and eased myself down. Henry finished dialing and held the phone to his ear. Looked at me a puzzle.

"Put that down," I said, and after a pause he did. We sat there for a moment in the dark, neither one of us moved or said a word. Finally he broke the silence. "What do you want?"

"Are you an evil man, Henry?" He didn't answer. "Am I? . . . Evil. I don't know what that means anymore. It's meaningless to me. All part of the madness. I've seen the darkest corners of my own madness, the demons waiting there, and it's quite a revelation, let me tell you."

"What do you want?" he said again but not as a question.

I gave his words such careful thought, took a deep breath and told him, "Right now all I want is to go home."

With slightly crazed disgusted eyes he said, "Then get the fuck out of my house. Now!"

I left through the glass doors leaving the gun behind. Kaval coughed under the tree as I approached.

"What happened? What did you see?!"

"I'll tell you on the way home. C'mon."

"Wait a minute! What did you do back there?! Did you kill him!?"

"Of course not! He's the wrong guy. It's not him. Please, let's just go home."

I started down the narrow road toward the main highway leading to the firehouse. Kaval stayed two steps back, apprehension in her shoes. "Kaval, if you don't believe me then go ring his bell. Watch him answer the door."

On the train I told her about seeing Henry through the window with his wife and the young daughter's birthday and my sudden change of heart. I didn't tell her about the dungeon or my journey. In the city we took a cab downtown and when we got into the apartment it had been robbed. Her stereo was missing along with most of her records, clothes on the floor and the mattress crooked the drawers and cabinets were searched and Kaval was angry near the point of tears. She growled about moving uptown and finally getting away from these wealthy trust fund junkies sleeping on the street and playing William Burroughs; as she began to get politic I went into the kitchen and turned off the gas, the stove had been left on. I opened the window and checked the refrigerator and all the shelves were bare. I let the door swing free and Kaval looked inside. Shut her gaping mouth.

"They must be vegetarians," I remarked and broke into a grin, started laughing. Reluctantly Kaval joined in and together we cleaned up the apartment and made robbery jokes and later that night I nailed the windows shut and we got undressed for bed and standing near the fire escape I asked her, "What are those bruises?"

"What bruises?"

"On your back. All over."

Kaval twisted her neck but still couldn't see them. Then she turned toward the mirror.

29

THERE WAS A KNOCK AT THE DOOR but no one had been announced. I peeked through the hole and opened the door.

"Detective Webster. Hello." I knew he would find me eventually.

"How are you? Can I come in for a minute?"

"Sure." I motioned him inside and he stepped into the middle of the room. Looking around he said, "Very nice place you have here."

"Thanks. I've been here about a month."

"Yeah, I know. You didn't leave any forwarding address. I had to ask around to find you. It wasn't that hard really."

"That's good. Won't you have a seat?" He sat on the couch and I sat on a chair opposite. Waited for him to begin.

"I want you to know how sorry I am to hear about your wife's death. It's a tragedy and I'm very sorry."

"That stove had been giving us problems for months, it was just a matter of time before it fucked up completely."

"Yeah, those old tenements . . ." he said and let it trail away.

"Actually, you can say 'Hi' to her if you like. She's up on that shelf. See the white box?" Webster didn't believe me but his eyes found the shelf and the box. "The funeral parlor sends you the ashes in a box these days, not even an urn. I thought Kaval would get a kick out of that."

Webster shifted uncomfortably on the couch and I thought she would get a kick out of that too.

"The reason I'm here," he began, "is twofold. I wanted to tell you that we're about to make an arrest in the homicide of your sister."

I stiffened. "You are? Who?"

"A former client." He raised his hand and added, "You don't have to pretend that you don't know what I'm talking about."

I didn't.

"He lives in the city. He's well-to-do, a family man; wife and kid. That's all I can tell you right now."

"He lives in *this* city?"

"Yes."

"How did you find him?"

"I'm afraid I can't tell you that. We'll probably make the arrest this evening. We're waiting on a search warrant."

The fact that he didn't mention Uncle Ted made me anxious, he must have known. The urge to set him straight tugged heavy on my tongue. Instead I said, "You said you were here for two reasons . . ."

"Yes. The second reason is a favor . . . It's about Agnes Demillow. CandyBar."

"Is she okay?"

"No, she's not. She's all alone in that hospital. Her friend disappeared a month ago, we're not sure if she went back home or what. Agnes just lies in bed all day, she won't work with her therapist, she doesn't speak to anyone, she isn't eating. The kid is slowly fading away. Look, I know that you know her. Would you visit her? Spend some time with her? Try and cheer her up?"

"Keep her happy so she can testify for your friends in court?"

"No, there won't be any court appearances. The case fell part when one of the main suspects was murdered." Webster looked into my face. "Her doctors aren't sure she can hold up for a trial anyway. I got no ulterior motive here other than she's a young girl, she's got nothing and no one. And it breaks my heart to see her like that."

"What if she doesn't want any visitors?"

"Let's chance it."

"You have a great view of the river."

"I wouldn't know."

"There's the garbage barge spilling trash into the water, smoke stacks spewing chemicals in New Jersey, mob hit victims floating near the piers. It's wonderful."

CandyBar refused to budge. The scowl on her face was warmly reminiscent.

"If you're not going to eat your Jell-O, can I have it?"

"Help yourself," she said, then added, "I sure can't." I slurped it from the cup then pretended I was puking it back. CandyBar was not amused.

"You know, you're a tough audience."

"Oh, is this entertainment?" she spit.

"Your snide remarks are not discouraging me. In fact, I'm enjoying them."

"That makes one of us."

"You know, for a kid you sure got a smart mouth."

"That's about all I got."

"Alright, stop it! I don't want to play this game with you. I know you got a fucked-up deal. Life sucks. It sucks a big fucking dick! But what makes you think death is any picnic? I have a feeling it's not all it's cracked up to be. You're making progress! You can move your toes, it's only a matter of time before . . ."

"I can take a shit!" she snapped.

A nurse came into the room wheeling a tray of medica-

tion. CandyBar didn't say a word as the nurse young naïv
and still thinking she could make a difference tried to brigh
en rainy day. CandyBar opened her mouth as the nurs
placed two capsules on her tongue and held a cup of wate
to her lips.

"There. That wasn't so bad, was it?"

CandyBar shot her a look that said it was. The nurse gave
me an uncomfortable glance, sealed it behind a smile, then
left the room. Once gone CandyBar produced the pills
between her teeth and I took them with water.

"Thanks."

"Don't mention it."

30

I STOOD AT THE LEDGE the water's jiggling flesh like naked
women running marathons. The first April Sunday chilly
sunshine breezes coming in from outer boroughs. A tugboat
red and black chugged along with an American flag blowing
in its wake. Driftwood trailing seaweed paper cups and
garbage washed up on the rocks, the angry breaking foam
brought her back in mind remembered. Lonely fingers
pressed my side as passion burns ephemeral; and ours had
blazed in chaos. A week before she died had made up with
her mother and made sure I was taken care of and when I
went to make the arrangements they had already been made.

I opened the box and held it to my nose, tried to smell
her scent of skin. Cardboard laced with sea salt air. My stomach tingled nervous as I sprinkled her ashes into the murky
green river, cried as she dissolved into nothingness. Looking
into heaven's gloomy realm I asked Him please to take care
of her. My wife and friend. Kaval.

I started west to Houston Street when passing a burnt out Buick lying sideways near the FDR a helpless whimper cried from inside. A small brown puppy trapped in the driver's door panel its paws wrenched underneath looked up seeking answers. I studied the eyes in case of recognition, but lately in remission visions and their counterparts confined themselves to dreams.

I freed the dog and walked along the LES an empty hole where heart should be when trailing close behind the dog wore happy innocence. We walked for miles and all the while that happy grin remained. Upward Seventh Avenue I passed the homeless drunks and junkies sleeping in the curb. I reached Jackie's with the puppy at my side and waited across the street, watching through the window. Inside were Dezmond and Wally and Paris and Harper with Old Man Costello and Jackie and life just went on in spite of its profanity. I wasn't sure I could participate anymore. A cab slowed down and in the back seat Camille was fixing her lipstick and I wanted to tell Wally his sister was alive but I didn't. Instead I searched strange faces for Denise and Kaval but spirits never smile when you want them to.

As sister killers roamed the streets where teenage girls gave tricks and treats I headed downtown with my loyal companion in tow. I reached Eleventh and Sixth as a tall man wearing overcoat walked briskly toward Seventh holding a bloody rag to his eye as plasma poured down the side of his face. Nobody said a word or tried to help him parting sea as he calmly walked into the hospital. I turned around and the puppy was gone. I stood on the corner alone as could be, watching little boys and girls play in the street; too soon for rules of genitalia.

The clouds turned gray and the wind blew harsh and through it came the ticking of a clock. I whirled around and the clock became strutting high heel shoes on dirty brown cement. I laughed out loud so safe secure with no one left to harm not even sleeping puppies. One by one the sounds and the smells of the city increased. As the poison fumes of traffic and the shrill horns blared with sirens taunting sobbing parents children having funerals, as racist gangs and homeless junkies drug deals killing innocents, unclaimed bodies burnt-out storefronts moving vans and women raped in burglary, old people eating dog food landlords clearing buildings pre-teen whores with bloated bellies, cops and killers switching places, like mutant cells of wounded plasma pissing in my brain; as the cacophonous soundtrack of Armageddon with its poverty murder and pestilence rained down upon me in all its muted damnation, drowning me in all this poetry and punishment, I decided to go visit CandyBar and tell her all I'd seen.